Living Proof

'We've read all of your books,' the woman in black was saying. 'They really made an impression.'

. 'And since it's your first visit,' her friend said excitedly, 'we've brought something for you.'

'Well, that's real nice,' Cathy Jordan said, giving it her best smile.

The woman raised the rucksack high and swung it towards the table: what was inside was a plastic container and what was inside that was blood. A lot of blood. It poured over Cathy Jordan's face and hair and down her front, splashing across what was left of the piles of books.

'We thought,' one of the women was shouting, 'you'd like to know what it was like.'

Living Proof is the seventh of John Harvey's Resnick novels, which have met with great critical acclaim and been translated into more than a dozen languages. He has adapted two of the novels for television and is currently adapting them for radio. His other television and radio work includes dramatisations of Arnold Bennett, A.S. Byatt and Bobbie Ann Mason. Since 1977 his Slow Dancer Press has published many contemporary English and American poets and a selection of his own poetry, *Ghosts of a Chance*, was published in 1992. After living for a number of years in Nottingham he now lives in London.

Also by John Harvey

Lonely Hearts*
Rough Treatment*
Cutting Edge*
Off Minor*
Wasted Years*
Cold Light*
Easy Meat

Ghosts of a Chance (Poetry)

* available in Mandarin

JOHN HARVEY

Living Proof

Mandarin

The lines from 'The Bad Mother' by Jill Dawson,
reprinted here in Chapter Thirty-five,
are from *White Fish with Painted Nails*
(Slow Dancer Press, London, 1994)
and are used by permission.

A Mandarin Paperback
LIVING PROOF

First published in Great Britain 1995
by William Heinemann Ltd
This edition published 1996
by Mandarin Paperbacks
an imprint of Reed International Books Ltd
Michelin House, 81 Fulham Road, London SW3 6RB
and Auckland, Melbourne, Singapore and Toronto

Copyright © John Harvey 1995
The author has asserted his moral rights

*Although this novel is set in a real city,
it is a work of fiction and its events and
principal characters exist only in its pages
and in the author's imagination.*

A CIP catalogue record for this title
is available from the British Library

ISBN 0 7493 1823 6

Typeset by Deltatype Ltd, Ellesmere Port, Cheshire
Printed and bound in Great Britain by BPC Paperback Ltd
A member of the British Printing Company Ltd

For Liz

One

The man running down the middle of the Alfreton Road at five past three that Sunday morning was, as Divine would say later, absolutely stark bollock naked. Poetic, for Divine, if not scrupulously true. On his left foot, the man was wearing a size eight, wool and cotton mix, Ralph Lauren sock, a red polo player stitched on to the dark blue. And he was bleeding. A thin line of drying blood, too light in colour to match the Lauren logo, adhered to the man's side, its source, seemingly, a puncture wound below his pendulous breast.

The surface of the road was hard; it bruised his feet and jarred his knees: his breath rasped harsh against his chest. Promises to give up smoking, take up swimming, resume playing squash – little in the man's past ten years had prepared him for this.

Still, he continued to run, past the Forest Inn and the Queen Hotel, the carpet tile shop and the boarded up fronts of the café and the fruit and veg shop, both long closed down; past Don Briggs Motorcycles, the Freezer Centre and Kit 'Em Out, all closed down; on past the Krishna Vegetarian Restaurant and Take Away and the tiny health food shop that offered vitamins and ginseng, athletic supports and marital aids.

Stumbling along the broken white line at the centre of the road, he passed the boarded-up branch of Barclays Bank, Tony's Barber Shop, the Bismilla Tandoori, the Regency Bridal Salon and the Running Horse pub, before finally, outside the vivid green front of Il Padrono

Ristorante Italiano, balance all but gone, arms flailing, he collided with a car parked near the kerb and cannoned sideways, falling heavily to his knees.

Under the changing glow of the nearby traffic light, his eyes were bright with tears. Not wanting to, he pressed his fingertips against his ribs and groaned.

The next time the light turned green, he pushed himself back to his feet and though at first his legs refused to move, he forced himself to carry on. Overweight, balding, middle-aged, a wound near the centre of his chest that had started to bleed again, the man had no idea where he was running to, only what he was running from.

Two

Across the city, Resnick was sleeping soundly, cats curled here and there among the humps and hollows of his bed.

He had spent the weekend in Birmingham, at a conference called to address the establishment of a national police force. More silver epaulettes and high-flown phrases than he had encountered in one place since Marian Witczak had dragged him along to a revival of *The Merry Widow* at the Theatre Royal.

'I feel,' one senior officer had said, 'that we are already moving towards the formation of such a force in a very British way.' Piecemeal, ill-considered and over-cautious then, Resnick had thought, somewhere between the re-organisation of the National Health Service and the building of the Channel Tunnel.

'Y' never know, Charlie,' Jack Skelton had said, when he pleaded a backed-up schedule and sent Resnick along in his place, 'might not do you any harm, putting yourself about a bit. Letting yourself be seen. After all, don't want to stick at plain inspector all your life.'

Didn't he?

Watching all the high fliers like Helen Siddons, Home Office approved, race past him in the fast lane, didn't make Resnick feel he had a great deal of choice. Although, truth to tell, if he had wanted promotion badly enough, he would have pushed for it by now himself. Got it, like as not, for all that he had long ignored the lure of the local Masonic Lodge and had maintained a steadfast preference for watching County over chipping balls on to the green, getting his handicap down below double figures.

No, the team he had working with him now – no one fussing overmuch with how he went about his job – thanks very much, Resnick liked it where he was.

The alarm aroused him a few minutes short of six and he padded, barefoot, towards the bathroom, cats, instantly alert, winding between his legs.

The shower head was in need of cleaning again and the water jetted out at him, unevenly, too hot or far too cold.

Before the cats could be fed, the caked residue of the previous day's Whiskas had to be prised from their bowls and Bud, the youngest, seized the opportunity to perfect that pathetic mew of hunger which, allied to the soulful stare of his eyes, would have served well amongst the young men begging beside the mural in the Broad Marsh bus station. What had someone at the conference called it, homelessness? A choice of lifestyle? As if, Resnick had thought, anyone would deliberately choose to sleep rough through the kind of wet winter they had just experienced.

He forked food into the four bowls, allowing the others to get a head start before letting Dizzy in through the back door, from where he had been patrolling the night. Tail angled high, the black cat stalked past him, green eyes narrowing against the extra light.

Resnick dropped a handful of Costa Rican beans into the grinder, sliced rye and caraway, set the kettle on to boil; he removed the outside layer from what remained of the Polish garlic sausage and cut thin slices from a stump of Emmental cheese. Behind him, through the glass at the top of the door, the sky was turning through purple and orange to red.

Resnick carried his breakfast through to the living room, switched the radio on low and sat with yesterday's paper on the arm of his chair, while Miles assiduously

4

cleaned himself on his lap, pink tongue licking deep between extended claws.

It was the time of day Resnick liked best, the quiet before most of the world had got under way. Even back in the days when he had been married – before the advent of the cats – he would slide from the bed early, careful not to disturb Elaine, and wander contentedly through the empty rooms before settling with a cup of coffee and a new record on the stereo, headphones to his ears.

These days he rarely used the headphones for fear he would fail to hear that first summons, hauling him into the working day – bit of an emergency, sir, something's come up.

This morning he got as far the sports round-up just ahead of the half hour – another England bowler laid low by a strained groin – before the phone rang and he swivelled towards it, Miles jumping to the carpet before he was pushed.

Divine's voice was loud with cynicism and wonder. 'Those blokes who were attacked a few months back in the red-light district, looks like we might have another.'

'Serious?'

'Serious enough. Lorry driver picked him up by Canning Circus, not far short of running all eight wheels right over him. Stretched out in the middle of the chuffing road he was, absolutely stark bollock naked.'

'Twenty minutes,' Resnick said. 'I'll be there.'

Three

Those blokes.

The first had been your average punter, run of the mill; confectionery salesman with a wife and kids in Hinckley and a four-year-old hatchback stuffed full with Snickers and liquorice chewing gum. Halfway along one of the alleys off Waterloo Road, lured by leopard-skin leggings and red high heels, and two men had suddenly been standing there behind him, quick and still from the darkness. Three weeks on the critical list, it had taken all the skills of the Senior Registrar and her neurosurgery team to reconstruct his skull, fragment by fragment, piece by broken piece. Every day his wife had come in on the bus to sit at his bedside, reading *Woman's Weekly*, filling in puzzles, eating his grapes. A couple of months later, one of his credit cards had turned up in Leicester, part of a job lot being offered for sale in a pub near the covered market.

The second victim had been an Italian soccer fan, jubilant after his team's victory in the Anglo-Italian Cup and celebrating on the open spaces of the Forest Recreation Ground with his friends, waving thousand-lire notes and singing Pavarotti's *Greatest Hits*. A young redhead, newly arrived on a Super Saver from Newcastle, had offered him a quick hand-job in the trees off the road, anything to stop him singing. A couple of early morning dog-walkers found him tied to a sycamore hours later, terrified, stripped of everything save his first-team replica

6

shirt. Seventeen stitches it had taken to mend the gash in his forehead. His plane ticket had been found in a rubbish bin near the Forest park-and-ride and his passport, torn in two and two again, finally surfaced floating on the duck pond by the entrance to the Arboretum.

The most recent occurrence had been at the nub end of March, another sales rep, in the city on a roll and booked into the Royal Hotel. He had met a woman in the penthouse bar, nice looking, good clothes, nothing garish but out for business just the same. Back in his room, she had undressed him on the bed, encouraging him, he said, to talk dirty to her all the while. Call her, you know, a slag, a dirty whore, stuff like that. When he was down to his Jockey's, she had pulled a knife from her handbag and stabbed him, once in the side, once through the flesh of the upper arm. Frantically, he had pushed her clear away and she had fled, off out of the room and down the hotel corridor, leaving him in no position to chase her. The description he gave of her, detailed as it was, matched no known prostitute on the Vice Squad's books. Just another housewife, most likely, eking out the Family Support.

Three incidents, probably unrelated, and now a fourth.

Resnick crossed the street from the centre of Canning Circus, early traffic already building up on its way along Derby Road towards the city centre. Time was, he would have bumped into Jack Skelton at this hour, the superintendent setting out on his regular three-mile run. But since early spring, Skelton's exercise had been restricted to pacing the four walls of his office. Whether the superintendent's relationship with DI Helen Siddons had progressed beyond an older man's fantasy or not, Resnick could imagine only too well the tartness with which Alice Skelton would have scolded him for his folly. And Siddons' accelerated promotion to the West Country had done little to ease the situation, leaving Skelton increasingly disgruntled and grey-haired, his girth thickening at a noticeable rate.

The CID office was close to the head of the stairs on the first floor, an L-shaped room with filing cabinets ranked along the far wall, below detailed maps of the city. A succession of desks and tables ran along two of the walls and down the centre of the room. Graham Millington's desk was on its own, adjacent to the thinly partitioned office which had the words *Detective Inspector Charles Resnick* on its door.

Behind Millington's desk were the kettle and mugs and the rest of the paraphernalia for tea- and coffee-making. Most of the other surfaces were clogged with official forms in a variety of shades and colours, typewriters and VDUs, here and there foil containers harbouring the remains of the previous night's chicken korma or lamb kebab.

In the usual way of things, only the officer on early shift would have been present when Resnick arrived, busy updating the files that logged the night's activities, after which the primary investigation of the inevitable break-ins would be his or her responsibility. This morning, though, Mark Divine had been there from first light, back aching after sharing the interior of a rusting blue Transit with Kevin Naylor, the pair of them peeing into old orange juice cartons and waiting forlornly for the Home-care warehouse on the Abbeyfield Industrial Estate to be raided for a third time.

'What buggers me,' as Divine was overfond of saying, 'is who'd go to all that trouble to liberate three gross of sink plungers and a couple of dozen aluminium ladders?'

The fourth night in a row in which they were no nearer to finding an answer.

Naylor had snuck off home to snatch a quick hour snuggled up to his Debbie, while Divine, for whom home offered no such luxury, had opted for a kip behind his desk. He had been snoring nicely when the duty officer rang up from below with details of a man who'd been brought in barely conscious from the end of the Alfreton Road. Soon after which, he had phoned his superior.

'Mark,' Resnick said, door swinging to behind him.

'Boss.' Divine swung his legs down from his desk and stood to uncertain attention.

'Best fill me in.'

Divine told him what little he knew about the man who was presently in a bed at Queen's Medical, barely conscious and temporarily restricted to fluids.

'This stab wound,' Resnick asked. 'Life threatening?'

'Seemed so at first, now they reckon he's going to be okay. Missed anything vital, by the sound of it.' Divine shrugged. 'Lost a fair bit of blood all the same.'

'And the nature of the attack, how much do we know about that?'

'Not a heck of a lot. I mean, when he first come round he was full of it. Tart and whore, over and over, blaming her, like, for what had happened.'

'It was the woman who stabbed him, that's what he's claiming?'

'No two ways about it. Aside from that, though, started asking him a few questions, clammed up tighter'n a virgin's arse. Wouldn't even tell us his name.'

Resnick frowned and shook his head. 'All right. Have a word with Vice, see if they had anyone on patrol last night, late. They might have noticed something that'll tie in. Minute Kevin arrives, pair of you can get up by the Forest, talk to the girls on the early shift. Meantime, I'll drop by the hospital. Maybe if our mystery man knows he's out of danger, he'll be more ready to talk.'

'Right, boss.' Divine was alert now, tiredness fallen away. It wasn't every day Resnick was prepared to trust the younger man's instincts and there was a grin around

the corners of Divine's mouth as he sat back behind his
desk, reaching for the phone.

Lynn Kellogg was on the stairs as Resnick went down.
After the traumas at the start of the year, she had had her
hair cut short, making her face seem less rounded, more
severe. More often than not now, there was a haunted
look, hunched at the back of her eyes.

'Morning, Lynn. Everything okay?'

'Fine.'

Neither of them believed it.

Resnick made a mental note to ask if she were still
seeing the police psychiatrist, and if she were, whether it
was doing any good.

Four

After circling the inner ring road twice, Resnick squeezed into a parking place at the rear of the hospital, close to the offshoot of the canal. Above, the sky showed a flat, unbroken blue, but the sun, for early summer, gave off little warmth. He thrust both hands deep into his jacket pockets as he walked.

That way in took him past the psychiatric wing and an image of his ex-wife, Elaine, slipped unbidden into his mind: the way she had looked the last time he had seen her, after spending God knows how much time in places likes this. And Lynn, he kept thinking of Lynn – two years without a relationship worthy of the name, and when she had come close to giving her trust to someone again, it had been the wrong man.

It had been a mistake that had cost her more than pride and self-esteem; it had very nearly cost her life. Resnick remembered how it ended: the mud that had sucked, thick, about her feet as he had run across the field-end, awkwardly towards her, helicopter hovering noisily above; the way the blood had pumped, jaggedly, from his heart when he knew that she was safe.

In the months since then, all conversation between them had been formal, withdrawn, as if what each had glimpsed in that despairing clutch of arms was more than they would dare acknowledge. And Michael Best was in custody awaiting trial for kidnapping and murder. His days in court – and Lynn's – still to come.

The single door which Resnick knew led through to the

rear of Accident and Emergency was directly in front of him and he pushed it open and went in.

They sat in small groups of relatives and friends or else they sat alone, staring off into that space where time, long since, had decided to stand still. For so many of the people here, Resnick thought, this was how they spent their lives; uncomfortably, on institutional chairs in institutional rooms, waiting for the number clicking slowly over to correspond to the one clutched in their hands. Social services, the housing department, medical centre, the dole; the bored clerk checking their answers, painstakingly scrawled upon this form or that. Rent rebate, clothing allowance, disability benefit. The women, pregnant, or with three kids under five who ran and chased between the lines of chairs, defying all the shouts and threats, sporadic and half-hearted, until finally they went flying, arse over tip, crashed into the wall and cried. Men with short moustaches, tattoos and sallow faces, shutting out all noise, clenching and reclenching their fists at their children's screams – the futility of dreams.

An Asian family sat off on its own, near the door, the man in a brown suit, bandage lopsided about his head, his wife in a sari, pale blue and green, carpet slippers on her feet, a small child, little more than a baby, sleeping fitfully inside her arms. Close to Resnick, a middle-aged man with tight grey hair and lined face, wearing someone's cast-off Fair Isle pullover pocked with holes and small burns, sat smoking a cigarette, after each drag carefully tapping the ash into the empty can of Strongbow cider clenched between his knees.

The nurse Resnick intercepted was wearing a sister's uniform and the badge on its lapel told him her name was Geraldine McAllister. Almost certaintly she was older, but all she looked was twenty-five or -six.

'Excuse me,' Resnick said. 'But you had somebody brought in earlier, a stab wound . . .'

'We had several.'

'This one . . .'

'Three, to be exact.' Resnick had expected Irish and what he got was Scots, not broad but unmistakable, musical.

'The one I'm interested in . . .' he began.

She was looking at the warrant card he held out in one hand. 'That would be John Smith, then, I expect.'

'Is that his name?'

She smiled. 'Probably not. But we had to call him something. He refused to give a name.' The smile was still there, broader if anything. 'Not very inventive, is it?'

'I'm sure you've got better things to do.'

'Than be inventive? I doubt that. Not round here.'

'Gerry,' a male nurse called from round a curtain, 'can you take a look at this a minute?'

'You,' she said to Resnick. 'Inspector. Don't go. Two shakes now and I'll be back.'

One small emergency extended into another and it was not so far short of half an hour before they were sitting in a cramped office behind the receptionist's desk. A polystyrene cup of lukewarm grey coffee sat, unwanted, between Resnick's feet.

Gerry McAllister held an X-ray in her hand, slanted up towards the light. 'You can see, the wound isn't very deep, a couple of inches at most. Even so,' she shook her head, 'a little bit higher and to the left . . .'

Her hair was not chestnut as Resnick had first supposed, but auburn, redder at the ends than at the roots. And she was older, a cross-hatch of worry lines around her eyes. Thirty-four or -five?

'Was it consistent with, I mean, did it seem to have been made with a knife?'

'Rather than what? A knitting needle, something like that?'

It hadn't been precisely what Resnick had in mind.

'A couple of weeks back,' Gerry McAllister said, 'we had this woman come in. She'd flagged down a taxi on the road; didn't have any money, but the driver brought her here just the same. There was a knitting needle sticking out from the corner of her eye.'

Automatically, Resnick cast his mind back, trying to recall whether the incident had been reported.

'There'd been a row at home, apparently. Things had got out of hand.'

Resnick nodded. 'Boyfriend or husband?'

The sister shook her head firmly. 'Mother. Should they go to the bingo or stay in and watch *Blind Date*.' She smiled. 'Alarming, isn't it, the way things get blown up out of all proportion? Arguing like that over something like *Blind Date*.'

'Our Mr Smith,' Resnick said. 'He didn't say anything about how he came to be stabbed?'

'My hand slipped a little on the needle,' Gerry said, 'when I was giving him his injection. Punctured the skin more than I'd intended. He didn't even open his mouth then.'

Resnick grinned and got to his feet.

'I've checked up on the ward, it's okay for you to go up and see him. Maybe he'll talk to you,' she said.

Resnick doubted that were true, but thanked Gerry McAllister and followed her out of the room. Immediately, three voices were calling her from three different directions, each as urgent as the next.

The anonymous victim had been put into a side ward which he shared with two men way past pensionable age and a nervous-looking youth whose bed was marked 'Nil by Mouth'.

He was lying on his side, face towards the wall, a tray of barely browned toast and soggy cereal on the bedside cabinet, untouched.

'Not hungry?' Resnick asked, pulling out a chair and setting it down close to the bed.

The man raised his head enough to look into Resnick's eyes, then rolled away.

'Whatever happened,' Resnick said, 'you were lucky. Lucky someone found you, brought you to us; lucky to be here. That whoever did this wasn't stronger.'

He reached out and, without force, rested his hand on the upper edge of the sheet, bone and flesh of the man's shoulder beneath. At his touch, the man flinched but nothing more.

'Listen,' Resnick said, 'if there's somebody out there attacking men, men who put themselves in a vulnerable position – we need to bring them in. If we don't, well, you understand what I'm saying. The next person might not get off as easy as you.' His voice was soft beneath the squeak of passing trolley wheels, the muffled inanities of breakfast television from the main ward. 'You wouldn't want to be responsible for that, would you? Someone dying?'

Beneath his hand, Resnick felt the muscles tighten through the loose flesh of the man's arm.

'Whatever you were up to, last night, no reason that shouldn't remain your business. No need to broadcast it around. Time to time, we all do things we'd rather nobody else knew. Family. Friends. It's something I can understand.'

For an answer, the man shuffled further across the bed, shrugging off Resnick's hand; sheet and blanket he pulled up until they half-covered his head.

Resnick leaned low across him, close enough to sense the damp ripeness of the man's sweat. His fear.

'Think on what I've said. Talk to us. Co-operate. You'll

15

find it easier all around.' Resnick raised his head and then, almost as an afterthought: 'There is a charge, you know, obstructing the police in the course of their duties.'

He took a card from his wallet and slipped it between the man's reluctant fingers.

'I'll be waiting for you to call me. Don't leave it too long.'

Five

'Yes, madam,' the uniformed PC was saying to the old lady at Enquiries, 'of course I can arrange for the Crime Prevention Officer to call round. If you'll just let me have your name and address and phone number, then he'll get in touch with you and agree a time.'

Resnick stepped around the woman as she fumbled in her handbag for the scrap of paper on which she had scribbled all the details down. 'I've just moved, you see, and I forget . . .'

Off to the right of the stairs, a repetitive yelling came from the direction of the police cells, the same two words, over and over, deadened of all meaning. 'Hold it down in there,' came the custody sergeant's voice. 'I said, hold it down!'

Resnick grinned into the silence that followed. The newly appointed custody sergeant had been transferred from Central CID; six foot three, boots that shone whenever he was on duty and shirts that were always freshly ironed. Most Saturdays he played alongside Divine in the Force's first XV and when he said hold it down, only the most drunken or foolish disobeyed.

Resnick turned left at the head of the stairs, towards the bird-like clamour of phones.

'CID. DC Kellogg speaking . . .'

'CID. DC Naylor . . .'

'CID . . .'

'Graham,' Resnick raised a hand in greeting as he

threaded his way between the rows of desks towards his office. 'Any chance of a cup of tea?'

'Kev,' Millington said, looking across at Naylor. 'Mash for us, will you?'

Naylor drew the telephone away from his face, one hand clamped across the mouthpiece. 'Mark, you're not doing anything.'

'Lynn,' Divine began, noticing that she was on her feet, 'while you're up . . .'

'Don't,' Lynn shook her head, 'as much as think about it.'

'Chuffin' hell!' Divine moaned, heading for the kettle. 'At least when Dipak was still here, you could count on him to fall for it.'

Overhearing, Lynn treated him to a look that would have stripped several layers of wallpaper. Although off duty, DC Dipak Patel had intervened in a brawl in the city centre and been fatally stabbed for his trouble: he had been a close colleague and a good friend.

'What I meant,' Divine grinned, seizing his chance to wind her up, 'one good thing about encouraging all these minorities into the Force, they're so grateful to be here, they don't mind doing a few chores.'

'Yes?' Lynn was out from behind her desk, blocking his path. 'All these minorities? Take a look, Mark. How many can you see?'

'Aside from you, you mean?'

'All right,' Millington said, setting himself between them. 'Shut it. The pair of you.'

'The pair . . .' Lynn began.

'Enough!' Like a referee about to issue a yellow card, Millington raised a hand in the air and glared. Lynn held his gaze for ten, twenty seconds, before turning aside, and grudgingly resuming her seat.

Blowing her a kiss over Millington's shoulder, Divine wandered across towards the kettle.

'And you,' Millington said quietly, coming up behind Divine as he was flipping tea bags into the pot, 'don't be so quick with your mouth. That way you might give what you call a brain a bit more of a chance.'

There were three Home Office circulars waiting on Resnick's desk for him to read, initial and pass on; a subscription renewal form for *Police Review* and information about a forthcoming course on the computer analysis of fingerprints at Bramshill College. Resnick pushed these to one side and shuffled through his drawer, searching for the flier from the newly refurbished Old Vic – the Stan Tracey Duo were playing that season and, if at all possible, he didn't want to miss them.

'Boss?' Millington knocked and entered, two mugs of tea precariously balanced in his one hand.

Resnick reached out and relieved him of one of the mugs, found a space to set it down; was it Millington or his wife, he wondered, who'd selected that particular shade of olive green from the suit rack in Marks and Spencer's?

'Ram raiding,' Millington said, helping himself to a seat. 'Buggers have come up with a new twist.'

Resnick sipped his tea and waited; over the past eighteen months there'd been a dramatic increase in the number of robberies carried out with the aid of stolen cars. As a method it was bog simple: drive the car fast through the front window of a city centre shop, jump out, grab what you can, either slam the car into reverse and drive back out or run like fuck.

'Bloke out at Wollaton, just back in from tending his begonias – holly-leafed, apparently, not so easy to grow ... anyway, sat himself down to watch a spot of racing, wife about to do the honours with the biscuit barrel and a pot of Earl Grey, when this four-year-old Ford Escort comes steaming up his front drive, detours across the lawn, smack into the conservatory at the side of the house.'

'After his prize blooms, then, Graham?' Resnick asked. But Millington was not to be diverted.

'Old boy grabbed the fire tongs and went off to repel boarders, while his missus phoned us. These three youths were into the house through the side door, knocked him flying, concussion, had the old lady tied up with the telephone wire and went out of there in five minutes flat. Half a dozen cups gone from his trophy cabinet, silver medals, jewellery box from the bedroom, her fur coat, watch, thirty-five-piece ruby wedding dinner service, didn't as much as bother with the VCR.'

'The couple, how're they doing?'

'Shook up, who wouldn't be? Keeping him in Queen's for a few days' observation. She's got a daughter, come to stay.'

'Leads?'

'Car was stolen the day before, shopping centre out at Bulwell. Found abandoned a few hours later, not so far short of Cinderhill.'

'Wouldn't be much left of it, then.'

'Four wheels and a chassis.'

Resnick had a mouthful more tea. 'Didn't Reg Cossall have something going over that way somewhere?'

'Broxtowe, yes. Still has. Urban Youth Initiative, that's the official name for it. Won't tell you what Reg calls it.'

'Have a word, then, Graham. Might tie in with something, someone he's got tabs on.'

'Right.'

'Meantime, description of what's missing . . .'

'On its way round today. Long as we can keep forgetting the photocopy budget.'

There was a knock and in response to Resnick's 'Come in,' Divine's head and shoulders appeared round the edge of the door.

'Kev and me are just off up the Forest. I was wondering, bloke in the hospital, anything useful?'

Resnick shook his head. 'Not as much as a name. How about Vice? Anything from them?'

'Low profile last night, as it happens. Promised to put the word out today, though. Turn up anything, they'll let us know.'

'Okay, Mark. Oh, and if Lynn's still there . . .'

But Lynn Kellogg was already in the doorway. 'Breakins in the Park. Five in total. Close enough to be the work of the same team. Several reports of an old post office van in the area, could have been using it to haul the stuff away in.'

Resnick nodded. 'Cool your heels on that for an hour, will you? Fellow who was stabbed last night, he's out at Queen's, refusing to say a word. Get yourself down there, see what you can do.'

'Right, sir, will that be Mata Hari, then, or Florence Nightingale?'

Resnick looked at her carefully and she was a long way from smiling.

'Don't suppose I'm allowed to ask any more if it's the time of the month?' Millington said, after Lynn had closed the door.

'No, Graham. You're not.'

Millington shrugged inside his olive-green suit and sucked on his upper lip. 'This party I'm getting up to go to Trent Bridge, first Saturday of the Test, you've not changed your mind?'

But Resnick was already shaking his head. Watching County of a Saturday afternoon through the winter was one thing – all the speed and excitement of plant germination, but at least it was over in an hour and a half. Whereas cricket . . .

'Oh,' Millington said, a last thought as he left Resnick's office. 'Skelton wants to see you. Something about shots in the park?' And he was off, wandering in the direction of the teapot, lips puckered together as he whistled thoughtfully through the opening verse of 'Sailor'. An early hit of Petula's, but a good one.

Six

When Resnick knocked and entered, Skelton was standing behind his desk looking at the first of several sheets of fax paper which were curling around his hand.

'Charlie, come on in.'

Resnick recognised neither of the other people in the room, a man and a woman rising to greet him, the man stepping forward with an uncertain smile.

'Charlie, this is David Tyrell, Programme Director of *Shots in the Dark*. Detective Inspector Resnick, CID.'

Tyrell was tall, taller than Resnick by an inch or more, bespectacled, his already slim body made slimmer by a suit that Resnick wagered cost more than a season ticket to County plus change.

'Inspector, good to meet you.'

Tyrell's handshake was strong, the eyes behind the glasses unblinking, but his skin had the pallor of someone who has spent too long out of the light.

'This is Mollie,' Tyrell said. 'My assistant.'

'Mollie Hansen. Assistant Director, Marketing.' Her grip was quick and cool and those five words enough to mark her as a Geordie, strayed from home. She stood there a moment longer, taking in Resnick with slate-grey eyes, the pinch of blood where he had nicked himself shaving, the speck of something yellow crusted to his lapel. A widening of her mouth, not yet a smile, and she stepped back – scarlet T-shirt, Doc Martens, jeans.

'You know this festival, Charlie? The one Mr Tyrell's responsible for.'

'Not really.'

Over by the side wall, Mollie Hansen sighed.

'Why don't we all sit down?' Skelton suggested. 'See what we've got.'

Tyrell crossed his legs, drew a cigarette packet from his pocket and, almost in the same gesture, pushed it back from sight. '*Shots* has been running four years. It's a crime and mystery festival, films mainly, TV, more recently, books as well. Each year we invite special guests, stars, I suppose you'd call them, to some extent built the programme around them. You know, Quentin Tarantino, Sara Paretsky, people like that.'

Knowing neither of them, Resnick nodded. He felt the strength of Mollie Hansen's gaze, weighing him up for what she thought he was.

'This year,' Tyrell continued, 'we've got Curtis Woolfe. The director. His first public appearance in fifteen years.'

'Sixteen,' Mollie said quietly.

Tyrell ignored her and carried on. 'For the book side of things, we've managed to get Cathy Jordan to come over from the States. Which is great.'

'Except . . .' began Mollie.

'Except she's been receiving threatening letters.'

'Which is why we've come to you.'

Cathy Jordan, Resnick was thinking. *Jordan*. He wondered if he should know the name, wondered if he did. The last crime novel he'd tried to read had been an old Leslie Charteris found inside a chest of drawers he'd bought in an auction at the Cattle Market. He had never finished it.

Skelton was holding the faxed copies out towards him and Resnick stood and took them from his hand. The words were typed and faint, not easy to read.

You know, I really do think you've been
allowed to pursue what is after all a very

24

> *limited talent altogether too far.*
>
> *It's one thing, of course, for people who should know better to be taken to the point where they will award you prizes, quite another for you to have the brazen effrontery to accept them.*
>
> *Remember Louella Trabert, Cathy, remember what happened to her?*

Resnick looked up, 'Louella Trabert?'

'She's in one of her novels,' Tyrell said. 'A character.'

'A victim,' Mollie said.

Resnick was watching her, the tilt of her chin, the flushing high on her cheeks. 'What does happen to her?' he asked.

'She gets dragged from a car in the middle of the night, with her children left strapped in the back seat. These guys haul her off into the woods, strangle and rape her. Next morning one of the kids gets free and finds her upside down, tied by her ankles to a tree, her body slit from neck to belly with a hunting knife. Gutted.'

'Not exactly,' Tyrell said.

'Jesus! How exact do you want it to be?'

Resnick glanced at the other letters and set them back down.

'You're taking these seriously? She's taking them seriously? Cathy Jordan.'

'Seriously enough to let us know,' Tyrell said. 'But not enough to prevent her coming.'

'They were posted in America?' Resnick asked.

Tyrell nodded. 'New York. Where she lives.'

'And she's no idea who sent them?'

'Apparently not.'

'Well,' Resnick moved back to his seat. 'Maybe she feels she'll be safer over here anyway.'

Tyrell looked over at Mollie, who was already reaching down towards the black leather bag by her feet.

'This arrived this morning,' Mollie said, the envelope in her hand.

Seven

Dear Cathy,

I keep waiting for you to make the announcement, go public, seize the moment during one of those chat shows you're always on whenever I switch on the TV. You know, one of those quiet moments, snuggled down on the settee with Letterman, or laughing with Jay Leno and then, out of the blue, leaving aside all the fun and the gossip – and you are funny, Cathy, I have to give you that – you'll come right out with it. Let me tell you something now, you'll say, looking right at us with those big, blue eyes of yours, the truth is, David, Jay, I am the most talentless bitch that ever got up on her hind legs and walked. Real talent, that is. Leaving aside self-promotion and back-stabbing – plagiarism – all the things I'm really good at. Oh, and of course it helps to have the morals of the well-known alley cat, best not forget that.

The trouble is, Cathy, the richer you get, the more units – isn't that what you call books nowadays, dear? – you sell, the less likely this is to happen. So I'm going to have to stop it now, myself, over here in England. Put an end to this farrago, once and for all. You do understand me, don't you, Cathy?

*You do realise I am serious? Poor little
Anita Mulholland, Cathy, remember what
happened to her.*

The letter was on a single sheet of white paper, A4 size,
unwatermarked, undated, almost needless to say,
unsigned. At first glance, a good bubble jet or laser printer
had been used. The envelope in which it had been
delivered was self-sealing, slim and white, manufactured
by John Dickinson and with the words 'Eurolope Enve-
lopes' printed over and over in a grey diagonal across the
inside. Centred on the front of the envelope, the words
'Cathy Jordan'. No postmark, no stamp.

'You found this where?' Resnick asked.

Tyrell glanced at Mollie. 'In the office,' Mollie said.
'At Broadway. It was there with the other mail when I
arrived.'

'What time?'

'I usually get in at around a quarter to ten. This morning
it was earlier, half past nine. I was sorting through the post
and I found this.'

'Who else was in the office beside you?'

Mollie gave it a little thought. 'The cleaner would have
been and gone. If the mail arrives before she leaves,
usually she'll put it on the desk, but this was still on the
floor. The only other possibility is Dick McCrea, he's the
finance director. He's sometimes in ahead of me, but . . .'

'But today he's in London,' Tyrell put in, 'a meeting at
the BFI. He would have gone straight to the station, the
7.38 train.'

'If he'd forgotten something, though,' Resnick said, 'at
the office, something he needed . . .'

'Dick McCrea,' Mollie said, 'got his memory in a direct
deal with God. Forget is a word he doesn't admit exists.'

'Miss Jordan,' Skelton said, 'you've told her about
this?'

'Not yet,' said Tyrell. 'We thought . . . I thought first of

28

all we should speak to you. See if there wasn't something you could do. Not a bodyguard, exactly . . .'

'Heaven forbid!' Mollie said, not quite beneath her breath.

'I don't know,' Tyrell continued, 'some kind of police presence, maybe. Low key. Something that would reassure her.'

'The last thing we want,' Mollie said, 'is for people to be put off attending because they think there's going to be some kind of incident.'

Or, Resnick thought, for one of your star guests to get back on the plane and fly home.

'When's Cathy Jordan due to arrive?' Skelton asked.

'Tomorrow,' Mollie said. 'The early morning flight. Her publisher's meeting her at Heathrow and taking her into London for lunch. She's continuing up here by train. She should arrive about a quarter to five.'

Resnick and Skelton exchanged glances. Aside from the recent stabbing, there were other serious crimes outstanding: a sub-post office that had been robbed at gun-point and the postmaster shot through the leg and shoulder when he tried to resist; a domestic incident that had left one partner with burns to the face and neck from scalding water, one of the children with badly bruised ribs and a closed eye; unsolved burglaries were up for the third year in succession, as were thefts from vehicles and taking and driving away without consent. The recruitment of new staff was on hold. Budgets were screwed down tighter than an Arctic winter. This was policing in the age of cost-effectiveness and consumer choice, when those at the top talked of minimal visual policing, counted the paper clips, put a ban on overtime and sat up long into the night massaging the crime figures. If Resnick and Skelton were in the business of selling sentences, less and less people were buying. The last thing they needed was a media celebrity in need of mollycoddling, a body to guard and protect against an unknown possible assailant during a festival at which the attendance might run into the thousands.

Skelton took a breath. 'Charlie, why don't you liaise with Miss Hansen? Arrange to meet this Cathy Jordan, talk to her, try and get a sense of how serious she thinks these threats really are. Assure her we'll co-operate as fully as we can during her stay. Without making promises we can't keep.'

Resnick nodded reluctantly and glanced over at Mollie Hansen who was already drawing a card from the back of her Filofax. 'My number's on there.'

'Meantime,' Skelton was on his feet now, 'I trust neither of you will say anything about all of this to the press. If there is anything to these letters, the last thing we need is a three-ring circus.'

'Of course,' said Mollie.

'Absolutely,' said Tyrell.

Unless, Resnick thought, they reckoned that instead of putting people off, a few good rumours might do wonders at the box office.

'Here,' Mollie said, pulling a paperback book from her bag and pushing it into Resnick's hands. 'You might like to take a look at this. It's meant to be one of her best.'

DEAD WEIGHT

An Annie Q. Jones Mystery

by
CATHY JORDAN

'One last thing,' Resnick said. 'The Anita Mulholland mentioned in the letter, is she another character in one of these books?'

'That's right,' Mollie said.

'Another victim?'

'She goes on holiday with her family, to Mexico. She's thirteen. One evening her parents go down to a barbecue by the hotel pool and leave her upstairs in their room. When they get back up, an hour or so later, she's gone. A few days afterwards, someone comes across this thing like a scarecrow in the hills outside the town; it's made from Anita's clothes, up high on a cross of sticks. The police get up a search and dogs find her body in a shallow grave.' The tension in Mollie's voice was tight now and undisguised. 'That's it,' she said, 'apart from the ways she's tortured before she dies.'

Tyrell was looking at her with concern, possibly anger. Quickly he shook Resnick's hand and then Skelton's. 'We should be going. Superintendent, Inspector, thanks for your time.'

'I'll expect to hear from you,' Mollie said to Resnick from the door. 'Meantime, enjoy the book. Let me know what you think.'

After she and Tyrell had left the room, Skelton fussed with a few things on his desk and cleared his throat. 'Quite partial to a bit of *Morse*, myself,' he said.

Resnick didn't answer. He dropped the paperback down into the already sagging side pocket of his coat and headed out along the corridor towards the CID room. Another task he was certain he didn't want.

Eight

Sharon Garnett took her time walking back up Forest Road West to where she had parked her car, a four-year-old Peugeot in need of a new clutch. She was wearing black ski-pants that emphasised her height, a red and yellow scarf pulled bandana-like across her hair; in one hand she was carrying a can of Lucozade, a paper bag containing a cheese and ham cob in the other. Relaxed, Sharon moved like someone at ease with herself, strength held in reserve.

The vehicle that slowed alongside her was a Vauxhall, almost certainly a fleet car, a dark blue Cavalier. The driver pressed the electronic switch to lower the window and leaned across. 'Working?' he asked.

She put him at thirty, no more than thirty-five, dark striped suit, white shirt, tie; expensive watch on his wrist, hair brushed down and across to compensate for its early loss. Sharon wondered if she had seen him there before and decided she probably had not.

'How about it?' he tried again. 'You working or not?'

'Sure,' Sharon said, without breaking her stride, 'though not the way you mean. Now piss off before I run you in.'

The Cavalier was off up the street and turning left into Southey Street with speed enough to leave tyre marks on the tarmac. Sharon shook her head: why was it some men were content with a jacket potato at lunchtime and for some it was a quick shag?

Back behind the wheel of her car, she popped the top of

the Lucozade can and tilted back her head to drink. A pair of girls – one in a short skirt and heels, the other in tight red trousers and boots – spotted her fifty yards along the opposite pavement, turned in their tracks and began to walk briskly back the other way.

The Lucozade was warm and fizzy and the cob was ten degrees short of stale; fragments of crust splintered over her legs and the seat. The Terry Macmillan she'd been reading lay open, face down, on the passenger side. The dashboard clock told her she had a good two hours to go.

Sharon Garnett had joined the police late, in her mid-thirties, a career move she had tried not to see as a sign of desperation. All her applications to CID in London had been rebuffed and it had taken a move north-east – to Lincolnshire – before she was able to join the ranks of detectives. After the best part of a year, she had known she wanted something closer to the cutting edge than investigating poultry fraud and pig rustling in King's Lynn. Moving here to the city had meant a move back into uniform, but almost immediately she had put in for a transfer to Vice, officially uniformed still but working in plain clothes, a step on the ladder towards the real thing.

The Vice Squad in this neck of the woods comprised one inspector, two sergeants and twelve constables, three of whom were women. What they hadn't had, until Sharon joined, was an officer who was black.

Leaning sideways, she wedged the can into the pocket of the passenger door, and what remained of the cob she stuffed back into its bag and placed on the floor. A grey Sierra crawled past for the third time, slowing almost to a stop at every woman it passed. In her notebook, alongside its registration, Sharon wrote the time. As she watched, the car turned right on to Waverley and she knew from there it would make a left on to Arboretum, then left again up Balmoral or Addison, squaring the circle.

This time she was ready. As the Sierra headed back

along Forest Road East, Sharon started up the car and drove diagonally across in front of it, headlights on full beam. The driver had two alternatives: run smack into her or stop. He stopped.

Sharon was out of her car quickly enough, not running, tapping at the near-side window for it to be rolled down.

'Police Constable Garnett,' she said, holding up her identification. 'I've observed you on three separate occasions in the past half hour, stopping to speak to known prostitutes.'

In the front of the Sierra, the two men exchanged glances and the one nearest to Sharon smiled. Divine drew his wallet from his inside pocket and let it fall open close to Sharon's face. 'Snap,' he said. 'Why don't we go and get a drink?'

The table was chipped Formica, the seats were covered in a dull red patched synthetic, and the television set above the bar was showing music videos, beamed in from somewhere in Europe. Hand-drawn posters on the walls advertised quiz nights, bingo nights and karaoke. Divine sat nursing what was left of a pint of Shipstones, Naylor a half of bitter; Sharon Garnett had drained a small glass of grapefruit juice and said no to another.

They had filled Sharon in on the events of the previous night, asked her if she had heard anything that might be useful, but she could only shake her head in reply.

'The girls you spoke to,' Sharon said. 'Any of them come up with anything?'

'Seen and heard sod all,' Divine said.

'And likely,' Naylor added, 'not to tell us if they had.'

'Then why bother going through the motions?' Sharon asked.

'Because if something happens,' Divine said, 'like this bloke in hospital takes a sudden turn for the worse and pops his clogs, or a couple of months down the line there's another incident, similar, maybe proves fatal, then at least we've covered our backsides.'

'And the guv'nor's,' Naylor said.

'Who is your DI?'

'Resnick.'

Sharon Garnett smiled, remembering. 'Not a bad bloke. Give him my best.'

Divine swallowed down the remainder of his pint. 'Don't you get brassed off with Vice?' he asked when they were back on the pavement outside. 'Spending all day chatting up scuzzy tarts and warning off kerb crawlers.'

Sharon shook her head. 'Half the rest of the squad, eight hours a day for the past twelve days, watching seven boxes of videos, clocking faces, trying to decide if what they're seeing's simply gross indecency or worse.'

'Dunno,' Divine grinned. 'Got to be worse ways of earning a living then watching dirty movies and getting paid for it.'

Sharon's mouth moved into a rueful smile. 'More than a few of those, I doubt you'd think that way. Even a horny bugger like you!'

Divine grinned, taking it as a compliment. Naylor laughed and thanked her for her time and he and Divine turned right towards where they had parked their car, while Sharon walked across the street to have a word with one of the girls who was loitering there, smoking a cigarette.

'Will you take a look,' Divine said, head turned to watch Sharon walk away, 'at the arse on that.' But he was careful to keep his voice low, so there was no danger of her overhearing him.

Lynn Kellogg knocked on Resnick's office door mid-afternoon, just as he was taking a bite out of a smoked chicken, tomato and tarragon mayonnaise baguette. Late lunch. A sliver of chicken slipped out on to his fingers and he ate it as delicately as he could, not noticing the tomato seeds which had sprayed across his tie.

'Our mystery man at the hospital,' Lynn said.

Resnick looked at her expectantly.

'He's done a runner.'

Resnick lowered the baguette on to the back of an already stained NAPO report and gave a slow shake of the head.

'There was some kind of emergency down at the other end of the ward. He stole some clothes and walked out without a word. I spoke to the nurse in charge; as long as he keeps the wound clean, changes the dressing, he should be fine.'

'Well,' Resnick said, 'one way of looking at it is that it's good news. No victim, no crime.'

'But?' Lynn said.

'If the similarity to that stabbing in March is more than coincidental, we've likely got someone out there with some kind of grudge. Could turn worse before it gets better.'

'That incident,' Lynn said, 'businessman from out of town, staying at one of the big hotels, wasn't that it?'

Resnick nodded.

'We could have a quick ring round, see if there's any with an outstanding account. I doubt he went back to pay his bill.'

'Worth trying,' Resnick said. 'See what you can turn up. Oh, and if Mark and Kevin are back . . .'

But he could already hear Divine's shout and raucous laughter as the two detectives entered the outer office. It didn't take long for them to make their report.

'We could have one last try tonight,' Naylor suggested.

Resnick nodded. 'Keep in touch with Vice, let them know you're around.'

'Reminds me, boss,' Divine said. 'One of theirs this

36

morning, one we spoke to, real looker, Afro-Caribbean.'
His tongue negotiated the term with exaggerated care, as
if stepping across a minefield. 'Wanted to be remembered
to you, Sharon Garnett.'

A memory flicked across Resnick's face. He had first
met Sharon early in the year: a cold January morning, the
ground rimed with frost, a body buried in a shallow grave.
One of the victims of the man who had held Lynn Kellogg
prisoner.

Resnick glanced over towards Lynn's desk, wondering
if she might have picked up on the name. But, directory
open before her, Lynn was talking intently into the phone.

'All right, Mark,' Resnick said. 'Thanks.'

Sharon, as she had made clear, was keen to move across
to CID; he would have a word with the inspector in Vice,
find out how she was settling in, couldn't do any harm.

'D'you know,' Millington said later. It was already well
past six and Resnick had been considering cutting his
losses, calling it a day. 'D'you know, for the price of a seat
at the Test, good one, mind you, up behind the bowler's
arm, you could see three films at the Showcase, nip into
the bowling alley for a couple of games and still have cash
left over for Chicken McNuggets and fries.'

Resnick was sure he was right. 'You read a bit, don't
you. Graham?' he said.

'I like the odd Ken Follett, Tom Clancy. Why d'you
ask?'

'Here.' He pulled Cathy Jordan's book from his pocket.
'Have a go at this. Might just be your kind of thing.'

Millington took the book, looked at the cover,
shrugged, tossed it on to his desk. 'Thanks. You coming
over the road for a quick pint?'

'Another night.'

'Suit yourself.'

It was the same old routine they went through most

evenings. Unless there was a special reason, Resnick preferred to let the team have the bar to themselves. Oh, he'd stop by for a quick Guinness now and again, buy a round and be on his way. Fancied a drink later, he would stroll over to the Polish Club, elbows on the table with a bottle of Czech Budweiser or Pilsner Urquell, listen to the gossip about who was in hospital, who had died, what Sikorski had said to Churchill in 1941.

Nine

Millington didn't stay long in the pub. Somehow he had managed to get himself wedged between Divine, making the usual extravagant claims about his sex life, and one of those ritual bores with a four-hundred-thousand-pound house in the Park. Sooner multiple orgasms, he thought, than a voice that spoke from generations of cold showers and good breeding, boring on and on about the way the working class was intent upon undermining the country's manufacturing base.

Millington wanted to tell him we hardly had a manufacturing base any longer, and most of that was due to the government or bad management – most likely by people like him. Most of the factories Millington knew that shut their doors never got round to opening them again. To say nothing of the pits. Hell and hullabaloo there'd been above a year back, marchers on the streets and speeches in the Square, whole bloody communities on the dole. Arnold Bennett! It was almost enough to make you vote Labour.

'Another?' Divine tapped his empty glass. Embellishing the story of his night out with a couple from Annesley, mother and daughter, had left Divine with quite a thirst.

'No, you're all right. Off home any minute.'

'Come on. Early days yet, just a half.'

Millington flattened his palm across the top of his glass and shook his head.

'Suit yourself,' Divine grinned and let out a low belch to get the barman's attention. 'Hey up!' he called, 'how about some service?' Divine, anxious not to lose his audience, hadn't even got to the bit about the snake yet.

A cos lettuce and half a cucumber were waiting for him in the salad spinner, a Marks and Spencer lasagne in the microwave. Millington guessed from the spoons on the dining room table there'd be dessert, like as not that Greek yoghurt with honey.

Madeleine called down from the bedroom to say she'd not be many minutes, wouldn't he like to make them a nice cup of tea? While the kettle was coming to the boil, he wandered off into the garden; this time of the year, all you had to do was turn your back and the bloody grass wanted cutting.

Trills and worse wafted down from the upstairs window; auditions for the local amateur operatics were in the offing and Millington could sense this year his wife was nurturing ambitions beyond the chorus.

'What would you think, Graham,' Madeleine asked a while later, showing the jar of Hellmann's low-calorie mayonnaise to her salad, 'if I said I were going to try out for the lead?'

'I'd say good luck to you,' said Millington, poking around in his lasagne.

'You don't think I might be, well, wrong for it? The part, I mean.'

'Depends what it is.'

'*The Merry Widow.* I'm sure I told you.'

'And that's the part? The one you're after? The merry, er, widow?'

Madeleine set down her fork and knife and prepared to look hurt. 'Yes.'

Beneath his moustache, Millington smiled. 'Not trying to tell me something, are you, love?'

'What? Oh, Graham, no. For heaven's sake!'

'Not been slipping down to the garden centre for the

odd half gallon of weedkiller? A little arsenic in the salad dressing?'

'Graham! Don't say things like that. Not even in jest.'

Millington went back to his lasagne, wondering what had happened to good old meat pie and chips.

'What I meant was,' Madeleine began. It was later and she was spooning yoghurt into two bowls. 'The character, the one I'd like to play, she's meant to be gay . . .'

'Gay?'

'Lively. Sort of sparkling, you know. Full of joy.' Madeleine paused, scraping stray yoghurt from the back of the spoon on to the edge of the carton. 'Sexy.'

'Well, that's all right, then.'

'What?'

'For the part. Sexy.'

Madeleine pushed her bowl away. 'That's what I mean.'

'What?'

'It's just a joke.'

'It's not a joke.'

'It is.'

Millington stood up from his chair, leaned across the table and kissed her on the mouth. When he eased away, some few moments later, there were honey and yoghurt in his moustache and neither he nor Madeleine knew who was the more surprised.

'I was wondering,' Millington said, turning away from a woefully unfunny situation comedy on the TV, 'if you fancied an early night?'

Across the room, Madeleine blinked across a pile of nine-year-olds' science notebooks. Thirty-seven drawings of a paramecium, all of which made it look like a hairy shoe. 'All right,' she said. 'Yes, I could. I'll just have to finish these first.' Already she was making calculations, dates and figures flying around her head, wondering if

41

maybe it was worth checking her temperature with the bathroom thermometer.

Chipper, Millington had put on the dressing gown his mother-in-law had bought him the Christmas before last and gone downstairs to make a pot of tea. Never mind Divine and all his bragging, Millington was prepared to wager it didn't get much better than that.

Madeleine, for whom it had actually been almost as satisfying a ten minutes as her husband had concluded, sat, propped up by a brace of pillows, searching for her place in *Lives of the Christian Martyrs* and still envincing a slight glow.

Millington brought the tea back up on a tray; best cups and saucers, green padded cosy, a small plateful of rich butter shortbread and custard creams. He remembered to stop whistling 'Don't Sleep in the Subway' out on the landing, not wanting to irritate her nerves.

'Graham,' Madeleine said, all smiling reproach, 'we'll get crumbs in the bed.'

'Not to worry,' he winked. 'Be changing the sheets tomorrow anyway.'

Biting her tongue rather than telling him not to be smutty, Madeleine reached for a shortbread biscuit instead. Millington settled the tray between them, poured milk and tea, set his cup on the bedside table and reached for the book that Resnick had handed him.

Madeleine's only immediate reaction was to shift a little on to one side, leaning her weight towards the light.

> *If anyone had told me, Annie Jones, you'll end up spending your seventh wedding anniversary alone in the front seat of a rented Chevrolet, outside of Jake's at the Lake in Tahoe City, I'd have told them to go jump*

right in it. The lake, that is. But then if that
same anyone . . .

'Graham,' Madeleine said, rolling towards him, 'whatever's got into you?'

'How'd you mean?'

'First, you know, and now this.'

'This?'

'You're reading in bed.'

'So?'

'You never read; not anywhere, never mind in bed.'

'I read that – what's his name? – John Grisham.'

'You bought the book when we were on our way back
from Devon, read the first two pages, put it in the bag for
Christian Aid and saw the film.'

'Two pages is about all I'll read of this as well, if you
don't let me get on with it. Try engaging you in
conversation once you're stuck into one of these door-
stops of yours and I get a look fierce enough to excommu-
nicate the Pope.'

'All right, Graham,' Madeleine said, giving it just a
touch of the long-suffering. 'I'm sorry. I won't interrupt
you again.'

'S'okay, love,' Millington said, fidgeting his backside
against her hip. 'Not as if it's anything serious, not like
yours. No one's going to set me an exam on it when I've
finished.' He opened the paperback wide and cracked the
spine a little, rendering it easier to handle.

> *But then if that same anyone had told me, the*
> *day I appeared, fresh out of law school, ready*
> *to start work at the offices of Reigler and*
> *Reigler, bright and full of promise in my newly*
> *acquired dove-grey two-piece with a charcoal*
> *stripe, skirt a businesslike three inches below*
> *the knee, that I would swap what was clearly*
> *destined to be a famous legal career for that of*

a lowly private eye, I would gleefully have signed committal forms, assigning them to the nearest asylum, and tossed away the key.

'You know, Annie,' my mother had said, the time I plucked up courage to explain, 'you can't really be a private eye, they only have them in the movies. And books. And besides, they're always men.'

My mom, God bless her, always seemed to have a vested interest in remaining firmly behind the times.

'Sure, Mom,' I said, 'you're right.' And inched back the business card I had proudly given her, stuffing it back down into my wallet. There'd be another time.

Madeleine turned with a start as Annie Q. Jones hit the floor with a small bump. Millington's eyes were closed and pretty soon, she knew, he would begin to snore. Leaning across him carefully, Madeleine lightly touched her cheek to his and then switched out the lamp.

Ten

The kids outside the amusement arcade at the end of Fletcher Gate stared back at Resnick with flat, hostile eyes. Fifteen, sixteen, younger: high-top trainers, T-shirts, jeans; cans of Coke and cigarettes and something in a polystyrene box from Burger King. Maybe they knew he was a policeman, maybe not; what they saw was someone older than their fathers, another version of their teachers, probation officers, social workers, another heavily built man in a shapeless suit.

A common incongruity, the windows in front of which they lounged or sat displayed pottery objects no one ever bought – shire horses, vases, bug-eyed dogs – all steadily gathering dust.

Resnick turned right towards Goose Gate, pausing for some moments outside Culture Vulture, looking with quiet delight at the display of extravagantly designed shirts he would never wear, black brothel-creeper shoes of the kind he had surreptitiously changed into almost thirty years before, ready to go out and about with his mates. Blown-up reproductions of Blue Note record covers hung as a backdrop: Big John Patton, John Coltrane; trumpeter Lee Morgan in his three-buttoned Italian jacket, neat shirt and knit tie; Dexter Gordon, leaning back from the curve of his saxophone and laughing on *A Swingin' Affair*. Inside Resnick's head a Hammond organ surged and Jimmy Smith set out on 'Groovin' at Small's', a blues solo Resnick had long savoured, even though the album itself had disappeared from his shelves without trace or

45

reason years before, the way favourite albums were sadly wont to do.

Crossing into Broad Street, the sound played on against a counterpoint of car horns and discordant voices, underscored by the insistent rap beat that came through the open doors of other hip, expensive clothing stores; only when he stopped outside Broadway's offices and pressed the buzzer did the music disappear.

'Charlie Resnick,' he said, head bent awkwardly towards the intercom. 'Here to see Miss Hansen.'

Too late, he thought Ms would have been more appropriate, awkward to pronounce as he always found it.

The door to Mollie's office was open, but Resnick hesitated long enough to catch her eye before walking in.

The scarlet had been replaced by a plaid shirt which almost matched the one on k. d. lang in the *Even Cowgirls Get the Blues* poster that was tacked up behind Mollie's desk. The desk itself held neatly labelled files, a stack of bright red plastic trays close to overflowing, several movie books, a battered A–Z map of the city, three purple mugs, each holding a residue of coffee and, at the centre, a desk-size Filofax with annotations in three colours.

'You found it all right, then?' Mollie said brightly, gesturing for him to sit down.

Resnick moved two telephone directories and eased himself down into the chair.

'Coffee? I can send out for cappuccino. You know the new deli at the end of the street?'

'If it's no trouble.'

Mollie called past him towards the open door. 'Larry, I don't suppose you've got a minute . . .'

He had.

Mollie drew a sheet of paper from one of the files and slid it towards Resnick. Her desk, he thought, lively and organised as it was, lacked the merest trace of anything purely personal – a photograph, a fading birthday card, a Post-it note reminding her to buy more flour, a pint of milk. He wondered where she kept her life and what it was like – or if this were all there was.

'This is Cathy Jordan's itinerary,' Mollie was saying. 'As you can see, we're trying to make as much use of her as we can. Some of these things . . .' leaning forward, she pointed with her finger, '. . . are arranged in tandem with her publisher. And here, and you see, here, she's taking a couple of days out. Stratford, I think, and Scotland. Or maybe it's the Lakes.'

Resnick ran his eyes up and down the page – press conference, Radio Nottingham, Radio Trent, Central TV, BBC Radio Four, several book signings, a reading, two panel discussions and her attendance was requested at a civic reception. Also there were the name and address of the hotel where Cathy Jordan would be staying, complete with telephone, fax and room numbers. He would study it all in detail later.

'Covering all of these isn't going to be easy.'

'Until we've talked to Cathy Jordan, we just don't know.' Only slightly mocking, she treated him to her professional smile. 'One thing we have to remember, she's not just our guest, she's a guest of the city as well.'

'And our responsibility.'

Mollie was still smiling. Resnick folded the list and slid it into his inside pocket.

Larry turned out to be a ruddy-faced youth of nineteen or twenty, ponytail dangling down beneath the reversed peak of his deep red Washington Redskins cap. The coffee, in white polystyrene cups, was strong and still hot. Mollie took a spoon from one of the used mugs and lifted chocolatey froth towards her mouth with such expectation that, for a moment, Resnick saw more than an efficient young woman whose life was strictly colour-coded.

'The letters,' Mollie said, 'what did you think? I mean, ought we to be taking them seriously or not?'

Resnick tasted a little more of his coffee. 'To a point, I don't see we have any choice. After all, Louella Trabert, Anita Mulholland – they may just be characters in books, but that doesn't mean the threats aren't real.'

Mollie smiled, meaning it this time. 'You've got a good memory for names.'

Resnick knew that it was true. Names and faces. There were others he could have added. Victims. Fact and not fiction. It went with the job, like so much else: a blessing and a curse.

'You don't like her, do you?'

'Who?' Mollie sitting back a little, on the defensive.

'Cathy Jordan.'

'I don't know her.'

'You know her books.'

'That's not the same thing.'

Resnick shrugged. 'Isn't it? I should have thought they must come close.'

Mollie was fidgeting with her spoon. 'Anyway, what I think's neither here nor there.' She leaned forward again, the beginnings of a gleam across the grey of her eyes. 'Unless you think I'm the one who wrote the letters.'

'Are you?'

Mollie flipped a page in her Filofax. 'If the train's on time, I could ask her to meet you at the hotel. There should be time before the opening reception. Say, a quarter past six?'

Resnick set down his cup. 'All right. Always assuming nothing crops up more urgent.'

'Good.'

He got to his feet.

'Here,' Mollie said, handing him a glossy black brochure with the *Shots in the Dark* logo heavily embossed on its cover. 'This is the press kit. There's a programme inside. And a complimentary ticket. It is a crime festival, after all. I should have thought you'd find quite a lot of interest. Especially if you like the cinema.'

For all his good memory, Resnick was having trouble remembering anything he'd seen since *The Magnificent Seven*. He took the brochure and nodded his thanks.

'I don't suppose you've had a chance to look at that book yet?' Mollie asked when he was at the door.

'No, afraid not.'

As he walked out along the narrow entryway and on to the street, Resnick noticed a freshening of the wind and when, back at the corner of Fletcher Gate, he tilted his head upwards, he felt the first drops of a summer shower bright upon his face.

Eleven

It wasn't as though Cathy Jordan had never been to England before. First, as a visiting student, on exchange from her state college in Kansas City, Kansas, she had been catapulted headlong into the heyday of British hippydom. Carnaby Street and the Beatles and the Stones and her first toke, four girls passing it between them, cramped inside one of the cubicles in the ladies' room at the Roundhouse. Could it really have been the Crazy World of Arthur Brown out on stage, singing 'Fire'? Or maybe that was later, underground at UFO? She couldn't remember now. The way her world had spun three hundred and sixty degrees beneath her, it was a wonder she remembered anything at all. Her family ringing nightly, after watching television newscasts of the French students setting fire to the barricades outside the Sorbonne; youngsters with long hair battling with police outside the US embassy in Grosvenor Square. 'Are you okay? My God, Catherine, are you sure you're okay? What is going on over there? The whole world seems suddenly to have gone mad.' One of her dad's Eddie Fisher albums playing steadfastly away in the background – 'Oh! My Papa!', 'Wish You Were Here.'

Her second visit had been made almost ten years later, when her first husband had been stationed at a US air force base in Lincolnshire and she had opted to join him for six months. In a number of ways, it had not proved such a good idea. From time to time, women old enough to be not

just her mother but her grandmother had chained themselves to the base's perimeter fence in protest at the
American presence. Sometimes when she was shopping in
the nearest town, angelic-faced young men wearing CND
badges or brandishing copies of *Socialist Worker* would
spit at her in the street.

Whatever else, her abiding impression of England was
not of cobbled streets, spied through the swirl of a quaint
Dickensian pea-souper; nor of some fading thatched roof
idyll over which the sun barely set and where the squire
and village bobby reigned supreme. England, for Cathy
Jordan, represented unrest and disruption, change – not
only for the country, but for herself.

Yet looking out now through the smirched window of
the Intercity train as it cleaved through the flat softness of
the Midlands landscape, she saw only field on field
washed by a perpetual grey drizzle – cattle standing
morose at hedgerows, a single tractor turning ever-widen-
ing circles to no purpose, knots of ugly houses huddled at
road ends – nothing to stir her heart or energise her mind.

Three days ago it had been Holland, before that
Denmark and Sweden, Germany: just another damn book
tour, that's what it was. A tour she had begun alone and
was ending with her second husband, Frank Carlucci,
asleep on the seat alongside her.

Frank, who had got bored minding his own business
back in the States and had flown out to mind hers. Except
that he had forgotten what it had become like for the pair
of them, on the road together – the sterile proximity of
hotel rooms and polite, translated conversation. More than
three days and Frank was floundering awkwardly in
Cathy's wake, bored, and Cathy, unable to stop herself,
was sniping at him without let-up or mercy.

This was already the sixth day.

The brittle plastic glass which held her Scotch now had
no more than a quarter-inch of once-iced water slopping

51

about at the bottom, and Cathy wondered if she had the energy to walk back through the train to the buffet car and order another.

'Do you think she'll be here on time?'

Mollie Hansen glanced up from her *Independent*. 'I don't see why not, do you?' There they were, twice on the Listings page, bare details under Events Around the Country and a boxed Daily Ticket offer – two pairs of seats for the opening night – complete with picture. Good old *Independent*! Saturday they'd promised a feature-length piece on the Curtis Woolfe retrospective, which would fit nicely with the Cathy Jordan profile they were publishing on Sunday. Coverage in the *Observer*, the *Telegraph* and *The Times*, all they needed now was the *Mail* for a pretty clean sweep.

As Tyrell watched the overhead screen, the arrival time disappeared. 'You see. Trouble.'

Moments later, it flashed back up: 5.18.

'Why are they never on time?'

'David,' Mollie shook her head. 'A minute late, I think we can live with that. Don't you?'

The woman who walked along the platform towards them was a good few inches above average in height, even allowing for the cowboy heels on the tan boots she wore below her jeans. Red hair, straight save for a slight curl at the ends, hung shoulder-length. She had taken the time to refresh her lipstick and the greenish shadow above what, even at a distance, were disturbingly blue eyes. A tweed jacket, predominantly green and tailored at the waist, hung open over a red silk shirt. She was carrying a medium-sized carpet bag in her left hand.

Rhonda Fleming, Tyrell decided, meets Arlene Dahl: though, close to, there was more than a touch of Lauren Bacall about the mouth.

Mollie was looking, not so much at Cathy Jordan, but at the barrel-chested man with cropped grey hair walking alongside her. He was carrying large, matching suitcases in both hands, a third tucked beneath one arm. Shorter than Cathy, what impressed immediately about him was his size. The bags he was carrying could have been toys.

For a moment, Mollie's face settled into a scowl: she didn't like surprises. Nevertheless, she was the first to step forward and hold out her hand. 'Cathy Jordan? Welcome to *Shots in the Dark*. I'm Mollie Hansen. We've spoken on the phone. And this is David Tyrell, he's the Festival Director.'

'Hi!' said Cathy. 'Hello.' Shaking hands. 'This is my husband, Frank.'

'Frank Carlucci. Good to know you.' His voice was pitched low and edged with something that might have been tiredness, but could have been drink.

Tensing instinctively, Mollie was surprised to find his grip so soft, not weak, almost delicate. 'We didn't know you'd be coming.'

Carlucci shrugged strong shoulders. 'Last-minute thing. Joined up with Cathy in Copenhagen. Nice little town. You know it at all?'

Mollie shook her head and they began walking towards the end of the platform, Carlucci falling in step beside her, while, immediately behind them, Tyrell was talking to Cathy Jordan.

'This hotel where we were just staying,' Frank Carlucci was saying, 'the Plaza. Oak panelling you'd kill for, leather books all round the bar, huh! They got this pillar in the lobby, names of all the celebrities ever stayed there engraved in gold. Well, maybe it was brass. But everyone, you know. Liza Minnelli, Paul McCartney, Jack fucking Nicholson. Michael Jackson. Well, maybe they'll be taking that one down. But Cathy, next time we go back, hers'll be up there along of the rest. Alongside of Jack Nicholson, ain't that something?'

Mollie made a sound that was strictly non-committal; Nicholson had been all right in *Chinatown*, but after that what was he? An overpaid actor with a paunch and falling hair.

Climbing the steps from the platform, Carlucci was still talking and Mollie realised he was the kind of man whose idea of a conversation was one-sided – he talked and you listened. She moved ahead on to Cathy Jordan's free side, Tyrell on the other telling her how excited he was she could be there, how much he liked her work.

Glancing across, Mollie put Cathy's age as late forties, certainly not a day under forty-five. Her bio sheet was surprisingly coy when it came to details like age. But whatever she was, Mollie thought, she was looking good.

Outside, on the station forecourt, waiting for a taxi, Tyrell assured Cathy that the civic reception would be no big deal, nothing exhausting. So far, neither he nor Mollie had said anything to her about the hand-delivered letter or its threat.

> *You do realise I am serious? Poor little*
> *Anita Mulholland, Cathy, remember what*
> *happened to her.*

Twelve

'Graham, you didn't get anywhere with that book, I suppose?'

Millington looked across the CID room hopefully, unable to pick out most of what Resnick had said. Two desks away, the world's noisiest printer was chuntering its way through a listing of the last six months' unsolved burglaries, broken down by the Local Intelligence Officer into location, time and MO.

Lynn set down the receiver, pushed herself up from her desk and stretched her shoulders and back. The last of her trawl around the city's hotels and she was no nearer to finding the identity of the mystery man who'd done a runner from the hospital. As one of the clerks had pointed out, with so many accounts prepaid by employers' credit cards, all some clients had to do was turn in their keys and wave goodbye.

'Sorry,' Millington said, having made his way to where Resnick was standing. 'Couldn't hear a bloody word.'

'That woman's book, the one I gave you . . .'

'How about it?'

'Thought perhaps you could give me some idea what it's about. Got to see her later.'

'Ah. Can't say I really got that far. All right, though. Not rubbish, you know what I mean. One thing pretty clear – she's not Agatha Christie, you'd have to say that.'

Resnick guessed that to be a compliment, but with Millington you could never be sure. This was, after all, the person who swore Petula Clark did a better version of

'Lover Man' than Billie Holiday. 'Not got it with you, I suppose, Graham?'

'Have, as a matter of fact. Reckoned I might give it twenty minutes in the canteen, but, of course, it never happened.'

'Best let's have it back, then. Take a look on the way down.'

'Suit yourself.' Millington shrugged and turned away to fetch him the book.

Minutes later, Resnick was on his way down the stairs, a copy of *Dead Weight* in his hand.

Cathy Jordan poured herself another shot from the one of the pair of kingsize bottles of J & B Rare they had bought on the plane. She and Frank buying silence with the usual share of booze in the usual bland hotel room, though here the walls were closer together than usual. Which meant that they were too. In a way.

Right now they were getting ready for the reception. Frank was wandering about morosely in a pair of striped boxers and a white shirt, the creases from where it had lain folded in the case pulled flat across the muscles of his arms and back; Cathy was wearing a couple of towels and a cream half slip, which she hated, but the problem with the dress she had chosen was the minute you stood in front of the light, it was the next thing to being featured in an X-ray.

For once it was Frank who broke the unspoken truce. 'So what d'you think?' he said. 'You worried or what?'

'About the reception?'

'Reception, hell. The letter.'

Examining a pair of tights, Cathy shook her head. 'Sticks and stones,' she said.

'That's it, sticks and stones?'

One leg in, one leg out, Cathy looked across at him. 'That's it.'

Frank breathed out noisily and shook his head. 'You're not scared? Spooked? Not even one little piece?'

Turning away, Cathy shook her head. Of course, she was scared. Not all the time, not even often, but, sure, step into a lift and there's a guy standing there, looking over at you in a certain way – walk out into the street to catch some air and the window of a slowing car slides down – who wouldn't be scared. The world was full of them, God knows, it wasn't just the pages of her books. Sociopaths. Psychopaths. Whoever was writing those letters wasn't *Dear Abbey*.

But admitting it to Frank, that was something else. The way it had become between them, everything was a statement of strength, not of weakness, neediness. It wasn't in her nature to be the one to back off.

'It's why you're here, isn't it?' Cathy said. 'Reason you changed your mind, flew over. Look out for me. Protect me.' She made *protect* sound like a dirty word.

Frank was having trouble with the knot of his tie. 'And if it is?'

'You needn't have bothered. They've got professionals for that.'

Resnick arrived at the hotel later than he'd intended and Mollie Hansen was already waiting on one of the leather settees in the foyer, her duty to escort Cathy Jordan and her husband to the reception. David Tyrell had claimed the task of collecting Curtis Woolfe, who had flown in earlier in the day from Switzerland, which was where he now lived. The third major guest, the octogenarian British crime novelist, Dorothy Birdwell, was being driven directly to the reception by her assistant.

Mollie, Resnick thought, was looking decidedly smart, rising to greet him in a loose-fitting pearl trouser suit which might have been silk. Something held him back from making the compliment out loud, a sense that, to Mollie, that kind of remark would be less than acceptable.

'Nice tie,' Mollie said, with a little nod. 'Interesting design. Paul Smith?'

'Spaghetti vongole.'

To his surprise, Mollie laughed and Resnick grinned back. 'What happened,' he asked, 'when you showed her the letter?'

'Oh, for a minute or two, I thought she was going to throw a wobbly, but then she just laughed and told me for all it was worth, I might as well tear it up. That was when I told her about you.'

Before Resnick could reply, the lift doors opened and Cathy Jordan appeared in an ankle-length, off-white dress from beneath the hem of which poked the toes of her boots.

Mollie moved quickly to meet her.

'Is there time,' Cathy Jordan asked, after Resnick had been introduced, 'for the inspector and me to have a chat?'

'Sure,' Mollie said. 'I think so.'

'Great!' Cathy said, appropriating Resnick's arm. 'Why don't we go to the bar?'

Perched on a stool, Cathy Jordan asked Resnick to recommend a single malt and, although it wasn't really his drink, after a quick glance along the bar he came up with Highland Park.

'Two large ones,' Cathy said. And to Resnick, 'Ice?'

He shook his head.

'One as it comes,' she said to the barman, 'one with lots of ice. That's L-O-T-S.' Turning towards Resnick, she made a face. 'What is it with this country? Is ice still rationed?'

He smiled. 'We're a moderate people. Maybe we don't like too much of anything.'

'That include crime?'

'Not necessarily.'

'Violent crime?'

'Well, we don't have guns on the streets . . .' He corrected himself. 'At least, not as many as you.'

'But you're getting there.'

'Maybe.' He said it with regret. He knew it wasn't only the more publicised areas of the country – Brixton, Moss Side – where weapons were increasingly easy to obtain, increasingly likely to be used. There were estates there in the city where firearms were heard being discharged far more frequently than gunshot wounds were ever reported. He didn't imagine their aim was always less than true.

Cathy clinked her glass against his. 'Cheers.'

'Cheers,' Resnick said. And then, 'Miss Jordan, about this latest letter . . .'

'Cathy,' she said. 'For God's sake, call me Cathy. And as for the letter, it's a crock, just like all the rest. Some scuzzbag shut off in a sweaty room, only way he knows of getting off, you know what I mean?'

Resnick throught that he might. 'Then you've no worries about security?' he said, after tasting a little of the malt.

Cathy rattled the ice cubes around a little inside her glass. 'I'm in a strange country, right. It wouldn't hurt to have someone watching my back.'

'All right. Mollie's given me a copy of your schedule. Maybe we could go over it and see which events you're most concerned about?'

'Sure,' said Cathy, but then became aware of Mollie Hansen hovering with intent and drained her glass in a double swallow. 'Gotta go. Look, couldn't we meet tomorrow? Go through things like you said?'

Resnick got to his feet. 'Of course.'

'Good. We Americans are big on breakfast meetings, you know.'

'Here?'

'Half eight, how's that sound?'

'Fine.'

'Good.' And Mollie steered Cathy Jordan away towards their waiting car, while Resnick sat back on the stool and nursed his way down the rest of his Highland Park.

Thirteen

Art Tatum and Ben Webster: they did it for him every time. Resnick lowered the stylus with care and watched as it slid into the groove; listened, standing there, as Tatum played his practised, ornate way through the first chorus of the tune, tightening the rhythm at the beginning of the middle eight, before stepping aside with a simple little single-note figure, falling away beneath the glorious saxophone smear of Webster's arrival. Resnick turned up the volume and wandered through into the kitchen: coffee was pumping softly inside the silver pot on the stove. He set a match to the gas on the grill, sliced dark rye bread and put it to toast. Cream cheese, not too much pickled cucumber, smoked salmon. While none of the other cats were looking, he sneaked Bud a small piece of the salmon. Some days he liked to drink his coffee, rich and dark, from one of a pair of white china mugs, and this was one of those.

Settled in his favourite chair in the living room, coffee and sandwich close at hand, album turned over and turned back down, Resnick lifted Cathy Jordan's book from the small table beneath the lamp and began to read:

> *If anyone had told me, Annie Jones, you'll end up spending your seventh wedding anniversary alone in the front seat of a rented Chevrolet, outside of Jake's at the Lake in Tahoe City, I'd have told them to go jump right in it. The lake, that is. But then if that same anyone had told me, the day I appeared,*

fresh out of law school, ready to start work at the offices of Reigler and Reigler, bright and full of promise in my newly acquired dove-grey two-piece with a charcoal stripe, skirt a businesslike three inches below the knee, that I would swap what was clearly destined to be a famous legal career for that of a lowly private eye, I would gleefully have signed committal forms, assigning them to the nearest asylum, and tossed away the key.

'You know, Annie,' my mother had said, the first time I plucked up courage to explain, 'you can't really be a private eye, they only have them in the movies. And books. And besides, they're always men.'

My mom, God bless her, always seemed to have a vested interest in remaining firmly behind the times.

'Sure, Mom,' I said, 'you're right.' And inched back the business card I had proudly given her, stuffing it back down into my wallet. There'd be another time.

And so there had. My first major cheque safely paid into the bank and cleared, two other clients waiting in the wings, I had invited my long-suffering mother out for cocktails and dinner at her favourite Kansas City restaurant.

I didn't mention that, did I? About my mother being from Kansas City. Well, that's an important part of it; it explains a great deal.

But back to cocktails. Emboldened by the second Manhattan, I had showed my mother my bank balance and launched into the spiel. Adventure, independence, the chance to be my

*own boss, run my own life – 'Mom, I'm a big
girl now. This is what I want to do. You see,
it'll work out fine.'*

*Which so far, pretty much, had been true.
During my time practising law I had made a
lot of useful contacts, in that profession as well
as the police. I was in pretty thick with a few
good working journalists, too – the kind that
still spend more time on the street than in the
office staring at their computer screen.*

*And Mom, I like to think, surprised herself
with a smile of pride when some new-found
friend asked over coffee, 'Marjorie, just what
is it that your daughter does out there in
California?' And my mom, smiling, saying,
'Oh, she's just a private eye.'*

*There were things about my life, though,
that I didn't tell her. A little knowledge may, in
some circumstances, be a dangerous thing, but
in my mother's case it's positively beneficial. I
didn't tell, for instance, about the six weeks I
spent in hospital after being stupid enough to
get trapped up an alley with three guys who
made Mike Tyson look like Mickey Mouse.
Nor the occasion I stepped in front of a light
and two .38 slugs tore past me so close I swear
I could feel the wind of their slipstream. And
the bodies. I didn't tell her about the bodies.
The one I had found tied upside down, offering
freebies to half a hundred flies; the little girl I
had discovered buried in a ditch. I hadn't told
her about any of these things on account there
was no need to upset her without cause –
which was why I had never told her about
Diane.*

My mom, you see, is strictly old school. The

63

reason she can come to terms with what I do for a job is because, when it comes right down to it, the job I do is not that important. At best it's a stage, a phase, it's what I do to fill in time before I finally settle down and get on with what the Good Lord set me on this earth for, get married, of course, and have children.

Somewhere, she has a picture of me, taken at a cousin's wedding when I was but thirteen. The same age as that poor child who ended her days in a shallow grave. There I am, on the left of the photo, wearing my pretty pink bridesmaid's dress and smiling through the jungle gym of my new braces as I cling on to the bride's bouquet which I have just caught.

When Miller and I were divorced, she took it pretty well. 'Everyone,' she said, 'is allowed one false start.' Since when, despite the fact that in child-rearing terms, the years are no longer exactly on my side, she has continued, optimistically, to wait.

As, I suppose, had I. Oh, you know, a dinner date here, a concert ticket there, but pretty much I'd laid low, let my work carry the load, kept my powder dry while making sure my underwear was always clean just in case.

Diane had been a columnist for the Chronicle when I met her, women's issues mostly, date rape, who has the key to the executive wash room, the right to choose, you know the kind of thing. Her byline and a photograph (not flattering) and five bucks a word. Someone had persuaded her, with all the women PIs appearing on the book-racks, she should do a piece on the real thing.

Diane rang me and after a couple of false

starts we finally got to meet in a bar out by the ocean in Santa Cruz. We hadn't shaken hands before my stomach was bungee jumping and . . . well, you're pretty sophisticated or you wouldn't have stuck with it this far, so you can guess the rest. That was almost a year ago – almost, hell! – it was eleven months, five days and around seven hours, and still, first thing I do once I've made sure my charge is seated safely at her table, is phone Diane's number just to hear her voice on the answer machine.

If that kind of thing happens in Kansas City – and I'm sure it does, both in Kansas City, Kansas and Kansas City, MO – then I'm sure my mother doesn't know about it. For now, for at least as long as Diane and I go on maintaining separate apartments, I intend to see it stays that way.

Right now I check my watch against the clock on the dash and they both tell me it's fifteen minutes shy of ten o'clock. The coffee the woman at the reservations desk organised for me is long reduced to a residue of cold grounds and, even in the expanse of my extravagant rental, my legs are beginning to cramp up and feel in need of a stretch.

At the desk the woman remembers me and says again, if I'd care to take a seat at the bar . . . But I assure her I'm fine and while she sends a waiter nimbly down the carpeted stairs in search of a fresh cup of coffee, I move close enough to the stained wood balustrade to see the young woman whose safety I am charged with protecting. She's sitting at a table, center room, pretty blonde head inclined towards the pretty young man who is *her dinner date, a poet from Seattle and a pretty serious one. A first collection already published by Breitenbush Books of Portland (he happened to have a copy with him and was kind enough to show me) and another from Carnegie Mellon on the way. They seemed to have reached the dessert stage, so we could be on the road by ten thirty.*

'They make a lovely couple, don't they?' The receptionist has come to stand next to me and I nod in agreement. 'Yes, they do.'

'Do you work for Mr Reigler?' she asks.

'Sort of,' I say.

By then the waiter has returned with my coffee so I thank them both and carry it outside, back into the parking lot. The air is warm enough for me to be only wearing a light sweater and even though we're close to the lake, it isn't too buggy. I stroll for a while between the cars, remembering the morning Reigler asked me to his office. It was only the second or third time I'd seen him since resigning from his law firm; the first time since his stroke. It had left him with some paralysis down the right side, not so bad that he couldn't stand, with help, and, although it was necessary to concentrate, he could speak and make himself understood. Once out of hospital and through his period of convalescence, he had insisted on coming to the office every day. Much of the time, I guessed, he just sat there and they ran things past him, playing up to the formality that all decisions were his.

What Reigler had wanted to talk to me about was a series of threatening calls, someone, anonymous, who felt their life had been ruined by some case or other Reigler's firm had handled.

'Now it ain't worth doing anything to you, you sorry bastard,' the last one had said, 'but you best watch out for your family, 'cause they can get hurt and there isn't a damn thing you can do to stop it.'

Aside from notifying the police, one thing Reigler did was to hire me. His daughter April was, I suspected, the one true love of his life. She was a beauty, of a fragile kind; she was bright, dutiful enough, but stubborn. She was prepared to humor her father by agreeing I could drive her places, keep an eye out, but made it clear this wasn't going to be like the secret service and the President. 'Besides,' she reminded her father, a little, I thought, unkindly, 'what could they do when Kennedy was shot? Reagan?'

Reluctantly, April agreed that I could go along on her trip to Tahoe, as long as I didn't get too close. This evening she has made it clear that any ideas I might have of sitting alongside herself and her poet while they share beautiful thoughts and a lobster and mango salad are not going to pan out. And in all honesty the only danger I suspect she might be a prey to in the midst of that crowded and fashionable restaurant rests in the depths of the poet's brown eyes.

Another turn of the parking lot and I'm back at the Chevy and there they are, April and her own Byron or Keats, stepping through the restaurant door. I set my empty cup down on the roof of the car and head towards them.

Seeing me, April's face breaks into a genuine smile and I am touched. She is a lovely girl.

'How was dinner?' I ask.

'Wonderful!' she enthuses. 'Wasn't it, Perry?' And she turns to where he has stopped, a pace behind as if suddenly uncertain of the etiquette of dating young women who have personal bodyguards. Which is when the shot rings out and April screams as she is catapulted into my arms and I know what is clinging to my face and hair, most of it, is blood, and at that precise moment I don't know if it is April's blood or mine and, in all honesty, right then and there, I don't care.

Aside from one of the cats purring somewhere out of sight, it was quiet. The record had long finished. Half the sandwich lay uneaten on its plate. Resnick sat where he was for several minutes more before closing the book, placing it on the arm of the chair, getting up and leaving the room.

Fourteen

'I read your book. *Dead Weight*.'

'You did? What did you think?'

'Well, maybe I didn't read all of it. Not yet. I'm sure I will.'

Cathy Jordan was looking at Resnick with amusement, her head tilted a little to one side, waiting for the truth. They were having breakfast at her hotel, sharing the decanted orange juice – produce of several countries – the pineapple chunks and the already solidifying scrambled eggs with a scattering of executives and Japanese tourists. The majority of visitors to the festival were saving their pennies elsewhere.

'The first few chapters,' Resnick said. 'One last night, the others earlier this morning.'

'I didn't think earlier than this existed.'

Resnick shrugged. 'The older I get . . .'

'I know, the less sleep you need. With Frank it's the opposite. I swear that man'd sleep twenty hours of any twenty-four if you'd just let him.'

'And Frank is . . .'

'My husband. But stop evading the issue – what did you think of the book?'

'I liked it.'

'You did.'

'Yes. You sound surprised.'

She smiled with her eyes. 'No, but I figured you might be.'

Resnick cut his sausage, skewered a section with his

69

fork and dabbed it in the mustard at the side of his plate. He knew she wasn't about to let him off the hook.

'It's direct, isn't it?' he said after a little chewing. 'Like you – like you talking.'

Cathy was pointing at him with her knife. 'Not a good mistake to make. Annie isn't me. A long way from it.'

'All right, then. Somebody who sounds like you.'

'Who'll talk with her mouth full over the breakfast table and threaten her guest with sharp implements?'

'Exactly.'

She laughed: okay.

'I suppose,' Resnick said a few moments later, 'I was expecting something more – I don't know – wordy. More description, is that what I mean?'

'Probably. Three quarters of a page detailing the stained glass window over the door, a couple more pages describing what our suspects are wearing, from the make of their brogues to the pattern on their pocket handkerchiefs, that kind of thing?'

'I suppose so.'

'Potential clues.'

'Yes.'

'Well, if that's the kind of writer you want . . .' Cathy was pointing her knife towards an elderly woman, slightly stooped, grey hair pulled back into a bun, waiting while a younger man in a navy blue blazer pulled out her chair. 'Dorothy Birdwell,' Cathy said, 'spinster of this parish.'

'She's a writer?' Resnick asked.

Cathy arched an eyebrow. 'Rumour has it.'

The waitress, a student on a six-month visit from Lisbon to learn English, offered them more coffee; Cathy Jordan spread a hand over the top of her cup, while Resnick nodded and smiled thanks.

'Toast,' Cathy said to the waitress, 'we could use more toast.' And then, to Resnick, 'One literary novel when she was at Cambridge or Oxford or wherever it was. Love between the wars; unrequited, of course. After that, nothing for a decade. More. Up to her scrawny armpits in academia. Then, out of nowhere, comes *A Case of Violets* and everyone's frothing at the mouth about the new Allingham, the new Marsh, the new Dame Agatha. Right from then till practically – what? – ten years ago, everything she wrote was guaranteed, gilt-edged bestseller.'

Resnick watched as the man in the blazer and light grey trousers carefully eased Dorothy Birdwell's chair into the table, bending low to enquire if she were all right before taking his own seat.

'Who's that?' Resnick asked.

Cathy lowered her voice, but not by very much. 'Marius Gooding. Her nephew. Or so she says. Of course, we like to think he's something more.' Cathy laughed, quietly malicious. 'Can't you see them, every night after she's taken her teeth out, getting at it like monkeys, swinging off the chandeliers?'

Resnick could not. Marius seemed fastidious, slightly effete, his moustache daintily trimmed. Resnick watched as he leaned forward to tip a quarter-inch of milk into Dorothy Birdwell's cup, before pouring her tea. Marius was possibly forty, Resnick thought, though he contrived to look younger – the kind of man you expected to find hovering around the edges of Royal Ascot, the Henley Regatta, though since Resnick had never been to either, that was a mixture of prejudice and conjecture.

'Dorothy Birdwell,' he said. 'What did puncture her career ten years ago?'

Cathy Jordan laughed. 'We did. Women. Marcia Muller, Paretsky, Grafton, Patsy Cornwell. Linda Barnes. Julie Smith. A whole bunch of others. Took old Dottie's space on the book-racks and wouldn't give it back.'

'Just because you're women?'

'Some say. Pretty much.'

'Dorothy Birdwell's a woman.'

'Another rumour. Nothing proven.'

Resnick smiled but continued. 'These authors you mentioned, they're all American? Is that the reason?'

'Maybe it used to be. Part of it, anyway. But not any more. Liza Cody, Val McDermid, Sarah Dunant – you've got people of your own, doing pretty good.'

'So what is the reason?' Resnick asked. 'Why the big change?'

Cathy pressed butter onto her toast and shattered it into a dozen brittle pieces. 'Okay. Fact: most crime readers are women. Fact: we give them protagonists they can identify with. Heroines. Never mind old biddies purling two and two together or chief inspectors with aristocratic leanings and patched tweed jackets, this is the age of the female PI. Smart, sassy, full of spunk, as likely to lay you out as get laid. On her terms. And enjoy it.'

'So she's out of date? Birdwell?'

'She was always out of date; that was the attraction. The thing is, now she's out of fashion. Which doesn't mean she doesn't still have her readers, just less of them and they're getting older all the time.' Cathy leaned closer. 'Rumour has it, her agent's on the hunt for a new publisher; after twenty years with one house. Something's hurting.'

Resnick set down his coffee and glanced round again at Dorothy Birdwell. 'You don't think, if she's got reasons to be jealous . . . ?'

'Dorothy? Behind those letters? I'd like to think she had it in her. But, no, not a chance. Malicious looks at thirty paces, that's her mark.' Cathy reached out and lifted up Resnick's tie, the end of which had been mopping up what remained of the mustard.

Resnick nodded and sat back, drawing the copy of Cathy's schedule from his pocket. 'This afternoon, you're signing books at Waterstone's; early this evening, introducing a film at Broadway . . .'

'*Black Widow*, d'you know it? No? Great little movie. Sexy. Debra Winger doing mouth to mouth with Theresa Russell, then busting her for murder.'

'After that?'

'There was something about a bunch of us going out to dinner. This director they've dug up. They're screening one of his films after mine. You should come. Some place called Sundays? David promised the food was pretty good.'

'Sonny's,' Resnick said. 'And, yes, it is.'

'Then you'll be along?'

'Maybe. I can't promise.'

'The policeman's lot . . .'

'Something like that.'

'Suit yourself.'

'How about earlier?' Resnick asked. 'The signing. Would you feel happier if I had someone there? Just keeping an eye?'

Cathy smiled. 'The author who got stabbed with a poisoned dagger behind the mystery shelves? Sounds too much like something out of a Dorothy Birdwell to me.'

'Okay. As long as you're sure.' Resnick checked his watch, then pushed back his chair and reached for his wallet.

'Don't bother,' Cathy said. 'It's covered.'

'No, I don't think I can . . .'

She covered his hand with hers. 'You're my guest. It's charged to the room. Which gets charged to the festival. Relax. It's not a crime. Not a bribe. Honest. Besides, young Mollie would be thrilled at the idea of buying you breakfast.'

'I doubt it.'

Cathy's half-snort, half-laugh was loud enough to turn heads.

'What?' Resnick said.

'You may be good at your job – I hope to hell you are – but you sure know shit about women!'

Flushing, Resnick tried for a smile.

'I'm sorry,' Cathy said, taking his hand again and giving it a squeeze. 'I didn't mean to be insulting.'

'That's okay.'

'Or just another brash American.'

'You're not.'

She held his gaze before replying. She liked the way the skin crinkled around his eyes when he smiled. 'Good. I'll look forward to seeing you tonight.'

'If I can,' Resnick said. 'I'll try.'

He was conscious of Marius Gooding watching him all the way to the dining room door – only one reason he didn't stop and look back at Cathy before passing through. He would check the roster, have a word with Skelton, see if they couldn't send somebody down to the bookshop in their lunch hour just the same. As for later, the invitation to the restaurant, he didn't know, though the last time he'd been to Sonny's, he remembered, on the occasion of his friend Marian Witczak's fortieth birthday, he'd had the rack of lamb and it had been very tasty, very sweet.

Fifteen

'Listen,' Divine was saying into the telephone. Not saying, shouting. 'No, listen. Listen. Listen up a minute. Bloody listen!'

Most of the CID room did exactly that; stopped whatever they were doing to stare at Mark Divine, standing beside his desk, brown hair pushed back from his forehead, blue shirt, dark trousers, tie twisted round, anger reddening his cheeks in ragged circles, telephone tight in his hand.

'For once in your life, just listen.'

Whoever was at the other end of the line chose to ignore the advice. Connection broken, Divine stared at the receiver in frustration before slamming it back down. 'Stupid tossing woman!'

'Nice,' Lynn Kellogg remarked. 'No wonder you're so successful at pulling. All that suave sophistication.'

Divine mouthed an everyday obscenity and kicked his chair back against the wall, stuffed both hands deep into his pockets and slouched out.

'Must be,' Lynn said, enjoying a little tit-for-tat retribution, 'his time of the month.'

'Time you weren't here, isn't it?' Millington said from the far end of the room. 'One of your snouts, give you a lead on those break-ins, didn't he?'

Lynn lifted notebook and ball-point from her desk and found space for them inside her shoulder bag. She was almost at the door when Resnick walked in, breathing a little heavily after hurrying up the hill from Cathy

Jordan's hotel, patches of mustard yellowing nicely on his tie.

'Off far?'

Lynn shook her head. 'Ilkeston Road.'

'How long d'you reckon?'

'An hour. Hour and a half.'

'Think you could get yourself into the city centre, middle of the day? Waterstone's, corner of Bottle Lane . . .'

'And Bridlesmith Gate. Yes, I know it. Why?'

'This American author who's over. Jordan, Cathy Jordan.'

'*Sleeping Fools Lie.*'

'Sorry?'

'One of her books. I read it last year.'

Resnick was quietly impressed. Aside from anything else, where did she get the time? 'There've been a few threatening letters. Offering her harm. Doesn't seem to take them too seriously herself and I'm not sure how far we should, but it might be no bad idea, to have someone around. She's doing some kind of book signing, one o'clock. Don't want to stick a uniform in there, scare people off.'

'Okay, fine. Be interesting to meet her, I should think.'

'Pop back in on your way down, I'll fill you in.'

Lynn nodded and was on her way.

Resnick beckoned Millington closer. 'Young Divine stormed past me and up the stairs as if you'd given him a good earful. Blotted his copybook again, has he?'

Millington shook his head. 'Mark? No, nothing I've said. Just off up the canteen, most like, have a good sulk.'

'What about?'

Millington's best malicious smile slid out from under his moustache like a ferret on the loose. 'Course of true love, never did run smooth.'

*

76

Kevin Naylor took two mugs of tea over from the counter, two sugars in Divine's, one in his own. 'Here. Drink that.' Divine continued glowering at a sausage cob, which sat encircled on his plate by a moat of brown sauce. Two tables away, three uniformed constables and a civilian clerk were arguing the merits of the present Nottinghamshire side. 'Give this lot a white ball with a bell in it, and they'd not top three figures against a blind school.'

'What's up?' Naylor asked. 'Lesley?'

Lesley Bruton was a staff nurse at Queen's Medical Centre. Divine had met her during the course of an enquiry and been immediately attracted. Nothing in itself unusual in that. Divine in the vicinity of an attractive woman was like a water diviner in overdrive. What had been unusual was that, despite her early indifference, he had stuck with it.

Months it had taken him to wear Lesley Bruton's patience down to the point where she would even talk about going out with him. Divine, week after seemingly thankless week, just chancing to be driving past the entrance to the hospital as she was coming off shift, more often than not still wearing her staff nurse's uniform beneath her outdoor coat. When finally he caught her at a weak moment and she conceded a quick drink, he had surprised her by making her laugh; surprised her more by not making a play for her when he dropped her at the house she shared with two housemen and three other nurses. Though she could see in his eyes it was what he was set on.

Since then she had put him through a series of arbitrary tests, from keeping him waiting one hour and forty-nine minutes due to an emergency admission, to holding a handful of her damp Kleenex as she sobbed her way through the sentimental bits of *Mrs Doubtfire*. Last night it had been an ordeal by association: Lesley had organised a leaving do for one of the other nurses on the ward and made it clear to Divine she wanted him along. It had all been fine until he'd lost count of his lagers and graphically propositioned one of Lesley's friends.

'Jesus!' Naylor said, hearing the story. 'Don't believe in asking for trouble, do you?'

'All I said was, one into two, how many times d'you reckon it'd go.'

'Pillock!'

Divine dipped his head and savaged the sausage cob. 'Wasn't as though I was trying to have it away behind her back.'

'Might've been better if you were.'

'Yes, happen you're right.' And then, eyes brightening: 'Got to admit, though, can't beat a threesome to get your hormones in an uproar. Remember those sisters whose caravan caught fire out at Strelley . . .'

But Naylor had other things on his mind, more compelling than his colleague's compulsive sexual shenanigans. Now that the baby was up and toddling, walking really, baby no longer, Debbie was only making noises about trying for another. As if eighteen months of post-natal depression had never happened. Perhaps blowing what little they'd saved on a trip to Florida would be worth it after all, shift her mind on to a different tack.

'I hope we're doing enough, Charlie, that's my concern. I'd not be happy coming out of this with egg all over our faces.'

Skelton held the milk carton up questioningly and Resnick merely shook his head; as it was, calling the superintendent's coffee black was asking to be summonsed by the Race Relations Board. 'If anything should happen to her, you know what I mean.'

Resnick set cup and saucer on the floor beside his chair. 'Watching brief, that's what I thought. Public appearances and the like. There's a dinner tonight, just informal, I thought I might go along.'

Skelton looked at Resnick with interest before fidgeting with the papers on his desk. 'No follow-up on that stabbing in Alfreton Road?'

Resnick shook his head. 'We've done a check of the hotels. Nothing. Bloke's likely off home, thanking his lucky stars, shooting a line to his wife about where the scar came from.'

The photograph of Skelton's wife, Resnick noticed, had still not found its way back on to his desk.

'Nothing else I should know about?' the superintendent asked. 'Advisory meeting's tomorrow.'

'Maybe just get some advice,' Resnick said. 'Like how are we supposed to increase the percentage of successful investigations when there's a ban on overtime.'

'Remember the old story, Charlie,' Skelton said, 'the one about the rabbit and the hat . . .'

Sixteen

Lynn had no trouble recognising Cathy Jordan. Red hair tied back with green ribbon, blue denim shirt, pale cord three-quarter skirt, tan boots, she stood, relaxed, alongside a table on which copies of her books had been piled high. A glass of red wine in her hand, she was chatting amiably to a pleasant-faced man in a dark suit whom Lynn took to be the Waterstone's manager. There were quite a few people already hovering in the general area of the table, glancing almost surreptitiously in the author's direction, waiting for the official business to begin.

Lynn stood by this month's best-sellers, making sure she had the layout of the shop clear in her mind: the main doors onto Bridlesmith Gate were at her back, a second entrance, from the foot of Bottle Lane, was in the corner of the travel section, several steps up to her left; around the corner at the far end, she remembered, were children's books and – what? gardening? – something like that, yes, gardening. Lynn moved through the steadily growing crowd and introduced herself.

Cathy Jordan took half a step back to look at her – Lynn with her newly short hair almost flat on her head, navy cotton jacket and dark skirt, black low-heeled shoes.

'Resnick, you work with him?'

'Inspector Resnick, yes, that's right.'

'Sent you along to hold my hand.'

'Not exactly.'

A line was beginning to form now, curving its way back between the other tables; those at the front coughing a

little nervously, wondering how it was Lynn had somehow got in before them.

'You're not armed or anything?'

Lynn shook her head. 'Should I be?'

'God, I hope not.' Cathy Jordan smiled. 'Just, if
someone's standing behind my back with a gun, I like to
know.'

'Don't worry,' Lynn said. 'I probably won't be at your
back at all.'

'Prefer to merge into the crowd, huh?'

'Something like that.'

'Good.' Still smiling. 'Good.' And, turning back
towards the manager: 'Shall we get to it?'

Derek Neighbour had made sure of getting there in plenty
of time. Parking, he knew to his cost, was always a
problem after mid-morning, so he had left his home in
Newark shortly after eight, called in briefly at the antique
shop he ran with his partner, Philip, and arrived in plenty
of time to find a space on the third floor of the Fletcher
Gate multi-storey. From there it was only a short walk
down the steps on to King John's Chambers and Waterstone's was just to the right – which was as well,
considering the weight of what he was carrying.

Derek hadn't discovered Cathy Jordan until *Shallow
Grave*, which, of course, was her fourth, the fourth Annie
Q. Jones, and, even then, he had almost never read it at all.
For at least six weeks it had lain on the nice Victorian
wash-stand below the bedroom window, six weeks when
Philip would say to him, 'Have you read that book yet?'
and he would reply, 'Well, no, not exactly. But I'm
getting around to it.'

What Derek normally liked was what the Americans,
who had to invent a category for everything, called
'Cosies'. Old-fashioned would have been another way of
putting it, but then, what was wrong with old-fashioned?

Craftsmanship, attention to detail, control. Dorothy Bird-well, now, she had long been one of Derek's favourites.

But Philip could be persuasive. 'Cathy Jordan, I do think you'd like her. She's good. The genuine article.'

Since some of Philip's bedtime reading was, well, dubious to say the least, Derek had remained noncommit-tal. Till, one day, or to be precise, two, he had been laid up in bed with flu. The Patricia Moyes he was rereading for the third time had come to its same, careful ending; Dorothy Birdwell had pottered around in the East Anglian fog to disappointingly little purpose, and there were just so many times you could reread the letters page of the *Telegraph*.

So, propped up on his pillows and with some Beechams and hot lemon close to hand, he had started *Shallow Grave*:

> *The first time I saw Anita Mulholland she was a happy twelve-year-old with braces on her teeth and a smile that would have knocked out the angels; next time I saw her was a year later, to the day, and she was dead.*

The voice, Annie's voice, had gripped him from that first sentence and hadn't let him go. The story, oh, the story was fine, perfectly fine, though in truth, there was little about it that was particularly original. But there were moments when Derek's skin had tightened about him, moments when the cold of shared fear slid along the backs of his already feverish legs and arms. And there was the disgust and shock of what had happened to that young girl. But without the voice, the sure, buttonholing quality of the voice, none of the rest would have been enough.

He finished *Shallow Grave* and, when he had recov-ered, set out to acquire the others. Philip had copies of the book that preceded it, *Sleeping Fools Lie*, and the one which came after it, *Dead Weight*. But now Derek had been well and truly bitten, he wanted to read all five Annie Q. Jones mysteries from the beginning. The second, *Uneasy Prey*, he finally found in an *Any two for 50p* box on the market, dog-eared and marmalade-stained, but, as far as he could see, intact. *Angels at Rest*, the first of the series, proved more difficult. It had been brought out in paperback in Britain by a firm that had rapidly gone into liquidation, and had been published in hardback in a small edition intended primarily for libraries. Derek had finally tracked down a copy through the *Books Wanted* section of Philip's *Guardian*.

Derek, of course, was more than a mere reader: he was a collector with a collector's mentality. Completism was his unquestioned faith. Inside the heavy cardboard box he was carrying were British editions of all five Annie Q. Jones mysteries, five American paperbacks, American first-edition hardbacks – the 'true' firsts – of everything except *Angels at Rest*, and, just for fun, a few assorted foreign-language versions he had picked up here and there – German, French, Danish, South Korean, Taiwanese.

A complete English-language set, except that it wasn't, to Derek's eternal chagrin, quite complete. Rumour had it that a mystery bookstore outside Phoenix had a first edition of *Angels at Rest* for sale at six hundred and fifty dollars, US, but it had proved sadly untrue.

Derek was still searching.

He turned his back towards the glass door into Waterstone's and eased it open, the box held tight in front of him on aching arms. The queue at the signing table was long, but that didn't matter in the least. If Derek only reached Cathy Jordan at the end of her session, so much the better, there would be more time to chat.

Lynn refused the glass of wine which the manager offered her and opted for mineral water instead, sipping it now from a vantage point by the side wall, close to the books on poetry and theatre.

She admired the way Cathy Jordan dealt with her fans; a smile for each one, not forced but seeming genuine, to each she offered a palatable slice of conversation; copies of her books she signed in black ink with a flourish, using a fat Mont Blanc pen she carried especially for the purpose:

> For Emily
> from Annie Q.
> & me!
> *Cathy Jordan*

The C was round and deep enough to contain, almost, the rest of her first name; the J swooped towards the bottom of the title page before sweeping through its final curve.

'Well,' Cathy Jordan said, 'it's good to meet you, too.' Her voice, American, slightly nasal, sounded overlarge within the confines of the store.

Lynn had decided she would buy a copy of *Dead Weight* for herself, but wouldn't bother, probably, to get it signed. The line was dwindling to an end: a youngish man wearing a black *Anthrax* T-shirt and with two gold rings in his right ear, one immediately above the other, was having his book signed now, and behind him two women waited together, deep in conversation. The taller of the two was wearing a brightly coloured ethnic dress, a green rucksack slung casually over one shoulder; her companion, several years younger, wore a black shirt over blue jeans, one hand resting on the leather shoulder bag slung from her shoulder. Behind them another man, older, with gingery hair and glasses, stood with an open cardboard box of books at his feet; and finally, a fortyish woman with a Warehouse carrier bag in one hand and a small child, already beginning to grizzle, clinging to the other.

Lynn glanced at her watch; she thought, I can be back at the station by half past two.

The man in the T-shirt moved away and the taller of the women swung the rucksack from her shoulder. The boy at the back of the queue had started to cry and his mother gave his arm a tug, causing him to cry louder. A couple of fourteen-year-olds, arms loose around each other's limber bodies, passed carelessly in front of where Lynn was standing.

'We've read all of your books,' the woman in black was saying. 'They really made an impression.'

'And since it's your first visit,' her friend said excitedly, 'we've brought something for you.'

'Well, that's real nice,' Cathy Jordan said, giving it her best smile.

The woman raised the rucksack high and swung it towards the table: what was inside was a plastic container and what was inside that was blood. A lot of blood. It poured over Cathy Jordan's face and hair and down her front, splashing across what was left of the piles of books.

'We thought,' one of the women was shouting, 'you'd like to know what it was like.'

Lynn pushed the two youths aside and in four paces she was at Cathy Jordan's side; Cathy standing, arms outstretched, blue of her shirt adrift in blood.

'Are you all right?'

'What the hell do you think?'

On his knees, Derek Neighbour was lifting books from their box as deftly and carefully as he could; those that had been lying on top were thickly spotted and stained.

Lynn part-swerved round him, part-vaulted over him; the mother with the Warehouse bag dragged her screaming child towards her and Lynn cannoned into the shelves avoiding him. Ahead of her she could see the two women pushing their way through the doors on to the street.

'Make way!' she called. 'Make way, police!'

Nobody moved.

Lynn ran between them, failing to notice the table opposite the cash desk until she struck it hard, somewhere between hip and thigh, her cry lost in the crash of books against the floor.

'Stop!'

They were running full-pelt down the middle of St Peter's Gate, ignoring the traffic, both pavements clogged with lunchtime shoppers, grazing on their take-away burgers or baked potatoes.

'Police!'

Halfway down, they separated: the one in black continuing on, actually gaining speed, the woman in the dress dodging her way into the arcade of fashionable shops that led towards the square.

Lynn ducked into the narrow alley higher up and emerged on to Cheapside before the woman was in sight; for a moment, Lynn thought she might have doubled back, but no, there she was, pushing between a knot of people outside Saxone's window.

'Right!' Lynn yelled, catching hold of the collar of the woman's dress. 'That's it!'

The dress ripped and, stumbling, the woman, all but bare-chested, fell across the kerb by the pedestrian crossing. A green double-decker bus pulled up not so far short of where she was sprawling.

Lynn seized one of the woman's arms and yanked her back on to the pavement; leaning over her, a crowd gathering quickly round, she drew out her warrant card and held it high in the air. 'I'm a police officer and I'm placing you under arrest. You do not have to say anything unless you wish to do so, but anything you do say may be given in evidence.'

Someone at the back of the crowd began a slow handclap and several more jeered; the majority started to drift away. On the ground, without bothering to pull the material of her dress around her, the woman began to laugh.

Seventeen

'Well, I suppose,' Marius said, pausing by the bathroom door, 'you could say that some kind of natural justice has been done.'

The door was open just a crack and he could smell the sweet, urine-like smell of baby powder, the kind with which Dorothy liked to dust herself after her bath. At first, Marius had found it almost repellent, but now he savoured it along with almost everything else – the small and delicate ways in which she kept her body sweet to the touch.

'Marius, dear. Hand me my dressing gown, would you?'

Quilted, pink, it slid around her shoulders like satin over old silk.

'Tea's ready,' Marius said. 'And I found some more of those nice little cakes. The butterfly ones with the cream.'

Stepping out into the main room of their small suite, Dorothy Birdwell smiled her thin-mouthed smile. 'Marius, you spoil me. You really do.'

'Not really,' he replied, smiling back. Not nearly enough, he thought.

'Now, dear,' said Dorothy, settling carefully into a high-arched chair. 'I want you to tell me all about what happened in the bookshop. And I don't want you to miss out a single thing.'

'Will you please state your name?' Lynn asked.'For the record.'

'Vivienne Plant.'

'And your address?'

'Flat seven, Ancaster Court, Bainbridge Road, Mapperley.'

Like all of the interview rooms at the police station, this was small and airless and hung over with the unmistakable pall of stale cigarette smoke. Vivienne Plant, with her bright dress and upright posture, the after-image of a sneer on her well-tended middle-class face, looked impressively out of place.

'What is your present occupation?' Lynn asked.

'I'm a lecturer in Women's Studies.'

'Here in the city?'

'In Derby.'

'And are you married or single?'

'Neither.'

'I'm sorry?'

'I have lived with the same partner for seven years; we have a three-year-old child. We are not married. Is that clear enough?'

As a manifesto, Lynn thought. 'Ms Plant, you do admit the assault on Cathy Jordan . . .'

'Demonstration. I was making a demonstration.'

'In relation to Ms Jordan?'

'In relation to her work.'

'You disapprove of her books, then? You don't like them?'

'Which question do you want me to answer?'

No wonder she didn't want a solicitor, Lynn thought, she thinks she is one. 'Aren't they the same thing?' she asked wearily.

'Disapproving and not liking?'

'Yes.'

'I like eating Terry's Chocolate Oranges, sometimes two at a time; I also like popping into McDonald's last

89

thing at night for apple pie. I don't really approve of either.'

Someone walked past along the corridor outside, heavy feet set down slowly and with purpose. Lynn tried not to look at her watch or the clock on the adjacent wall. 'Can you tell me,' she asked, 'why you disapprove of Cathy Jordan's books so strongly?'

'Which version do you want? The fifty-minute lecture or the single-paragraph outline?'

Lynn was reminded of those times she had been lectured by her head teacher at school. 'The outline will be fine.'

'Right. What I object to about her books is that they rely on an almost exclusive portrayal of women as victims, usually victims of violent and degrading assault. Their degradation and pain are in direct proportion to Jordan's profit. She's got rich on women's suffering. She should know better.'

'And your intention was to teach her that lesson?'

'I thought it was appropriate.'

'Covering her with paint?'

'Yes, don't you?'

'Then you do admit to throwing paint over Ms Jordan?'

'I thought of it more as pouring, but yes, all right. I do.'

'You assaulted her.'

'Surely that's for the court to decide?'

'You want this to go to court?'

'Of course.'

Oh, God, Lynn thought, spare me from people who know what's right for me better than I do myself. The whole Greenpeace, civil liberties, feminist bunch of them. 'This action, was it carried out on behalf of some group or organisation?'

'Not officially, no. It was an individual act.'

'Aside from your accomplice.'

Vivienne Plant's shoulders braced back even further. 'There was no such person.'

'Ms Plant, I was there in the shop. I saw you standing in line with another woman, talking. A woman wearing a black shirt and jeans. You came into the shop together. Approached Ms Jordan together. After the incident, you ran out together. You were not acting on your own.'

'Well, that's going to have to be your word against mine.'

Lynn shook her head. She could have thought of places she would rather be than shut up with Ms Self-righteous, plenty of them. 'All right,' she said, 'we'll come back to this again.'

'Look,' Vivienne said, leaning forward, holding Lynn with her eyes, 'the responsibility for what happened is mine. Okay? But what I did, I did for all women, not just me.'

'All women?' Lynn said.

'Of course.'

'I don't think so.'

'No?'

Lynn pushed back her chair and got to her feet. 'You didn't do it for me.'

Vivienne pitched back her head and laughed. 'Well, you really do need the fifty-minute version, don't you?'

Lynn reached sideways, towards the Off button on the tape machine. 'This interview stopped at thirteen minutes past three.'

Once Naylor had settled him down, assured him that in all probability he would be able to drive back to Newark ahead of the evening rush hour and allowed him to make a call to his partner, Derek Neighbour had proved a good witness. He had seen Vivienne Plant's actions clearly and described them with accuracy. Yes, she and the other woman, the one in the black shirt, had chattered away all

91

the time they were waiting in the queue and although he hadn't heard a great deal of what they had actually been saying, the impression they gave was not of two people who have only just that moment met. Absolutely not.

'So it was your impression that the two women were friends? That they knew one another quite well?'

'Very well, more like.'

'And their names? Did you hear either of them address the other by names?'

'No. Come to think of it, no. Not that I can recall. I don't think they did.'

'All right, Mr Neighbour. Thanks a lot. We've got your address and if we need you again we'll be in touch.'

Naylor got to his feet. Derek Neighbour continued to look up at him, uncertain.

'Was there something else?' Naylor asked. 'Something you wanted to add?'

'It's just, well, you know, the damage . . .'

'To Miss Jordan? Apart from the shock, I don't think it was too serious. Her clothes, of course, and . . .'

'No. To me. My books.'

'Well, I don't know. Perhaps Waterstone's, in the circumstances . . .'

'You don't understand. There's a first edition of *Uneasy Prey*, absolutely ruined. I don't even know if I'll be able to find another one, and if I do, the cost is going to be close to three hundred pounds. More.'

Three hundred, Naylor was thinking, for one book. Only a crime book, at that. Debbie's mum got through four or five a week from the library, large-print editions in the main. Debbie reckoned she could get one finished between *Neighbours* and *Countdown*. Why would anyone pay three hundred quid for something you could get through in a few hours and never want to look at again? It didn't make a scrap of sense.

*

'The stuff with the paint she's ready to admit to. Eager. Not that she could do anything else.' Lynn was at her desk in the CID room, talking to Graham Millington. Vivienne Plant she had left to stew a little in the interview room. 'The woman who was with her, though, she won't give us a thing. Denies knowing her altogether.'

'No chance she's telling the truth?'

Lynn looked up at him. 'None.'

'Charlie,' Skelton said, 'we're not going to let this woman wrap us round her little finger, commit time and money, all so's she can garner free publicity for whatever cockamamie idea she's spouting. Women's Studies, that's her, isn't it? Jesus, Charlie! Women's Studies, Black Studies, Lesbian and Gay Studies, what in God's name happened to good old History and Geography, that's what I'd like to know?'

Resnick couldn't oblige. Though he had recently been taken to task for carelessly using the masculine pronoun by a very intelligent and thoughtful young woman, who, it had turned out later, believed Norwich to be located in the middle of Hampshire.

'What about the American?' Skelton said. 'Is she keen to press charges?'

'We don't know yet . . .'

'Then it's about time we bloody did!'

Right, Resnick thought, getting to his feet, and it's about time you went back to running before you have some self-induced heart attack. Whatever was going on behind closed doors in Skelton's executive home, it wasn't happy families.

Lynn was waiting outside Resnick's office. 'Graham and I had another go at her. Still won't budge. Didn't know the other woman from Adam. I mean Eve.'

'She's lying?'

'Not just that. She knows we know she is, but at the moment there's not a lot we can do to prove it. Loving that, isn't she? Clever cow!'

'Not your favourite person, then?' Resnick smiled.

'Women like that,' Lynn scowled, 'whatever their intentions, just end up making women like me feel inferior.'

'Well, looks like you can have the pleasure of kicking her free. Last thing the old man wants to do is contribute to her publicity campaign.'

'What about Cathy Jordan? Suppose she wants . . .'

'To lay charges? I doubt it. Wouldn't exactly help her, would it? But if she does . . .' Resnick shrugged. 'I don't suppose Ms Plant's about to do a runner, do you? Suddenly turn into a shrinking violet?'

Lynn looked back at Resnick, concerned; unless she was very much mistaken, he had made a joke.

Eighteen

'Catherine, dear. How awful for you. How perfectly awful.'

How Cathy Jordan hated being called Catherine; especially by Dorothy Birdwell, wattled hands flustering all around her, smelling her old maid's smell of face powder and malice.

'Yes, well, you know, Dottie, it really wasn't so bad.'

'Perhaps you should consider following my example, dear, and have a nice young man to look after you.'

Marius Gooding was standing a short way off, blazer buttons glistening. For the first time, Cathy noticed his manicured hands, long fingers flexing slightly at his sides. Catching Cathy's gaze he made a quick dipping gesture with his head, somewhere between a nod and a bow, a token smile of sympathy passing across his face. Without her understanding exactly why, something deep inside Cathy shuddered.

'I don't need a nice young man, Dottie,' she said, 'I have a husband.'

'So you have, dear, sometimes I forget.'

'What in hell's name happened to you?' – Frank's first words when Cathy had appeared back at the hotel in borrowed clothes, face oddly aglow, hair clotted red. 'Something go wrong at the beauty shop?'

'Screw,' she'd said, pushing past him on her way to the bathroom, 'you!'

'Nice idea, Cath, if you could remember how. Wait for

you to screw me, might as well hand my dick to Lorena Bobbitt for surgery.'

The only answer was the sound of water bouncing back from the shower. Frank poured himself a drink and took it across to the window, looking out. There was a plane rising slow between the small, off-white clouds and for a moment, wherever it was heading, he wished he were on it. Then he laughed. The thing that had most fascinated him about the whole Bobbitt affair, the way the guy had made a living later in a Californian nightclub, women handing over good bucks to dance with him in the hope of scooping ten grand by giving him a boner.

For Frank, whose childhood had been spent in cast-offs and hand-me-downs and who had stolen his first quarter at age five, it was eloquent testimony to what made his country great. The ordinary American's ability to make entrepreneurial capital in the face of any adversity.

Tyrell had insisted on living as close to the centre of the city as his and his wife's combined salaries would allow. After all, he had reasoned, the one thing we don't want to add to my already antisocial hours is a lot of unnecessary travelling time, right? And Susan Tyrell had nodded agreement and said nothing about the fact that buying a house where her husband was suggesting would give her a forty-five-minute drive each way to the comprehensive where she taught.

Besides, she had liked the house: substantial, large without being sprawling, one of those late-Victorian family homes near the Arboretum which she and David had redecorated and were steadily filling with books and videos instead of children.

Another of those decisions that Tyrell had talked her into with his usual mixture of enthusiasm and dodgy rationalisation. She had, Susan knew, allowed it to happen too often, agreed to far too much for too long and in favour of what? A quiet life, contentment? When most of their friends were already into their second divorce or separation, what was she trying to prove? That she was a survivor? That, despite all the odds, she and David still loved one another, that they had found a way of making it work?

The first time she had spoken to him, really spoken, had been after a seminar at the University of Warwick, where they were both doing Media Studies. The only one of the group not majoring in Film, Susan had sat there for eight weeks, listening, contributing very little. Finally, she had plucked up her courage and launched into a mild attack on the film they had been watching, a fifties musical called *It's Always Fair Weather*. Pretty enough, she had said, but pretty vacant. Fun, but why all the fuss? David had told her in no uncertain terms and after twenty minutes she had bowed her head and agreed with him and a pattern had been set.

On the way out of the seminar, he had invited her for coffee; in the coffee bar he had invited her to a movie. The movie turned out to be two, an Elvis Presley double bill, and David had made them sit on the front row. *King Creole* was okay, he pronounced, but the really interesting one was *Change of Habit*, Presley's last feature, 1969. And Susan had kept her thoughts to her popcorn, watching Dr Elvis falling sanctimoniously in love with a speech therapist she had only later identified as Mary Tyler Moore.

'Didn't you think it was great,' Tyrell had enthused later, 'the way our sense of Presley as star bifurcates the diegesis of the narrative?'

'Um,' Susan had said. 'Yes. Absolutely.'

She looked up now from the pile of books she was marking, hearing the front door open and Tyrell's voice calling her name from the hall. 'Susan, you there?'

She would, he thought, be in the long kitchen which

doubled as dining room, marking another thirty-three pastiches of *EastEnders*, ever ready to pop another frozen pizza into the microwave.

'My God! You won't believe what happened. In the middle of the day, broad daylight. Must have been like that scene in *Carrie*, the one with the pig's blood, you know.'

Susan was on her feet, filling the kettle. 'I heard about it on the car radio.'

'National?'

'No, Radio Nottingham.'

'Oh,' Tyrell sounded disappointed, ferreting in the cupboard for what was left of the packet of custard creams. 'I thought at least we might've got some good publicity out of it.'

'I wonder if she felt the same? The woman – what's her name?'

'Come on, Susan. Cathy Jordan, how many more times? You'll meet her tonight at Sonny's.'

'I'm not sure if I'm going.'

'What? Don't be ridiculous, of course you're going.'

'I don't know, I think I'm getting a headache. I've got all this work to do.'

Tyrell swore as the last biscuit crumbled between his fingers and fell to the floor. 'Susan, it's all booked. Arranged. Besides, you want to meet everybody, don't you?'

'Do I?'

'Of course you do. You'll have a great time once you're there, you always do.'

Susan reached for the tea bags. 'Earl Grey or ordinary?'

'Ordinary.'

What Susan could remember was sitting at one end of the table, drinking glass after glass of Perrier while the conversation spun around her.

Tyrell smiled. He had found a cache of plain chocolate

98

digestives. 'I don't want to go without you, you know that. Still, if you've really got your mind made up . . .'

When she looked at him, what Susan saw was relief in his eyes; he would be so much happier not having to bother about her. 'Yes,' she said, pouring boiling water into the pot, 'you go on your own.'

Tyrell shrugged and sat down at the pine table, reaching for the *Guardian*. First chance he'd had to look at the paper that day.

Nineteen

Angel Eyes. The first film in the Festival's Curtis Woolfe season and, to Tyrell's mind, the best. Made in 'forty-five for Republic, and photographed by John Alton, it featured Albert Dekker as a middle-aged businessman lured to destruction by slinky, wide-eyed Martha MacVicar who, a year later, her name changed to Martha Vickers, would come to brief fame as Lauren Bacall's thumb-sucking, promiscuous sister in the film of Raymond Chandler's *The Big Sleep*. Woolfe, who collaborated on the script with an uncredited Steve Fisher, persuaded 'Wild Bill' Elliott, a Western star under contract to the studio, to shed his buckskins and play the honest cop who investigates Dekker's murder and almost falls for MacVicar's wiles himself.

Despite the film being almost unknown, Mollie had garnered enough publicity around Curtis Woolfe's re-emergence to ensure a three-quarter-full house. Woolfe had limited his spirits intake to a half-bottle of vodka and rather less of gin. The plan was for Tyrell to introduce him briefly to the audience before the screening and invite anyone who wished to remain behind for a question-and-answer session at the end.

As the house lights dimmed and the stage spot flicked on, Tyrell dabbed sweaty palms against the sides of his black suit and with a whispered, 'Let's go to work,' set out down the sloping aisle towards the microphone.

At about the same time that Tyrell was introducing Curtis

100

Woolfe, Peter Farleigh was stepping out of the shower and sipping the Dewar's and ginger ale he had poured for himself earlier. A little something from the mini-bar to set him up for the evening. And why not? Whatever he was about to treat himself to, Farleigh thought that he deserved it. He had had a good day. Now it was a few drinks in the bar, a meal and then he'd see. But one thing was certain, even if he ended the night back in his hotel room watching a Channel Four documentary about Tibet, it was preferable to driving the relatively short distance home; better than enduring Sarah's pained indifference and cold back.

Even before his seven-thirty alarm call that morning, he had been wide awake, eager to go. *Telegraph* and *Mail* delivered to his room, he had browsed the front pages between buffing his shoes and shaving, the sports and financial sections he had read over breakfast – the full English as usual when he was travelling, but careful to use sunflower spread instead of butter, pour skimmed milk into his coffee, half a spoonful of sugar, no more. Time to telephone his wife before leaving, remind her the Volvo had to be taken in for service; maybe she could check the wardrobe, see if any of his suits needed dropping off at the cleaner's while he was in town.

His hire car was a new Granada, almost pristine, one of the perks of the job. His first meeting, at Epperstone Nurseries, had been over by lunchtime. Oh, there'd been one or two potentially dodgy questions about increased resistance to the new systematic fungicide he was pushing, but that was what he was paid to deal with. A few fancy charts prepared by the research department, a joke about not going back to the bad old days of mercury pollution, and they had been falling over themselves to sign on the dotted line.

Farleigh had joined them for a swift half in their local before driving to a little place he favoured just this side of

Loughborough; very nice smoked mackerel with goose-berry sauce. By twenty past two, he had been steering the Granada into the car park at the University School of Agriculture, Sutton Bonington.

Whenever people asked his line of work, more often than not he would temper sales executive with a wink and a self-deprecating smile: fifteen years in fertilisers, best make sure you're sitting downwind.

He had been back in the city by six and by seven had written up his sales reports, called his secretary on her home number and checked his appointments for tomor-row, thought about phoning his wife – got halfway through dialling the number – before deciding against it. One of the things he couldn't stand, men who behaved as if they were on some kind of leash.

Peter Farleigh sucked in his stomach beneath the hotel towel, made a fist to circle steam from the mirror and leaned forward to examine his face; he could leave shaving till morning. A splash of aftershave would do.

Dry, he put on clean socks, underpants and shirt, the same suit and tie. In the lounge bar, he ordered a G & T, evinced enough of an interest in the forthcoming test series to have the waistcoated barman smiling, tipped in the rest of his tonic and carried his glass over to a table near the smoked-glass window. Blurs of light passed along the street outside, trailing orange smoke.

When Farleigh turned his head, she was sitting across from him, relaxed into one of the easy chairs near the piano, leaning back. Black dress, dark hair curling away from the nape of her neck. Thirty? Thirty-three? He watched as she bent forward to pick up her bag, the way the button-through dress eased itself a little higher above her knees when she sat back. Oblivious to anyone around her, the woman tapped a cigarette from the pack, clicked her lighter, no response, gave it a shake and tried again,

102

finally dropped the lighter back inside her bag and began rummaging for a match.

'Here,' Farleigh said, walking towards her. 'Allow me.'

'Thanks.' Perfume, red nails matching the dark of her lipstick; smoke that moved soft across her face.

'Staying here at the hotel?'

Shaking her head, she smiled. 'No. I'm meeting a friend.'

Back at his seat, Farleigh thumbed through the menu, vacillating between the steak and the salmon. A light-toned Afro-Caribbean sat down at the piano and almost immediately began with 'Over the Rainbow', sleeves of his lightweight cream jacket pushed high above his wrists. For some moments, Farleigh was nagged by the thought that he had missed his daughter's birthday; once they were off at university, it was so difficult to keep tabs. At the edge of his vision, the woman shifted her position casually, leaning forward to the ashtray and back, crossing and recrossing her legs.

If she looks at me when I get up, Farleigh thought, I'll speak to her again. Instead, her head was turned towards the pianist, who had eased the microphone over the keyboard and was lightly crooning, 'Me and Mrs Jones'. For God's sake, Farleigh told himself, stop being so bloody pathetic!

In the dining room, he decided fish twice in one day wasn't a good idea and ordered the steak. One bite and he knew that hadn't been a good idea either.

'Everything satisfactory, sir?'

'Fine, thank you.'

As compensation, he sent back his glass of house red and ordered a bottle of good Bordeaux. Before now he'd paid the earth for stuff that tasted more like the copper sulphate fungicide known to the trade – his trade – as Bordeaux Mixture, but this was the real thing.

By the time he had risen to his feet, one bottle later, his

head was slightly muzzy and it had taken him a while to realise that the dark-haired woman from the bar was now sitting at a corner table of the restaurant, evidently still alone.

That's all right, Farleigh lectured himself, keep on walking; couple of phone calls, early night. Just as long as she doesn't look up. But it hadn't even taken that.

The woman was surprised when Farleigh stopped beside her table. 'At least you made the right choice,' he said, nodding towards her plate.

'I'm sorry?'

'The salmon. I had the steak. Like the proverbial, I'm afraid.'

'The proverbial what?' There was just a hint of lipstick, dark against the white of her teeth.

'Old boots.'

Farleigh smiled and she smiled back with her eyes; she was older, he decided, than he had first thought, but not by too much. Still the right side of forty.

'It was never an issue,' she was saying. 'The steak. I'm vegetarian.'

'Ah.'

'All that stuff they pump into the poor animals, mad cow disease and everything.' She smiled, more fully this time. 'Perhaps you think that's foolish?'

'Not at all.' Things I could tell you, he was thinking, put you off your food for a lifetime. 'What happened?' he asked, indicating the empty chair.

Vaguely, she waved a hand. 'Oh, you know . . .'

'It's difficult to imagine.'

'What's that?'

'Anyone standing you up.'

He had hoped for some response, a laugh, an explanation. Instead, she looked down at her plate and pushed at a piece of pink flesh with the edge of her fork. Farleigh knew he had blown it. 'Well, enjoy the rest of your meal.'

She waited until he had almost turned away. 'Why don't you sit down? Join me for a drink.'

Twenty

Curtis Woolfe's film had been well received. Of course, there were always those who wanted nothing more than the latest glossy mishmash of unarmed combat and special effects, and who found anything pre-seventies slow and dull and boring. 'Nothing happens,' they would say, mooching down to the bar for their designer lager. Nothing happens. Well, nobody's head came off, nobody's blood spurted a perfect technicolour parabola across the screen, nobody humped naked in the shower or the kitchen sink; there was no Chuck, or Steven, or Cynthia, no Jean Claude, Arnie, or Sly; not even (the heavens forfend) Bruce Willis. But the moment when Albert Dekker steps into the darkness of his hotel room, twists the key in the lock behind him, slides the bolt and turns back into the room to see Martha MacVicar's feral face illuminated through the slanting blinds by the light across the street, still had most of the audience catching its breath. The smile that died in her eyes as her teeth bit down into her lower lip.

In the auditorium, Curtis Woolfe had been pleased with the audience's reaction and had answered questions with self-deprecating charm. What had it been like working with Mitchum? 'Delightful, especially when he was stoned.' Who was the most beautiful *femme fatale*? 'Gail Russell – ask John Wayne.' What was his favourite *film noir*? 'Aside from my own, *Out of the Past*.' Why hadn't he made a film in over twenty years? 'Nobody asked me.'

Here in Sonny's restaurant, he was even more relaxed. Gesticulating over the food in his assumed Gallic manner, almost anxious to talk about the other films in the season, Woolfe was lavish in his praise for Tyrell and the festival.

Resnick had arrived early, drunk a Beck's alone at the large reserved table and been about to leave when, through the curved corner window, he had seen Mollie Hansen leading the group along Carlton Street, past the George Hotel. There were a dozen of them in all, Dorothy Birdwell the last to arrive, leaning on Marius Gooding's arm. Cathy Jordan, her hair trimmed back and partly covered by a black velvet beret, had taken a seat alongside Resnick; her husband, facing them, sat beside Mollie.

'So how was the film?' Resnick asked, starting on his second beer.

Cathy Jordan speared a piece of bread, spread it lavishly with butter and took a generous bite. 'I had an aunt once, lived all her life in this town near Jackson, Wyoming. So small it didn't even rate a pimple on the map. You could turn up there any time, day or night, unannounced, nothing in her store cupboard to speak of, yet inside half an hour you'd find yourself sitting down to the tastiest snack you could ever have imagined.' She brushed a crumb from the side of her mouth and tried the wine. 'Well, Curtis's film was like that. Considering what he had to work with, it was a small miracle.' She lifted the menu towards the light. 'How d'you think this rack of lamb would be? I'm good and tired of steak and chicken.'

Across the city in his hotel, Peter Farleigh and the dark-haired woman were back in the bar. Michelle – she had told him that was her name, Michelle – had developed a taste for blue cocktails afloat with tinned fruit and Farleigh had kept pace with her, drinking brandy now and talking in a voice that was just this side of loud. On and on about crop yields, fertilisers, EEC farming subsidies.

When Michelle's eyes began to glaze over he changed the topic to his family, his three kids – the one at university, the one who was already an accountant, the one who had gone off with a bunch of travellers and sent them marigold teas and pictures from the I-ching. The pianist had trawled his way from *Cats* to *Carousel* and eventually given way to piped music: bland arrangements of the Beatles for saxophone, six strings and a drum machine.

From behind the bar, a voice called last orders. Farleigh looked hard at Michelle and she looked away; he let his hand drift down towards her leg and with a look she stopped it well short of her knee.

'I hope, Peter, you're not going to make a move on me.'

'I'm sorry, no, look, I . . .' He could feel his face reddening and that only made it redden more. What was he doing sitting there, blushing like a schoolboy whose mother had chosen the wrong moment to come into the room?

'What was going to be the next step, Peter?' She was leaning towards him, almost touching her shoulder to his arm. 'Asking me up to your room?'

'Look . . .'

'Well . . . ?'

'Michelle, I . . .' Suddenly he became aware of his own sweat, sweet and rancid; the muscles of his stomach tightened and refused to let go.

'Was that it?' her voice rising. 'Because if it was, Peter, well, I have to say you'd have been disappointed.'

Farleigh was certain everyone else in the bar could hear. 'All right, look, it's been a nice evening, let's just forget it.'

'Forget it?'

'Yes.' He pushed an almost empty packet of cigarettes down into his pocket, brushed the heel of his hand across the eyebrow of his right eye. 'I think that's best, don't you?'

'Best?'

'Yes.' Standing now, while she leaned back into the comfort of the chair and surveyed him with amused eyes.

'Peter?'

'Mmm?'

'You know I'm teasing you, don't you?'

He could still smell himself, hear his own breath.

'I am teasing you.'

'Yes, well, like I say . . .' All the while, backing away.

'I would – if you asked me – I mean, I would like to . . . go with you, you know, to your room.'

Farleigh looked clumsily round. A man with a shock of almost pure white hair was staring back at him from a stool at the corner of the bar. As Farleigh continued to look, the man smiled, more a simper than a smile, and Farleigh quickly looked away.

'Unless,' Michelle said, 'you've changed your mind.'

He sat back down. There was a mole, a small one he hadn't noticed before, just to the right of her cheek, and her eyes, what would you call that shade of brown?

She inclined her head towards him. 'Have you changed your mind?'

The answer, not instant. 'No.'

'Good. Let's not waste any more time, then, down here.' She was on her feet now, holding out her hand.

Peter took it, but as soon as he was standing she pulled it away.

'After you.'

As they were waiting for the lift, she slipped her arm through his. Another couple stood waiting, a little behind them, younger, the woman fidgeting with the cuff-links on the man's right sleeve. They had been out to some formal occasion and were wearing evening dress. The woman was pretty in an obvious kind of way and somehow reminded Farleigh of his daughter, not the one at university, the other one. The one who sent him tea and blessings

109

and whom he rarely saw. She was wearing a silver dress cut low and once they were in the lift, despite Michelle's proximity, he found it difficult not to stare at the tops of her breasts.

'A hundred and fifty,' Michelle said.

At first, Farleigh wasn't even sure she was talking to him.

'A hundred and fifty.'

'What about it?'

'That's what it'll cost.'

'What?'

'Me. For the rest of the night. A hundred and fifty pounds.'

Farleigh was still staring at the young woman, unable to look at Michelle. The young man, embarrassed, was staring at the buttons beside the lift door.

'Well?' Michelle said. 'Don't you think I'm worth it?'

Close to Farleigh, the young woman suddenly threw back her head and laughed. The lift stopped at the sixth floor and the couple scrambled out. After a moment, the doors sighed shut and the lift continued its ascent.

'I thought you knew,' Michelle said. Farleigh shook his head and she smiled. 'Knew that I was working.'

'No, how could I?'

The lift stopped again and they got out into the empty corridor.

'What did you think was going on then?'

'I don't know. I suppose I just thought, you know . . .'

'That I'd let you pick me up? That I fancied you?'

'Yes.'

'Marvellous, isn't it?' Michelle said. 'The way we deceive ourselves.'

Threading through the sounds of the restaurant, the voice of a woman singing 'Someone to Watch Over Me.' Resnick thought it might be Carmen McCrea, but he

110

couldn't be sure. Whoever had decided, ten years or so ago, that jazz was a good accompaniment to fashionable eating, he felt he owed them a vote of thanks.

Beside him, Cathy Jordan was tucking into an unhealthy portion of sticky toffee pudding, while Resnick, with unusual restraint, confined himself to his second large espresso.

'See that?' With her spoon, she made a dismissive flicking gesture across the table. 'Lothario in action.'

Oblivious, Frank Carlucci was engaging Mollie Hansen in intense conversation; if he got any closer he would be eating his creme caramel out of her lap.

'Doesn't bother you?' Resnick asked.

Cathy glanced across at them and then away. 'Not any more.' The look in her eyes suggested she might almost mean it. 'Besides, that young woman can handle herself.'

Resnick drew breath slowly and nodded. About that, he thought she was right. Along the table, Dorothy Birdwell, back upright, head tilted forward, sat quite asleep.

'That was all it took,' Frank Carlucci was saying to Mollie, 'a little investment here, little advertising there. One minute I'm the guy who won silver snatching the big one at the Games, face all over the sports pages for weeks. The Olympics, right? A big deal.'

Mollie yawned.

'A while after that,' Frank said, 'things got kinda slow. That's till I met Cathy there. Married her. Wake up and what am I? Mr Cathy Jordan, that's what.'

Oh, God, thought Mollie, here we go. Another everyday story of emasculation. Tennessee Williams without the style.

'I could only take that for so long,' Frank was saying. 'I knew I had to do something for myself. Something big. So I look around, talk a little here, a little there, a favour to be called in, you know what I mean? Now here I am, heading up the fastest-growing catering franchise on the West

111

Coast. Shops everywhere, those little carts, signs – Carlucci's cappuccino, the coffee with muscle. Truckers pull over and drink my stuff without there's guys looking at 'em strange for drinking something with a fancy name, bunch of froth on top. You understand what I'm saying?'

'I understand,' Mollie said quietly, 'if you don't take your fucking hand off my leg, I'm going to stick this fork right through it.'

There was a scar on one of her breasts, curving beneath it, a thin ridged line, small and white. Peter Farleigh lay on his back and Michelle knelt above him, straddling his thighs. She was still wearing skimpy bikini pants. They had fooled around for a while earlier, Michelle finding some baby oil in her bag, and now a small pool of it floated in one of the folds of his stomach, glistening a little in the light from the window, the only light in the room.

'Are you ready?' she said.

She could see he was ready.

'All right,' she said, 'just a minute.' And leaned sideways, reaching down again to where her bag lay beside the bed.

Bloody condoms, Farleigh thought, shifting his position to accommodate her move. Still, better safe than sorry.

But then he saw what was in her hand, the look in her eyes, and he knew that wasn't true.

Twenty-one

Resnick had just walked into the CID room when the call came in, Millington picking up and listening only long enough to beckon him over, pass the phone across.

'Right,' Resnick said, a minute later. 'We've got a body. Graham, you come with me. Mark . . .'

'Boss?'

'I shall need you and Kevin knocking on a few doors.'

Divine didn't need telling twice.

'How about Lynn?' Millington asked. They were in the corridor, heading for the stairs. 'Seeing the shrink, isn't she? Could always get her to cancel. Reschedule.'

'For the sake of fifty minutes? No, I don't think so.'

Millington pushed open the rear door to the car park. 'How long till all this psychobabble business is over and done with, that's what I'd like to know?'

'Graham,' Resnick said, with a slow shake of the head, 'I doubt it ever is.'

To say the body was in the bath was not quite accurate. The left arm and leg and most of the trunk were hanging inside, the right leg outside, trailing at an awkward angle to the floor. The right arm stretched along the bath's rim, the head resting, open-mouthed, against the crook of the elbow. From the position alone, it was unclear whether the dead man had been trying to climb into the bath or crawl out.

A patchy trail of blood contoured its way across the carpet, leading from the bed into the bathroom; blood had dried in tapering lines down the plastic-coated side of the bath beneath the body and more had collected around the plughole like a pressed rose.

'Dragged there, d'you reckon?' Millington asked.

Resnick's mouth tightened. 'Possible. Dragged himself, could be.'

'Why the bath, then? Not the door?'

'Might not have known. Just getting away. Disorientated. Then again, maybe it was deliberate. Wanted to wash it off.'

There was a uniformed officer outside the door, another further along the corridor, shepherding curious staff and guests on their way. From the hotel register, it had been established that the occupant of the room was a Peter Farleigh, with an address Resnick recognised as one of those villages in the Wolds, north of Loughborough.

The clean towels which the maid had been carrying were in a heap near the door where she had dropped them; the maid herself was lying down in one of the vacant rooms, according to the manager, in a right old state.

'We don't know, of course,' Millington said, 'if this is Farleigh or not. Not for a fact.'

Resnick nodded, stepping back into the main room. Both he and Millington were wearing plastic coats over their street clothes, white cotton gloves on their hands.

A wallet lay on the table beside the bed, nudged up against the base of the lamp. Cautiously, Resnick fingered it open. Whatever money it might have held was gone. Surprisingly, though, the credit cards seemed to be in place. Behind a kidney donor card was a membership card for a squash club in Melton Mowbray which bore a small, coloured photograph above an address and the name, Peter John Farleigh. The man poised over the bath looked different, in the way that dead people do, but Resnick had no doubt that he was one and the same as the person pictured in the photo.

Resnick stood where he was, focusing on the bed, the ruck of clothes, darkly stained; under the almost silent hum of the air conditioning, the scent of sweat and blood were unmistakable. He tried to imagine what had happened in that room, tried to magic words, expressions out from the walls. If that address were still correct, then Farleigh lived no more than an hour's drive away, so why opt for the hotel in preference to going home?

Sex, Resnick thought.

A lover.

A liaison, bought and paid for, bought and sold.

Sometimes this was what it cost.

The door opened from the corridor and Parkinson, the pathologist, came in: tall, bony, thinning hair, neat in a mossy tweed suit. Automatically, he fingered an extra-strong mint from the roll in his side pocket and slid his glasses from their case. 'Now then, Charlie, what have we got here?'

Lynn thought, this room always smells of flowers. Roses, though there were none that she could see. She sat in the same chair, wooden arms and a curved back, comfortable, but not so comfortable that you would drift off to sleep. Not even through these long silences. Petra Carey, Dr Petra Carey, sitting near to the window, seemingly relaxed. There was a desk, but the doctor ignored it, except sometimes at the beginning of the session when Lynn arrived, she would be there, finishing writing up her notes, glancing, perhaps, at Lynn's file. 'Lynn, it's good to see you. How are we today?' Petra Carey, today in a short jacket and loose, long skirt, white blouse with a slight frill, wedding ring wide on her hand. Scrubbed face and careful hair, attentive eyes. 'What would you like to talk about today?' Lynn supposed she might be five years older than herself. Quiet, she could hear the ticking of the clock.

*

There were seven wounds in all: four to the chest, one between the ribs to the left-hand side, two low in the stomach, approximately two inches above the line of pubic hair. All but one of the chest wounds were scarcely more than superficial; the deepest seeming the one which had passed between the ribs, close, Resnick guessed, to where the heart had been still beating.

After the scene-of-the-crime team had finished shooting off several rolls of film and videoing Farleigh's body *in situ*, it had been removed from the bath and laid on thick, opaque plastic sheeting.

'What time are we looking at?' Resnick asked.

Parkinson wiped the thermometer with care and returned it to its case. 'Ten hours, give or take.'

'Midnight, then?'

'Round about.'

Resnick grunted. At midnight, he had been leaving Sonny's restaurant, exchanging handshakes and goodbyes with David Tyrell, hoping that the heated words being exchanged between youths outside the pub opposite would not escalate into blows, causing him to intervene.

'Any chance you'll get to my panel tomorrow?' Cathy Jordan had asked.

Resnick had replied non-committally, uncertain; now it was clear that he would not.

He had picked up a cab across the street from Ritzy's and, home, had poured himself a half-inch of bison grass vodka and read a little more of Cathy Jordan's book. So far, the most likely culprits behind April's murder seemed to be a former ex-criminal client of her father, a rejected would-be lover, or – just out of the woodwork – April's half-brother by one of her father's previous liaisons. Resnick's money was on the brother. In the book, it was easier; in the book it didn't matter if he were wrong.

'Nothing else for me here now,' Parkinson said. 'You'll be at the post?'

Resnick nodded.

In a room along the corridor, Kevin Naylor was patiently questioning Marie-Elisabeth Fournier, having to remind her almost every other sentence to speak in English, not French. Earlier, he had tried a few remembered phrases from his schooldays and she had looked at him blankly, as if he were speaking another language. Then finally she told him everything she knew.

Divine had found two of the guests with rooms on the same floor, still lingering over their breakfast in the dining room, but they claimed neither to have seen nor to have heard anything. Names and addresses of the other guests he obtained from the hotel register.

Computer records showed that Farleigh had stayed at the hotel on three occasions in the past eighteen months, the first time for a single night, the others – of which this was the last – for two. Always a single room, always on his own.

'Visitors?' Millington asked. 'You know the kind I mean.'

'We try not to encourage it, but . . .' The manager shrugged. 'People do what they do.'

'And Farleigh, you don't know if . . .'

'I've no idea.'

'No gossip amongst the staff? No . . .'

'You'll have to ask them yourself.'

'We will.'

The first of the night staff to respond to urgent requests that they make themselves available for questioning, was one of the waiters from the restaurant. Yes, he recognised the man's photo and, no, he had eaten alone, but after he had finished his meal he had sat down again with somebody else. The description the waiter gave was backed up by the barman when he arrived some forty minutes later. Late thirties, early forties, dark hair, black dress. On the game? Could be, nowadays it was increasingly difficult to tell.

Had either of them seen the woman there in the hotel before?

No, they didn't think they had.

If they were to be shown some photographs?

Oh, surely, they'd be happy to oblige. Tickled pink. Couldn't let the likes of her be running around free, now, could they? Was it true, as they'd heard, she'd stabbed him fifteen times or was it just the twelve?

'Sure you're up for this?' Resnick asked.

Lynn was looking through the car window at alternations of hedgerow, sunlight catching silver along arable fields. 'I'll be fine,' she said.

At the outskirts of the village, Resnick slowed behind a dozen sheep, a lad no older than fourteen herding them slowly through a farm gate. When Resnick glanced across at Lynn, the skin around her eyes was drawn. He knew he shouldn't have asked her to come with him; knew also that in situations such as this, she was irreplaceable.

The house was well back from the road, a small Fiat parked in the drive.

'Mrs Farleigh,' Resnick said to the middle-aged woman who came to the door. 'I'm Detective Inspector Resnick and this is Detective Constable Kellogg. I wonder if we might come inside?'

Twenty-two

Sarah Farleigh had gone through all the normal reactions to her husband's death: disbelief, shock, anger, finally tears. Lynn had moved to hold her and the older woman had shrugged her off, stumbling from the kitchen in which they had been talking, through the French windows of the living room into the garden, which was where Resnick found her, squatting in the middle of half an acre of lawn, face in her hands.

For several minutes he hunched there beside her, while a blackbird noisily disputed their presence from the branch of a nearby apple tree. When the worst of the crying, the kind that scrapes against the chest, tears the back of the throat, had stopped, to be replaced by intermittent, stuttering sobs, Resnick reached for her hand, the one in which a sodden Kleenex was tightly balled, and she clutched at his fingers as if they were all that could prevent her from falling. Clung to them until they hurt.

'Do you know,' she said a little later, letting go of Resnick's hand, accepting the handkerchief that he offered her, wiping her face and blowing her nose. 'Do you know, he would never lift a finger in this garden? Not as much as mow the lawn. These trees, the flower beds, all of the shrubbery down along the south wall, that was all me. My work. I even used – of course, he used to get it at a discount, he would do that – I even used the fertiliser the company made, you know, the one where he worked. Whose goods he sold. It could have been anything, you

119

see. Kitchenware, clothing, anything, just as long as it was something he could sell. It didn't matter that . . . it didn't matter that . . . it was used to make things grow.'

Resnick was ready; he shifted his weight and caught her as she half-turned, her body, stiff and thickening into middle age, falling across him, his arms supporting her, her brown hair harsh and soft against his neck.

Over the top of her head, he could see Lynn standing in the doorway, watching; after a while she turned back into the house.

The telephone rang and then was still.

Sarah Farleigh straightened and, shakily, got to her feet. 'I'm sorry. Thank you. I shall be all right.'

Resnick smiled a wan smile. 'I shouldn't be surprised if Lynn hasn't made some tea.'

She looked at him. 'No. I expect she has. It's what women are good at. It's what we do.'

Resnick walked with her, back to the house.

The scene-of-crime team had lifted seventeen good prints from the hotel bedroom, the bathroom had yielded eight more. Likelihood was that most of the prints would have come from Farleigh, others either from the hotel staff or previous occupants of the room. So much for cleaning. All these people would have to be contacted, checked and eliminated. If everything worked out the way it did in the textbooks, if luck and logic were on their side, any prints unaccounted for would belong to Farleigh's attacker. If that person had a record, well, while not exactly home free, the police would have a suspect, clear in their sights.

Everyone involved in the inquiry knew things were rarely that simple.

'Any sign of those photographs? From the hotel?' Resnick was barely into the office, loosening his tie, undoing the top button of his shirt.

'Promised half-hour back,' Millington said, looking up from the computer printout splayed across his desk.

'Give them a chase.'

'Right. Mark . . .'

'Boss?'

'Ten-by-eights from this morning, find out where they are. And while you're about it, check out the arrangements for viewing the scene of crime video.'

'On it now.'

'Good lad.'

Resnick was reading the printout upside down. 'From the hotel,' Millington explained. 'Three lists. Guests registered for the past two nights, previous occupants of Farleigh's room, going back two months, and all staff on duty in the past forty-eight hours.'

'Any headway?'

'Kevin's got a couple in now, running through photos with them. Maybe they'll pick out the woman, maybe not. If not, best haul our tame artist in, get a composite.'

'How about the hotel?'

'We've got three lads out of uniform, questioning the staff as they clock in.'

Resnick picked up the list and let it fall. 'We'll need more bodies.'

'Too right. I can hear 'em bleating about overtime already.'

Resnick sighed. 'I'll have a word with the old man. He can lean on the ACC. Budgets should be their problem, not ours. Meantime, we should get the names on this list checked with Intelligence at Central. Never know your luck.'

Millington nodded. 'Next thing up.'

In his office, Resnick wondered if it weren't time to call down to the front desk, see if someone wasn't nipping across to the deli.

*

They were getting tired, Naylor could see that; losing concentration. Time and again he was having to stop them, not leading, not wanting false information, but slowing them down, bringing them back. Not wanting their eyes to gloss over another page of photographs without discriminating, letting individual features sink in. Known prostitutes, working the city centre, with a possible preference for hotels.

'Jesus,' the waiter said. 'How much longer are we going to be?'

'Not too long now.'

'Yes, but how long?'

'Till we're done.'

'Don't worry,' the barman said, winking. 'I know him. This is how he spends his breaks; feet up in the bogs back of the kitchen, looking at pictures of women. Only difference, these've got more clothes on.'

'Up yours!' the waiter said, cheerily feigning offence.

'No, ta. Not today. It's Friday and I'm a good Catholic, remember?'

'Here,' Naylor said, turning the page. 'Take your time and have a careful look at these.'

Resnick had the scene-of-crime photographs spread across his desk; the gorgonzola and radicchio sandwich he was eating lay on a paper bag in his lap. What held his attention most, aside from the unfocusing depth of the dead man's eyes, was the haphazard pattern of stab wounds in the chest, the single blow – the first to be struck, or delivered later, after the fury of the first assault? – that had penetrated the ribs and found the heart. Resnick imagined Farleigh struggling from the bed, endeavouring to escape, only to fall across the mattress-end before the blade was driven home again. Was that how it had been? And then the slow crawl towards the bath . . . ?

Resnick looked again at the pictures of Farleigh's face,

the spread of his overweight body. What had he done or said, Resnick wondered, to provoke such an outburst?

He brought the remaining half-sandwich to his mouth with both hands and chewed thoughtfully. Catching a stray drip of mayonnaise on the back of his hand, he looked around for something to wipe it on, finally resorting to licking it away; the last thing he wanted to do was get splotches all over the photographs.

'There!' the waiter said.

'Where?'

'There.'

The face he was pointing to, finger wavering stubbily above it, was of a woman who was probably in her forties, with dark hair that hung, puppy-dog-like, around her ears and over equally dark eyes. There was no humour in those eyes. For all the world, she looked as if she had been willing the police photographer to shrivel up and – yes – die.

Marlene Kinoulton.

'You're mad.' The barman said, shaking his head. 'That's never her.'

'I say it is.'

'She's too old, way too old.'

'You didn't see her as well as I did. You were never as close.'

'She was at the bar.'

'How many times? Twice? Once? You think how many times I was over to the table, bending over to serve her ...'

'Gawping down her front.'

'Never mind that. You know what I'm saying. I had a better sight of her than you. And for my money, that's her.'

The barman swivelled away in his chair, gestured towards Naylor. 'The hair. It's wrong.'

'What d'you mean wrong?' the waiter asked.

'It didn't look like that at all.'

'So what? Aren't women changing their hair all the time?'

'But this – look – it's thicker, bushy. Can you not imagine feeling that? What it'd feel like? Coarse, am I not right? Where that one last night in the bar, her hair was fine, well looked after, finer than this. No, no way, this is never her.'

For several moments there was silence, both men sneaking glances at Naylor and Naylor not wanting to influence either of them unduly.

The barman finally jumped to his feet. 'Well, I don't care what you say. I reckon that's her and I'm sticking to it. And now, if there's anything you want me to sign or whatever I'll sign it, because then, I don't mind telling you, I've had quite enough and, if it's all right with you, I'm out of here, so I am, now.'

Kevin Naylor was looking at the photograph. Marlene Kinoulton. The name meant nothing to him. He would pass it on down the line and, as long as she was still working the city, they would bring her in. He knew that both men were looking at him, waiting for him to say something positive, send them on their way. His back was aching from bending over the albums for so long and he knew he could do with a pint, but it was at least an hour before he would get one, possibly longer. Always, jarring at the edge of his mind, the conversation he had had with Debbie over breakfast, over children, another baby.

'Thanks,' he said. 'Thanks for all your time. You've been very helpful.'

Twenty-three

Frank Carlucci had picked up the first edition of the local paper on his way back from the municipal pool. Thirty minutes of steady lengths, interrupted only by the arrival of the first batch of schoolkids of the day. Juice and coffee hadn't been as difficult to find as the last time he was in the country, ten years before, but even so, his request for a caffe latte had been treated with disbelief and the cappuccino he ordered instead was weak and boasted no more than a quarter-inch of froth. Let me into this market, Frank thought, and I could clean up.

Cathy was in the shower when he got back, between the groans and the splashes singing one of those old Brill Building songs by Carole King, Neil Sedaka, one of those. Later that day was when *Shots on the Page*, the literary segment of the festival, began, and she would be at her busiest, fans simpering round her for autographs, coming off with the same stupid questions – 'Who are your favourite mystery writers, Ms Jordan?', 'Where do you get all your ideas?', 'Just how much of you is there in Annie Q. Jones? Is she really you?' One major difference between them, Frank knew for sure, no way his wife was a dyke.

The water stopped and a few moments later Cathy came through from the shower, a towel about her hair.

'Jesus H. Christ!' Carlucci whistled in wonder. 'You still got a great body, you know that?'

'Frank,' Cathy smiled, her voice slipping into the

mock-innocent tone with which she often teased him, 'you didn't drown. You're back.'

For once, Frank refused the bait. 'Maybe it's 'cause you never had kids, I don't know, but you're in as great shape now as when you was twenty-one.'

'Bullshitter! You didn't know me when I was twenty-one.'

Carlucci laughed. 'More's the pity.' He cupped one of her buttocks with his hand and she slapped him away.

'Hey, you don't want to get felt up, shouldn't walk around that way.'

'What's that, Frank, rape defence A? Your honour, she was asking for it.'

'What you talking, rape? Husband pats his wife's ass, that's not even sexual harassment. Not even today.'

Cathy pulled on a pair of white underpants and began sorting through her tights. 'I know, Frank, you're right. It's just, well, sometimes I have difficulty remembering – that you're my husband, I mean.'

'Listen,' said Frank, serious now. 'I ever force myself upon you?'

Cathy straightened away from the bed. 'No, Frank, I can't say you have. Not recently anyway. Not since that time in Atlanta I broke your nose.'

'You didn't break my nose. A few seconds maybe, it was out of joint. Hey, you even helped pop it back, remember?'

'And got snot and blood all up my arm for my trouble.'

She had her back to him, snapping on a brassière, and he waited until she turned, wondering if she were really mad, remembering. She didn't look mad. Standing there, white bra with some cleavage and a little lace, blue jeans, even with her snarled-up hair, she looked great.

He told her so.

'Look,' he said. 'I'm serious. You don't think we could . . .' Eyes straying towards the bed.

126

'Come on, Frank. I just got out the shower. And I've got this radio interview in less than half an hour. Mollie's coming by to pick me up.'

Right, thought Frank, always something. He tossed her the paper and Cathy caught most of it, the second section sliding from the bed down to the floor. 'Maybe you should take a look at this before you go. Hung on to your front page spot, but only just. I'll see you later,' he said and left the room.

The piece describing the affray in the bookshop was boxed towards the bottom of the page, two columns. Beneath the headline, **STAR US CRIME WRITER ATTACKED**, Cathy Jordan's face smiled out from one of her standard issue publicity shots. '*Presumed feminist protest . . .*' it read. And: '*Although clearly shaken by the unprovoked assault, the visiting best-selling American author insisted she would not be curtailing her very full programme during the city's top film and fiction festival. This evening, Miss Jordan is appearing on a* Shots on the Page *panel discussing the future of crime fiction.*'

Terrific, Cathy thought, every weirdo and closet voyeur coming out of the woodwork, eager to see what I'm going to get doused in this time.

But she didn't think about that for long; her eyes kept being pulled back to the top of the page:

Police Probe Hotel Slaying

DEAD MAN FOUND NAKED IN BATH

Police launched a major inquiry today after the body of 53-year-old Wymeswold man, Peter Farleigh, was found in his hotel room earlier this morning. Farleigh, a married man with three grown-up children, who worked as a sales executive for Myerson Chemical and Fertiliser, had been stabbed a number of times in the chest and abdomen. His body was discovered when Marie-Elisabeth Fournier, a maid employed by the hotel, entered Mr Farleigh's room. She found Mr Farleigh's naked body lying in the heavily blood-stained bath.

Miss Fournier, who is nineteen, and studying English here in the city, works at the hotel on a part-time basis. She is understood to have been sedated and treated for shock.

An incident room has been set up at Canning Circus police station and the inquiry is being headed by Det Insp Charlie Resnick.

A police spokesman said they were not sure if there was any link between Mr Farleigh's murder and a recent incident in which an unidentified man, apparently naked, was found with stab wounds in the Alfreton Road area of the city. This man, whose injuries were treated at Queen's Medical Centre, has since disappeared without trace.

Forensic experts are continuing to examine the room in which Mr Farleigh was found for clues and a post-mortem examination will be carried out by Home Office pathologist Prof Arthur Parkinson.

Det Insp Resnick declined to give any further details of the death until the post-mortem has been carried out, or to *detail any lines of inquiry being followed.*

Speaking from her five-bedroomed detached home in the village of Wymeswold, a grief-stricken Sarah Farleigh said, 'Peter was a model husband and a perfect father to our children. We are all heartbroken at the news of what has happened.'

Well, Cathy Jordan thought, that puts the occasional pot of paint into perspective, doesn't it? She slid a green silk shirt from its hanger in the wardrobe and held it against herself in front of the mirror. Radio, for God's sake, she was about to do radio. What did it matter what she looked like? Now that he had his very own murder inquiry, she doubted that good old Charlie Resnick would have much time left over to think about her.

Mollie Hansen was waiting for her in the lobby, one of Cathy's books and a folder of publicity material under one arm.

'The car's waiting. It isn't far.'

'Fine. And, look, I hope you made it clear. I'll talk about anything but that stupidity with the paint.'

'Of course,' Mollie said, holding open the door. 'I've spoken to the producer twice.'

Cathy Jordan sat in front of the goose-neck microphone, a plastic cup of water near her right hand. Across the broad desk, the morning presenter picked his way through several cassettes before finding the trail for that evening's live broadcast from Mansfield Civic Centre and slotting it into place. A recording of 'Up, Up and Away' by the Fifth Dimension was coming to an end. He had already checked Cathy's voice for level.

'More music later. But now I've been joined here in the

studio by the American crime writer Cathy Jordan, one of the people most responsible for the amazing increase in the popularity of women in this field. Good morning, Cathy.'

'Hi.'

'Tell me, Cathy, while it's true that your books have proved almost as popular here as back home in the States, this hasn't been without some opposition. I believe, for instance, there was an incident yesterday involving some paint . . .'

Twenty-four

The questions didn't finish there.

Even without the additional publicity, the hotel's principal convention room would have been full for Cathy Jordan's evening panel, but, as things had developed, it was close to overflowing. Delegates who had been unable to get seats were standing at both back and sides, or leaning against ledges and walls; several more were sitting cross-legged between the front row and the platform. Cathy, herself, was sitting to the left of Maxim Jakubowski, the chairman; the young Scottish writer, Ian Rankin, sat, toying with his water glass, alongside her. On the chairman's right, Dorothy Birdwell and the tall figure of South Londoner and ex-Who roadie, Mark Timlin, sat in unlikely alliance.

'Excuse me, I have a question...' The voice was articulate, middle-class, used to making itself heard. 'I have a question for Ms Jordan...' From the chair, Jakubowski leaned forward and acknowledged the speaker from the floor.

The woman was standing now, a few seats in from the central aisle near the back of the room – rimless glasses, greying hair pulled back, a perfectly unexceptional print dress. Alongside Jakubowski, Cathy Jordan had poured water into her glass; everything had been going smoothly up to now, as predictable as discussions on the future of crime fiction tended to be.

'I should like to ask Ms Jordan if she shares my

concerns about the way women are increasingly being represented in crime fiction?'

Cathy sipped her water and counted to ten. Ian Rankin coughed and winked. 'Here we go,' he whispered.

Cathy set down her glass. 'Well,' she said, 'doesn't that depend on what those concerns are?'

'Those of most women.'

'*Most* women?'

'Yes.'

There was an uneasy stirring amongst sections of the audience; some, having heard of the bookshop incident, had come anticipating conflict and so far had been disappointed, others were inwardly flinching, steeling themselves against embarrassment.

Cathy took her time, waiting until the hum of expectation had faded into an expectant silence. 'Now I don't know, of course, how you're calibrating ''most''. I mean, is that most women in this country? This city? Or are you claiming to speak for most women in this room?' She paused and looked slowly around and heard a few disclaimers from amongst the crowd. 'Maybe, you mean most of your own little circle of friends?'

There was a sprinkling of laughter, mostly self-conscious, during which the questioner stepped out into the aisle. For the first time, Cathy caught Marius Gooding's eye. He was sitting four rows back, staring not at Dorothy Birdwell, but at her, staring hard.

'No,' the questioner was replying, her voice louder now, more openly aggressive. 'I mean any women. All women.'

Again there were mumbles of dissent, but not many, not enough to deflect shouts of acclamation which seemed to come strategically from around the room. Cathy glanced towards the chairman, who undemonstratively shook his head, happy to let things proceed.

'I'm speaking for any woman who has any sense of her

own strength or dignity, her own independence or sexuality . . .'

'Oh, come on!' Cathy Jordan said. 'Spare us the speeches.'

'. . . and who could not fail to be appalled and threatened by the excessively violent way . . .'

'Always did like a bit of violence myself,' Timlin said, as much to himself as anyone else.

Dorothy Birdwell, much like the Dormouse in *Alice*, seemed to be sleeping.

'. . . the violent ways in which you and others like you, serve up women as a series of passive victims at the hands of men.'

'Hang on a minute now,' Cathy protested, as Ian Rankin leaned towards her with a few words of encouragement.

Amongst the growing hubbub, a handful of people were heading for the exits and a number of women – half a dozen now, several others prepared to join them – were on their feet and pointing towards the platform.

'I intend to make my point . . .'

'You made your point.' Cathy said, louder now, close to losing her temper. 'The same old tired point I've heard half a hundred times before. Women as victims. Poor damned women! What is the matter with you? Don't you live in the real world?'

Some of those standing had begun a slow handclap, drowning Cathy's words. The expression on the questioner's face was a satisfied sneer. Marius had still not taken his eyes from Cathy's face.

'Pick up a paper,' Cathy said into the din, so close to the microphone that it distorted her voice. 'Any paper, switch on the news, what do you see? Women *are* victims. You think I invented that? You think I made it happen?'

'Yes!' they chorused back. 'Yes!'

Cathy Jordan sat back with the gasp of mock surprise and shook her head.

'Every time you attack a woman in your books . . .' another voice from another part of the room. 'Every time you rape, or kill, or maim . . .'

'*I* rape?'

'Yes, you. You! You! You!'

Beside Cathy, Ian Rankin was shaking his head in a mixture of bewilderment and anger, and at the far end of the table, Mark Timlin was smiling happily. Dorothy Birdwell had awoken and, like the Dormouse in *Alice*, was looking around in dazed surprise. The chairman tapped a warning on the end of his microphone, but to no avail.

'Every time you do those things, one woman to another . . .'

Cathy Jordan was on her feet, pointing. 'I do not *do* those things.'

'Yes, you do!' It was the original questioner, closer to the stage now and pointing. 'And as long as you go on perpetrating this myth of female weakness, it will go on happening.'

'That's a crock of shit!'

'Is it? Is it, Ms Jordan? Well, I hope next time you open your paper and read about some poor fifteen-year-old, or some old woman of eighty being raped and beaten, you should think about that a little more carefully.'

'Jesus!' said Cathy, slamming back down into her chair. 'I don't believe this is happening.'

'All right,' Jakubowski said, raising both hands in an appeal for calm. 'Thank you very much, thank you very much indeed. I'm sure we all appreciate your point, but now I feel we should move on. Yes, thank you, there's someone over there . . .'

Cathy continued to sit there, taking no further part in the discussion, staring at the blank sheet of paper in front of her as her anger began slowly to subside.

Twenty-five

The photographs of Peter Farleigh had been enlarged and pinned, head height, to the wall. Slightly below them, to left and to right, the other, earlier, non-fatal victims: Paul Pynchon, from Hinckley, stabbed in the red-light district near the Waterloo Road; Marco Fabrioni, beaten and tied up on the Forest; Gerry McKimber, the sales rep stabbed in his hotel room; a quick drawing from memory of the still-anonymous man who had disappeared from hospital after being found, stabbed and naked, on the Alfreton Road. The one they were now, thanks to the rare flash of inspiration from Divine, calling Polo after his sock.

Maps, dates, approximate times.

Details of wounds, weapons used.

Data.

Three colour ten by eights of Marlene Kinoulton, left profile, right profile, full face: the woman identified by the waiter in the hotel where Farleigh had been killed.

There were twenty officers in the room, most with mugs or styrofoam cups of tea, Players' Silk Cut between their fingers, Benson King Size; expectation adhering to the walls like yellow smoke.

Skelton, straight-backed, stood near the main door, watching. His responsibility, not his show. Resnick rose purposefully to his feet.

'Pynchon, Fabrioni, McKimber, Polo, Farleigh: five stabbings, one fatal. Five male victims, all of them – and this is not entirely confirmed, but I think we can assume it

135

for now – engaged in some kind of sexual activity involving prostitution.'

Resnick paused, making sure of everyone's attention.

'Now if we look at where the attacks took place, they break down into two basic groups: outside, in the red-light area, and inside, in one hotel or other. From that first group, two attacks – those on Pynchon and on the Italian – were carried out by more than one person, male as well as female, and the injuries received were more general. Personally, I think we can disregard these as having any direct connection with Peter Farleigh's murder. Our friend, Polo, I'm not so sure about.

'We think he was running from his attacker, that's the only reasonable assumption, and that would place the attack in the same general area as those on Pynchon and Fabrioni. But what have we got? A single wound, no more. Nothing to suggest the kind of group attack that took place in the earlier cases. So, let's presume, one assailant. All the other evidence suggests a woman, some kind of assignation that went wrong. Likely, but only conjecture. The wound is interesting, though; a single blow with a sharp implement, most likely a knife, in an area that closely corresponds to where most of the stab wounds in Farleigh's body were found. So, although Polo's stabbing is the incident about which we know least, and therefore it might be convenient to push it to the back of our minds, I don't want that to happen. Not yet. It may connect.'

He paused, glanced over towards Skelton, who avoided his eyes and fidgeted instead with the knot of his tie. What did that mean, Resnick wondered? That I'm going on too long and he's bored? Or does he think I've got it wrong? Barking up the wrong tree? Maybe his tie was simply too tight.

'Now,' Resnick said, moving towards the photographs, heads turning to watch as he pointed with the first two fingers of his right hand. 'These pair, McKimber and Farleigh, this is where our main focus has to be. Look at the similarities. Both men attacked in hotel rooms, attacked with knives, stabbed more than once. In both instances, the most likely scenario, the assailant was a woman. A woman who was there for the purposes of prostitution, though it's only in McKimber's case we know that for a fact.'

Lynn Kellogg's arm was raised. 'Surely, sir, we don't even know that? The woman he claims stabbed him, she's never been identified.'

'That's right.'

'So, he could be lying. I mean, we've only his word.'

'Right, he stabbed himself,' Divine called out, sarcastically.

'No,' Lynn snapped back. 'But it could have been a man, right. A boy. Men are prostitutes too, you know.'

'Okay,' Resnick raised his hand for silence. 'We're going to be talking to McKimber again. I'm seeing him myself. I'll bear what you've said in mind. You're right, it wants double-checking. No harm.'

He moved across to the pictures of Marlene Kinoulton. 'This is the woman identified by the waiter in the hotel restaurant as the one Farleigh was talking to earlier on the evening he was killed. They'd been eating at separate tables till Farleigh went over and joined her. Afterwards they went out, the waiter thinks, into the hotel bar, and although the barman confirms that Farleigh was there with a woman, sat there with her until past eleven, he wasn't able to confirm the identification. His general description of the woman Farleigh was with is close enough though, for us to take this woman, Kinoulton, very seriously.

'She is a known prostitute, here in the city, we've established that. Also works in Sheffield, Leicester and Derby.'

'Anywhere she can get a Cheap Day Return,' some-body said.

Resnick waited for the laughter, what there was of it, to fade. 'On five previous occasions, she's been issued a warning for soliciting in the big hotels. She wants finding and fast. Mark, Kevin, you're already liaising with the Vice Squad, she's your target, down to you. As I've said, I'm talking to McKimber. The rest of you, we have to keep checking other guests at the hotel, the rest of the staff, so on. We really need another ID to back up the one on Kinoulton. Or some positive forensics. We're also going to do a little digging into Farleigh's work, appoint-ments kept on this trip, general background. Why he chose to stay in a hotel in the city when an hour's drive at most would have seen him home.' He looked around. 'All right. Questions? Sergeant Millington's got your assign-ments. Let's be diligent. Not miss anything. Let's get this wrapped up as fast as we can.'

'You think I'm wrong?' Resnick asked. He and Skelton, out in the corridor, officers spilling past them, voices raised from the stairs, banging of doors, the same old chanting of telephones.

'No, why?'

Resnick shrugged.

'If I thought you were going down the wrong road, as your superior officer, I'd say so. Only . . .'

Resnick looked at him expectantly. A shout, distant, from the area of the cells, was followed by a metallic slamming sound, then silence.

Skelton stood back, nodding, still fiddling with his tie. 'Not wanting to chuck a spanner in the works, Charlie, not at this stage. But like you said, tunnel vision, it's a dangerous thing.'

'Yes,' Resnick said. 'Thanks. Thanks, I'll keep it in mind.'

*

Breakfast had been a rushed affair, needing to be in at the station early, make certain everything was up and ready for the briefing. Now, Resnick stood in line behind a pair of purple-shirted tax accountants, waiting for the assistant at the deli to make him a couple of sandwiches for the drive down into the neighbouring county, something tasty on dark rye and caraway, an espresso for now and another for the journey. The tape machine in his car had been on the blink for weeks, all he'd been able to listen to was GEM-AM, recycling the glorious moments of some-body's youth, though rarely, it seemed to Resnick, his own. But now it was fixed and he could play the new – to him – Joshua Redman to his heart's content: 'Moose the Mooche', 'Turnaround', 'Make Sure You're Sure'.

Clicking the seat-belt into place, Resnick turned the key in the ignition and switched on the stereo, tenor sax loping in at mid-tempo as he eased out into the mid-morning traffic.

Twenty-six

The pub was flat against the main road, a thin line of
pavement all that separated its windows from the heavy
lorries shuddering down towards the A5, the M69, the
M6. Inside four men, worn down by middle-age, sat at
four separate tables, nursing pint glasses through until
lunchtime. All four looking up when Resnick entered, but
none looked up for long. The landlord, restocking shelves
behind the bar, paused to glance at Resnick's warrant
card, listened to his question and pointed towards the
stairs. 'First floor, back.' If the radio had been switched on
and if it had been playing David Whitfield or Perry Como,
Resnick would not have been surprised.

There were three boards, bare along the landing, and
each one of them creaked.

'Gerry McKimber?'

A tall man, spindly with a nose like a wedge that had
been driven hard, and not quite straight, into the centre of
his face, McKimber stared at Resnick's identification,
then stepped back, shaking his head. 'Christ! It's not taken
her so bloody long!'

'Her?'

'I told her I'd pay, Jesus, she's knows I'll pay just as
soon as I can. She knows I've lost my fucking job, for
Christ's sake, what does she expect?'

'Mr McKimber?'

'I've told you . . .'

'Mr McKimber . . .'

'What?'

'You're talking about maintenance, child support?'

'No, I'm talking about winning the fucking pools!'

'That's not why I'm here.'

'Not? Not the pools, then?' He laughed, more a bark than a laugh. 'Not here to tell me that? Half a million quid? Am I going to let it change my life?'

Resnick shook his head.

'Well, thank Christ for that. 'Cause I forgot to post the sodding coupon.'

'Mr McKimber, can I come inside?'

There were two beds pushed back against the far wall, narrow divans low to the floor, only one of them recently used. On the other, McKimber had piled, not neatly, some of his possessions, cardboard boxes, motoring magazines, clothes. A wardrobe, a table, what might euphemistically have been called an easy chair. The single window, with a view over beer crates and barrels and an outside urinal, was open a crack.

McKimber stubbed out the cigarette that had been smouldering in the ashtray and lit another. He held the packet towards Resnick, who shook his head.

'If it's not that cow, then what is it?' But then he saw Resnick's face and thought he knew. 'You've caught her, that cunt as stabbed me? You've got her, right?'

'Afraid not.'

'Then what the fuck . . . ?'

'There's been another incident . . .'

'Like that? Like what happened to me?'

'Similar. Enough to make us think there might be a connection. I need to talk to you again.'

McKimber walked towards the window and looked down, pushing fingers back through his unkempt hair. 'You know, at first she never believed me, the wife, I don't know why. It was a fight, she said, you were in a fight. Some pub or other. Same as before. Why bother making up an excuse? Why bother lying?'

McKimber turned back into the room, cigarette cupped in his hand. 'As if what I'd said, you know, what really happened, the hotel and that, as if somehow she'd never have minded so much.'

He went over to the bed, sat down. 'I used to get into these scrapes. Once in a while. You know what it's like, on the road. Travelling. Well, you can imagine. Chatting up people all day, trying to. Half the time getting doors closed in your face. Abuse. You wouldn't believe the abuse. Come evening, had a bit of a meal, too far to go home, too tired, what do you do? Well, me, like a lot of men, I like a drink. Trouble is, when I drink I suppose I get careless 'bout what I say. Don't care who hears me, either. Gets me into trouble, I admit it. The firm, they'd warned me, Gerry, this has got to stop. So many last warnings, I never believed them and then they gave me the push for something else altogether, but that's another story.'

He drew on the cigarette, releasing the smoke, slow, down his nose. 'The wife, see, she'd been on at me, an' all. Forever on at me. Just once more, Gerry McKimber, you come home looking like you've been in a brawl and you're out of my house. My house!' McKimber repeated his barking laugh. 'Not now. Not when she's crying out for me to pay something towards the sodding bills. Oh, no. Now it's our house again. Our house!'

He looked across towards Resnick, who waited, listening, prepared to listen, saying nothing.

'This business with the woman, the one as cut me, the wife, she thought I'd made it up. Of course, I never told her, what I never told her, that I was, like, paying for it, you know. Christ, I wasn't about to tell her that now, was I? Paying for it. Give her that satisfaction. No, what I said was, what I told her, this woman and I, we get talking in the bar, one thing rolls into another, I've had a few too many to know properly what I'm doing, next thing she's with me, up in the room. Would she believe that? Not for weeks would she fucking believe that, blue in the sodding face from telling her. Well, it was the truth, more or less the truth, I didn't want her mingeing on at me for something I'd never done. Jesus! When I finally get it through her thick head I'm not lying, what does the stupid cow do? Fucking slings me out!

'All my stuff, clothes, everything, out the window, out the door. Out the house. Receipts, samples, God knows what, all over the front garden, next door's, up and down half the bloody street. Some of it I never even bloody found. "You believe me now, don't you?" I said. "You're filth," she says. "You're scum. You're never setting foot in this house again." The kids upstairs, hanging out of the upstairs, taking it all in.'

He ground the nub end of his cigarette into the threadbare carpet with his heel. 'What was it you wanted to know?'

Sharon Garnett had been on court for the best part of an hour and a half; two games down in the fourth set and any rhythm in her service had gone. A couple of double faults, an attempted lob off her backhand which had landed closer to the next court than the one on which they were playing, and it had been over.

'Thanks, Sharon. Good game.'

'Sure,' Sharon grinned. 'I was crap.'

Her opponent laughed. He was a nice enough bloke, sergeant in Surveillance, wife and two-point-four kids, semi-detached south of the city at Ruddington. 'Time for a drink after?'

'After?'

'Shower, change, whatever?'

'Thanks, no. Maybe some other time. I'm going to shower at home.'

She was almost at her car before Divine spotted her, Divine and Naylor, leaning up against their own vehicle,

143

taking in what there was of the sun. The rhododendron bushes thick along the perimeter of University Park behind them.

'Will you look at that?' Divine said. 'Legs that go all the way up to her arse!'

'Right,' Naylor said. 'New design. Don't know if it'll catch on.'

'Clever bugger!'

Naylor gave a shout and Sharon turned and saw them, no more than a couple of big kids, standing there in shirtsleeves, grinning. She wished she had stopped for a shower now, changed; aware of her sports shirt sticking to her, the sour-sweet smell of her own sweat.

'Called in at the station, said you might be here,' Divine said.

'Day off.'

'Win?' Naylor asked.

'Not exactly.'

'This bloke copped it in the hotel,' Divine said. 'You heard about it?'

She nodded.

'Witness made an ID . . .' Naylor said, taking over. 'Waiter, works in the hotel restaurant.'

'She's a tom,' Divine said, interrupting.

'Local?'

'So it seems.'

'Name?'

'Kinoulton. Marlene.'

Sharon wished they weren't having this conversation out there, cars driving in and out of the tennis centre behind them. Sweat growing cold.

'Know her?' Divine asked.

'I've not been here long enough to know all the girls.'

'But this one, this Marlene?'

'I might.'

They waited.

'You know the girl I contacted you about? Doris. The one said she might have something interesting to tell me, about the night that man was knifed near the Alfreton Road? Well, turns out, as far as Marlene Kinoulton's got a best friend, she's it.'

Divine grinned across at Naylor and Naylor winked back: at long last they might be getting somewhere.

Resnick had taken McKimber back through the evening in low gear, beginning to end. 'Never occurred to me at first that she was on the game. Never cottoned on. I thought, I suppose, nothing special, even so, not going to let themselves get turned into a knocking shop. But then I thought, yes, well, why not? Where all the money is, isn't it, after all? Blokes with time on their hands, money to spend.'

'So, as far as you were concerned, at the beginning, it was what? Just a casual chat?'

'Well, no, not exactly. Way she was coming on to me, right off like, knew it was more than that. But, well, like I say, I suppose I thought I'd clicked, you know. Pulled.'

'And when did she make it clear that wasn't exactly the case?'

'When we got to the room.'

'Once you were inside?'

'No. I was just, like, about to use the key. One of them bits of plastic, not really a key at all. She leaned past me, hand against the door. "You know this isn't your birthday, don't you?" That's what she said.' He looked over towards Resnick. 'She was there, then, wasn't she? What was I supposed to do?'

'What kind of a woman would you have said she was?' Resnick asked. 'Based on that first part of the evening.'

'Woman? She was a tart, wasn't she?'

'Yes, but before you knew that. I mean, was she pleasant, well-spoken? How did she come across?'

McKimber shrugged. 'Just sort of normal, you know.'

'Intelligent? Bright?'

'Bright enough to know she had my balls in her pocket.'

'But, aside from what you've already said, were you surprised to find out she was apparently a prostitute?'

'Surprised?' McKimber shook his head. 'One way or another, they all are. I mean, that's the way it works. If you can get someone to pay for it, why give it away?'

Resnick showed him six sets of photographs, six different women, all similar, all with dark hair.

'Look,' McKimber said, 'you're wasting your time. I've already been through this.'

'Humour me,' Resnick said. 'Let's try again. Just these few.'

McKimber lit another cigarette. A good minute before he answered, Resnick could see that he'd stopped really looking. 'I'm sorry,' McKimber said. 'It isn't any good.'

'You're quite sure.'

'Yes, I said. The only one . . .'

'Go on.'

'The only one it just might possibly be . . .'

'Yes?'

McKimber transferred the cigarette to his mouth and jabbed a finger – 'That one. That's the only one, if you told me I had to pick out one of these, had to, that's the only one comes close. Only one that's near.' And he picked out, not Marlene Kinoulton, but the woman in the set of photographs immediately above her, gazing into the camera with a slight squint.

Divine and Naylor had driven Sharon Garnett back to her flat and waited while she had cleaned up and changed into tan leggings, a purple T-shirt, black cotton jacket. Together, Naylor driving, they trawled the red-light district looking for Marlene Kinoulton and her friend

Doris Duke. Nowhere to be seen. None of the girls out working claimed to have seen them for several days. A week. Sheffield, try Sheffield. Leeds.

'Sorry,' Sharon said eventually. 'We're wasting our time. We'd be better trying again later tonight. Late.'

'Fair enough,' Divine said and Naylor pulled in towards the kerb.

'I might have a problem,' Naylor said. 'With later. I'm supposed to be off round Debbie's mum's. She's got this relation over from Canada. Nephew or something. Having a bit of a celebration.'

'Sounds,' Divine said with a smirk, 'like the kind of thing you wouldn't miss for the world.'

'Yes, well. I'll see what I can do.'

Sharon opened the car door. 'Half ten in the Arboretum then, okay?'

'Get there first,' Divine grinned, 'and mine's a pint of Kimberley.'

'You wish! I'm the one doing you a favour, remember? And mine's a Bacardi and Coke. Large. Ten thirty, right?'

Divine watched as Sharon walked away. 'Second thoughts, why don't you go hobnobbing with the in-laws after all. Leave this to me.'

'Thought you were being faithful this month?' Naylor said. 'One-woman man.'

'Yeah, so I am,' Divine grinned, grabbing his crotch. 'It's just this that doesn't understand.'

Twenty-seven

'Honey, you sure you're up for this?'

Cathy Jordan hesitated in what she was doing, adjusting her silver Zuni earrings in front of the mirror; her favourites, the ones she had bought in Santa Fe. 'God, Frank, I wish you wouldn't do that.'

'What? Show a little concern?'

'Call me honey that way. Makes me feel like something out of Norman Rockwell.'

'Not *The Shining*?' He came up behind her with arm raised, as if holding a knife, leering his manic Jack Nicholson leer. 'Honey, I'm home!'

'Jesus, Frank.'

'What?'

'All that's been going on, that's not so funny.'

Dipping his head towards her shoulder, an oddly tender gesture, he slid both arms around her. 'That guy, huh? The one in the paper. Poor bastard!'

She was looking at his reflection in the dressing table mirror, both their reflections: familiar and strange.

'Frank?'

'Umm?'

'Did you read any of the new book?'

'Your new book?'

'Uh-huh.'

'I didn't think you'd even shipped it off to the publishers yet.'

'No, but . . .'

'You're still working on it, right?'

'Fiddling, that's all. The manuscript.'

'You remember one time you caught me reading these pages you'd left lying around? I thought you were going to go crazy.'

Cathy Jordan smiled into the mirror. 'That was a while back. I was more cranky then. Nervous, I guess.'

'What you mean is, back then, you cared what I thought.'

'That's not what I mean at all.' Looking at him, defiance and concern in his eyes, the stance of his body, strength of his arms. So easy to have turned inside those arms.

'Anyway,' Frank said. 'I didn't look at it, not a peek. How come you ask?'

'Oh . . .' Her voice drifted off and she looked away; how strange desire was, months in which she had felt – God! – nothing, at best a mixture of comfort and irritation, and now this. 'It doesn't matter,' she said, and moved her mouth over his.

They kissed until it was difficult to breathe.

'Jeeze,' Frank said, as she released him. 'What's got into you?'

Cathy let her smile spread wide and when she laughed it was down and dirty. 'Recently, not a whole lot.'

He reached for her and she reached for him.

'Well,' Cathy said, eyebrow arched. 'Have you been working out?'

They were midway between the dressing table and the bed when the phone rang.

'Leave it,' Frank said.

'All right.' But she could see the time, winking at her, green-eyed, from the clock radio beside the bed.

'Cathy, come on.'

She reached out a hand and the ringing stopped. 'Hello,' she said, listening a moment before dropping the receiver back down. 'It's Mollie. She's in the foyer, waiting. We have to be there in thirty minutes.'

Frank rolled clumsily round and leaned forward, elbows on his knees, fingers pressed against his temples.

'Don't, sweetheart,' Cathy said, giving his arm a squeeze. Her voice tenderly mocking. 'Don't have a headache.'

'What do you suggest?' he said. 'A shower? Maybe there's time to jerk off? I know, I could jerk off in the shower.'

Already she was on her feet, reaching her coat from the hanger. 'You could come with me to the store, that's what you could do. Protect me from any more militant paint-throwers. Radical *femmes*. With this murder on their hands, I doubt the police will have officers to spare.'

Frank looked across at her from the bed, still undecided how grouchy he was going to be.

'Don't be mad,' Cathy said. 'Do this for me. Once it's over, we've got the rest of the afternoon to ourselves. We can come back here, what do you say?'

But Frank knew, they both knew, whatever he replied, the moment was gone.

Cathy hadn't known what to expect, but the city centre on a Saturday lunchtime wasn't it. The way people pushed, wall to wall, along the pedestrianised street leading towards the Victoria Centre, all Cathy could think of was one of those paintings by – who was it? – Brueghel. A medieval vision of Hell.

The bookshop, where she and Dorothy Birdwell were to do a joint signing, was on the ground floor of the shopping precinct. Signing with Dorothy, needless to say, had not been Cathy's own choice, but it was at the shop's request and, as her publisher had been quick to point out, the shop was capable of shifting a lot of product. Cathy presumed she meant books.

Mollie steered Cathy and Dorothy between groups of teenagers wearing high-tops, reversed baseball caps and T-shirts, Frank and Marius, unspeaking, following close behind. Between River Island and HMV they passed several mothers, dragging squawking children in their wake, fathers striding several paces ahead, the fuss and commotion no concern of theirs. Cathy saw one woman spin a small boy, no more than three, out of the path of a pushchair and give him a slap, hard, across the backs of his bare legs. 'There! Now stop scraighting, you mardy little sod, or I'll slap you again.' For a moment, Cathy caught her eye: blonde hair tight like copper wire, cigarette, eyes hard as coal. Pregnant again. No way was she more than twenty, twenty-one. A moment, then she was gone.

'Here we are,' Mollie said cheerfully. 'And look, there's a queue already.'

Cathy's face beamed back at her in full-colour from a poster in the window. Inside the shop, it was reproduced many times: smaller posters on the walls, dumpbins at the ends of aisles, a whole shelf of paperbacks and hard-covers, book back to front, displaying the same image. How did she look to all these people, Cathy wondered? Sunny, smug, self-satisfied. American. But, in truth, most of the people pushing round her seemed quite oblivious, not to care.

In contrast, the publicity for Dorothy Birdwell, who stood talking now to Marius, was noticeably less prominent, her books less visible.

'Cathy Jordan?' She shook hands with a surprisingly young woman in a light grey suit with a faint stripe. 'It's a pleasure to welcome you. We've got you set up over there.' Cathy shook her hand and she turned aside to Dorothy. 'Miss Birdwell, how are you? If you'll excuse me, I'll be with you in just a moment.'

Leaving Dorothy and Marius stranded, she led Cathy

151

past the line of fans towards a table piled high with yet more copies of her books; those waiting to speak to Dorothy Birdwell were far fewer and mostly older.

'Is that her?' one woman said of Cathy as she passed.

'That's never her.'

'Bet you it is.'

'Some of those photos don't do her any favours, do they?'

'Not much. Lop a good ten years off her age, that's all.'

'Get away!'

The manager saw Cathy installed and moved swiftly across to deal with Dorothy Birdwell and an increasingly irate Marius, who was quick to complain about what he saw as second-rate treatment.

Responding to Cathy's request, Frank had positioned himself midway along the queue, feigning an interest in a shelf of books dealing with railways. If he went and stood right behind her, he'd only succeed in looking like a semi-pro bodyguard, with his brains firmly in his biceps.

'Hello, Miss Jordan. It's really nice to meet you. My husband and I've read all of your books, haven't we, Trevor? I wonder if you could just sign this for me? Yes, that's it. Janice and Trevor. That's lovely. Oh, yes, and the date. Ta ever so much. Bye-bye.'

The first railway in Britain, Frank read, was a simple set of wooden beams laid on the ground in Nottinghamshire in the reign of Elizabeth I, to transport coal from the coalfield.

Mollie drifted off towards the contemporary fiction shelf and thumbed through the latest Michèle Roberts.

'You're not going to stop writing them, Miss Jordan? I mean, you won't pack it in will you? You'll not get bored with Annie? You can't, not while there's so many of us, all waiting for the next.'

Confused between the LMS, the GWR, the Southern and the LNER, Frank set the book back. Mollie moved on to find something that would do for her mother's birthday. Fay Weldon or Joanna Trollope, perhaps. Something that would take away the taste of the Jeanette Winterson she had given her the year before.

Cathy Jordan's hand was beginning to ache and she still hadn't got to the additional copies she was sure the manageress would want her to sign for stock. But at least the end of the line was at hand, and not a single troublemaker in sight.

The queue to Dorothy Birdwell's table had long since dried up and she was still sitting there, straight-backed and hopeful, Marius gently massaging away a little stiffness in her shoulders, whispering in her ear.

'What name would you like me to put?' Cathy asked for the umpteenth time. And, 'How do you spell that?'

With only a few people still to go, Frank had seemingly got bored with watching over her and was chatting to Mollie instead, the pair of them up at the front of the shop, near the cash desk. Cathy dipped her head to sign another book and the next time she looked up, there was Marius, immediately in front of her.

Cathy jumped, surprised at his being there, disturbed by the intensity of his stare. 'Marius, you don't want me to sign a book for you, I suppose? For Dorothy?'

She forced herself to smile, but Marius was not smiling back. Instead, unnervingly, he slowly leaned towards her, the table edge gripped with both hands. His stare was fixed on Cathy and would not let her look away. 'What I want,' he said, his voice intense and low, 'is for you to understand what's happened here today. All these people, foolish, small-minded people flocking around you, I want you to understand what that is about. It's not you. Not talent. Not originality, not skill. That woman over there has more of those qualities in her little finger than you'll ever have in the whole of your life. No, what this . . . this charade is all about is publicity, media, money. That and

153

the sordid muck you wallow in every day of your writing life. Sensationalism of the kind that real writers would never for one moment soil their hands with. Or their minds.'

He held her gaze a moment longer, straightened, and turned away, leaving Cathy shaken and pale.

'What the hell did he want?' Frank asked, moments later, glancing over to where Marius was now helping Dorothy Birdwell from her chair.

Cathy shook her head. 'Nothing,' she said. 'Nothing important.' But the coldness that had spread along her arms and the backs of her legs was still there and although Marius now had his back to her, she could still clearly see her image, reversed, reflected in his eyes.

Twenty-eight

Back in the Book Dealers' Room at the festival hotel,
business was in full swing. Derek Neighbour had spent
some time moving from stand to stand and had finally
come upon Ed Leimbacher, from *MisterE Books* in
Seattle, who had assured him that he could he could lay
his hands on a first edition of *Uneasy Prey* in mint
condition. Something of a snip at four hundred and sixty
pounds. Plus commission. And handling. And packing.
And insurance. 'And a bargain at that,' Leimbacher had
smiled reassuringly.

Neighbour wondered why he wasn't reassured.

There was no getting round the fact, though, that the
damage to the copy of Cathy Jordan's book he had taken
with him to Waterstone's was even worse than he had
feared; as many as fifty pages were stuck together
irretrievably with paint, many of the others spotted and
splotched. And the dust-jacket . . .

'Look,' Neighbour had finally said, fingering his
cheque-book nervously inside his jacket pocket, 'I'll have
to think about it a little longer. I'm sorry.'

'You could be,' Ed Leimbacher said. 'Pass it up and by
the time you've done another circuit of the room, it could
be gone.'

'I know, it's just . . .'

But the book dealer had turned aside and was no longer
smiling – not until the next potential customer came along
moments later. Books may be books, but business, well,
that was business.

Dorothy Birdwell was leaning back in the armchair of their hotel suite, a damp cloth lightly across her eyes. Marius had helped her to remove her shoes and stockings and now was slowly massaging her feet, first one and then the other, each held close against his chest as he worked his fingers around the ball and carefully across the instep, knowing exactly when and where to apply pressure, when his touch should be little more than a breath.

'Marius, my dear . . .'

'Mmm?'

'When you went across to speak to the American, you didn't say anything too, well, distressing, I trust?'

'Oh, no. No.' Sliding one of his fingers along the delicate curl of her toes. 'Of course not. Nothing like that.'

'I know. I know. Some people, some men, if they were annoyed, they could be a little crude. But not you. I don't think you could ever be crude in the slightest.'

Mouth curved into a smile, Marius bent forward and lightly kissed the underside of her foot.

'How'd it go at the signing?' Tyrell asked. It was mid-afternoon and he was snatching the chance for a quick sandwich and a pot of tea at the convention hotel.

'Okay,' Mollie said. 'At least as far as Cathy was concerned. It was Dorothy Birdwell I felt sorry for. I doubt if she had more than half a dozen people standing in line. Still, I'm arranging transport for her and Marius to go out to Newstead Abbey. Apparently she's got this big thing about Byron.'

Tyrell's eyes brightened. 'Did you know Curtis was going to make a film about Byron? Ages ago. Late fifties biopic. Script, locations, everything. Apparently, some of his original drawings are around somewhere. Sounds like a really interesting project. James Mason as the man himself – can't you just see it? Mad, bad and dangerous to know. Patricia Medina. Vincent Price as Shelley. Aside from that Steve Reeves thing he did in Italy, it would have been the only costume piece he made.'

'How is Curtis?'

Tyrell inclined his head in the direction of the bar. 'Keeping himself topped up.' He lifted up the pot and gave it a gentle shake, offering it towards Mollie, who shook her head.

'What amazes me,' Mollie said, 'he seems able to drink all the time and never get drunk.'

'He explained it to me the other night,' Tyrell said. 'Claims he attained a state of perfect equilibrium in 1965 and he's been balancing there ever since.'

'What crap!' Mollie said. 'All Curtis has done, like a lot of other pissheads, is attain a state of being perfectly unemployable.'

Tyrell was on the verge of arguing back, but thought better of it; no sense in taking on Mollie when he didn't have to. Easing his slim body back into the comfortable chair, he opted for enjoying his tea instead.

As soon as the signing was over, Cathy Jordan had decided what she wanted most was to walk. She didn't know where and perhaps it didn't matter. She just wanted to walk.

'Want me along?' Frank asked.

Cathy gave a suit-yourself shrug and began to push her way through the crowds entering the Victoria Centre. Crossing the road in dangerous defiance of a black and white cab and a green double-decker bus, she hurried past the Disney shop on the corner and plunged into the Saturday afternoon throng.

Frank knew his alternatives: let her go her own way and head off back to the hotel and watch TV; or do what he actually did, tag along several yards behind and wait for her to slow down, for whatever was irking her, gradually to become less troublesome.

With no clear idea where she was heading, Cathy found herself on a recently re-cobbled road that led towards the castle; dropping down below the sandstone rock, she turned past the Trip to Jerusalem, local bikers and Japanese tourists sharing an uneasy space outside the proclaimed oldest pub in England. Beyond Castle Boulevard, Cathy crossed the bridge above the canal and walked down towards the lock.

Pigeons roosted in the broken windows of abandoned warehouse buildings. Brickwork blackened and cracked. Iron gates bloomed rust. Idling past, a freshly painted longboat leaked colours onto the oily surface of the water. Mallards, unconcerned, rocked and resettled in its wake.

'I'm sorry,' Cathy said, pausing.

'No problem.'

Ruefully, Cathy smiled. 'Why do we say that? No problem, all the time. Waiters in restaurants, cab drivers, clerks. You. Especially when it isn't true.'

'Hey, I didn't mean anything.'

'Exactly.'

'You mean there is a problem? That's what you think?'

'Don't you?'

They were walking slowly now; heels of Cathy's boots clipping the uneven concrete of the canal path.

'It's not that guy, Marius, is it?'

'Marius? What about him?'

'I don't know. Just the way he came up to you at the end, there. I thought maybe he had you spooked.'

'Jesus! It'd take more than a creep like Marius to spook me.'

They walked on. Between the buildings on the far side of the canal, traffic shunted eastwards in a slow line.

'Is it the letters?' Frank asked.

Cathy sighed. 'I've hardly thought about the damned letters.'

'Then it's somebody else.'

Cathy laughed, short and humourless. 'You mean, a man?'

'Unless you've changed a lot more than I thought.'

She shook her head. 'You know you amaze me, Frank. There you are, shaking your dick at anything in sight, telling me it doesn't mean a goddamn thing, where if it's me . . .'

'There is somebody then.'

She stopped, folded her arms across her chest. 'Frank, you have my word, I have not been screwing the home help.'

'Maybe not. But that might have been better than banging that plastic surgeon.'

Cathy didn't respond. She set off walking again, watching as a pair of ducks, grey-green, floated past along the canal. 'Water under the bridge, Frank. Old water under an old bridge. And, besides, he was interested in offering a little liposuction, that was mostly all.'

'I can imagine.'

'God, I hope not, baby.'

'What?'

'The two of us hacking at it in that hotel room, the size of a domestic freezer. Me struggling with my thermals and Mr Plastic with the kind of all-over body hair that puts King Kong in the shade.' She shuddered. 'Not a pretty sight.'

Frank strode on ahead, putting some distance between himself and his wife's revelations. He didn't know how much she was joking, if at all. After twenty or thirty yards, Cathy caught up with him, touching the fingers of her left hand to his neck, the ridge of muscle just above the collar. 'I'm sorry, I'm a bitch. You don't deserve that.'

'I do,' Frank said.

'Okay,' Cathy agreed, laughing. 'You do.'

Thirty minutes later and they were sitting at one of the

159

wooden tables outside the Baltimore Exchange, staring off towards the water with a couple of beers. Away to the east, where the canal disappeared between low, suburban houses on its way to join the River Trent, the sky was suddenly thick with clouds and the near horizon had misted over with slanting rain and violet light.

'How many years,' Cathy asked, 'have we been together?'

'Seven,' Frank said, not looking at her direct. 'Eight.'

'I wonder,' Cathy said, 'if that isn't long enough?'

Twenty-nine

Resnick's friend, Ben Riley, had never been much of a ladies' man. Back in the late sixties, early seventies, when they had been young constables there in the city, there had been girls, certainly – nurses from the old city centre hospital, since rationalised out of existence, workers from the hosiery factories strung out along the roads north-east of the city, long since pulled down for DIY stores and supermarkets, Toys R Us. But the drinking, hobnobbing with the lads, to Ben they had always been more important. Until Sarah.

Sarah Prentiss had been a librarian who worked at the central library when it was on Shakespeare Street, close behind the Central Divisional police station. It was a place Resnick himself had liked to wander through, sit in sometimes, reading through the jazz reviews in back issues of the *Gramophone*. A solid building, thick stone walls, monumental, long corridors and high ceilings, shelves of books that seemed to stretch on forever, a pervasive silence – to Resnick, it was the essence of what a good library was about. Some years back, it had become part of the new university and the main library had moved even closer to the city centre. Now you had to push your way through a conglomeration of sales goods, advertising, magazines, videos and CDs before coming face to face with a good old-fashioned book. As far as marketing went, Resnick was sure it was successful, he was certain the library boasted a greater number of clients than before; he just wasn't one of them.

Neither was Ben Riley, who, to Resnick's continuing regret, had relocated to America some ten years ago. He doubted whether Sarah Prentiss visited the library much either, now that she was Sarah something else, and living in Northamptonshire with a husband, kids, and a couple of cars. He had learned this from Ben, with whom she had, for some years, exchanged the obligatory Christmas cards.

Why was Resnick thinking of all this?

Betty Carter was singing 'Body and Soul' on the car stereo as he drove, mingling the words and tune with those of a second, similar song, so that the final, climactic chorus seemed forever delayed, but that wasn't it. Not exactly. More confusing still, the words of yet another song were worrying away at some part of Resnick's mind.

'Send in the Clowns.'

He had heard Betty Carter live just once. A rare trip to London, a weekend in early spring, and she had been at Ronnie Scott's. A striking black woman, not beautiful, not young; warm and confident, good-humoured, talking to the audience between numbers with that slight show-business *bonhomie* that set Resnick's teeth painfully on edge. But when she sang . . . He remembered 'But Beautiful', 'What's New?', the way she would move around the stage with the microphone, her body bending to the shapes of the words with a combination of feeling and control that was unsurpassable.

Scott himself, nose like a hawk and gimlet-eyed, his sixty-odd years showing only where the skin hung thinly at his neck, had been leading his quartet through the support slots on the same evening. Tenor saxophone, piano, bass and drums. After several rousing numbers, Scott had played a two-chorus version of Sondheim's 'Send in the Clowns', almost straight, bass and drums dropping out, the tone of his saxophone ravishing and hard, one of the best ballad performances Resnick had ever heard, silencing the club and striking him straight to the heart.

Ben Riley's heart.

Resnick had never known his friend fall for any woman the way he had fallen for Sarah. 'Don't know what she sees in me, Charlie, but thank Christ that she does!' And soon after, 'Not going to believe this, Charlie, but I think we're going to do it. You know, yes, tie the knot.' During the preparations for the wedding, little by little, Resnick had sensed Sarah withdrawing; the way she would react sometimes when he saw them together, snatches of conversation that were reported back. He tried to say something about it once and it was the first and only time Ben had come close to hitting him. Three weeks before the ceremony, Sarah had told Ben there was somebody else.

When Ben had scraped himself back off the ground days later, he sent her flowers and a telegram – *I guess they sent in the clowns* – a line from the song, which was popular at the time. With Sarah, certainly. She had bought Ben a record of it, Judy Collins.

He didn't know her response, whether she laughed or cried. He wouldn't talk to Resnick about her for months, years, wouldn't hear her name; then, one day, Ben said she had phoned him, from nowhere, out of the blue. Almost, he had failed to recognise the voice and the name; of course, it was no longer the same. Feeling low, lonely the way only marriage can make you feel, she had got to thinking about him. What he was doing. Where he was. They met once on a country road and she held his hand but turned aside from his kiss; there were things she wasn't telling him about the marriage, she made that clear, a tiny hook that bit deep. Then came the Christmas cards: *With love from Sarah and family*. The last few were returned to sender: Ben Riley had gone to the States.

Why was Resnick thinking of all this now?

*

163

She was out in the garden and hadn't heard the bell. Resnick let himself in through the side gate and walked along the gravel path. Honeysuckle climbed the wall. She was bending over one of the flower-beds, using a tool Resnick recognised but couldn't have named, to lever out weeds. As she straightened, she put her hand, no more than a moment, against the small of her back.

'I didn't think you'd recognised me, Charlie,' Sarah Farleigh said.

'I hadn't.'

She smiled at the ground. 'When did you realise?'

'Today. Oh, no more than an hour ago.'

She paused in pulling off her rubber gloves to look at him, asking the question with her eyes.

'I don't know,' he said. 'I mean, exactly. It came to me suddenly, I don't know why.'

'Why don't we go inside?' Sarah said. 'It's getting cold.' This time the smile was fuller, more real, and for the first time he saw her as she had been, the woman with whom Ben Riley had fallen in love.

The interior of the house was not ostentatious, but neat. Comfortable furniture, wallpaper Resnick would have guessed came from Laura Ashley, not an Aga but something similar dominating the broad, flagstoned kitchen where they now stood.

'Do you really want tea?'

'Coffee?'

'All right,' she set the kettle to boil, balanced coffee filters over two green Apilco porcelain cups, and reached the sherry bottle down from between glass jars of puy lentils and flageolet beans. Resnick shook his head and she poured a good measure for herself, tilted the glass and poured again.

'You'll think I'm becoming an alcoholic,' she smiled.

'No.'

Her hair was thick the way it had always been, streaked now with grey. The skin around her eyes was red from too much crying, but the eyes themselves were green, the green of slate that has stood fresh in the rain, and bright. Her wrists were thin, but strong, and her calves and ankles fleshed out and solid. She had aged more heavily, more hastily than Resnick had ever imagined she would.

'Will you come to Peter's funeral, Charlie?'

He took a first sip of his coffee, surprised.

'Isn't that what they always do, Morse and the others? I've watched them on television, standing in the background at their victims' funerals, looking for suspects among the guests.'

'I don't think that would be appropriate,' Resnick said. 'Not in this case.' He looked into her eyes. 'But, yes, if that's what you want. Yes, I'll be pleased to come.'

'Thank you,' she said. And then, 'Peter has family, of course, had, but I can't say we ever really got on.'

'You have children, though.' He had seen their photographs in the hallway and on the mantelpiece in the living room when they had walked past.

'Yes, three.'

'All grown up?'

'All grown.'

Sarah took her sherry to the window; it was darkening steadily outside and somewhere was getting rain. 'Do you ever hear from him at all?'

'Ben?'

'Yes.'

'Not for a while. He's in America, you . . .'

'Yes, I know. Montana, isn't it? Nebraska? One of those western states.'

'Maine, he moved to Maine.'

'Married?'

'There's someone, yes.'

'Children?'

165

'Yes, there's a child. A boy. I . . .'

'Charlie, I don't want to know.' There were tears in her eyes, but she was damned if she was going to cry. There had been crying enough lately and with good reason. What was the point of crying over impossibilities? Spilt milk gone sour.

'Sarah, what happened to your husband, I couldn't be more sorry.'

'Thank you. I know.' She smiled again, a generous, smile, almost a laugh. 'You always were a sympathetic man.' Turning, she rinsed the sherry glass beneath the tap. 'Maybe I should have married you.'

'I don't think so.'

She did laugh then. 'No, neither do I. Why don't we sit for a while in the other room? Have you got time, before you need to be getting back?'

Resnick got to his feet. 'A little, yes.'

They sat in armchairs on either side of an open fireplace which had a centrepiece of dried flowers in the grate. The curtains, full and dark and with a recurring motif of leaves, were closed. There was one photograph of Peter, arm around one of his daughters, laughing into the camera. The others were of the children, none of Sarah herself. On the polished coffee table lay copies of *Good Housekeeping* and *Vanity Fair*, several paperback books.

'Did you marry, Charlie?'

'Uh-hum.'

'Elaine, is that what she was called?'

Resnick nodded. 'Yes.' Christ, he didn't want to talk about this.

'What happened, Charlie?'

'We divorced.'

'For better or worse.'

'Something like that.'

'Which was it for you?' Sarah asked.

166

'Oh, worse. I suppose it was worse.'

'And now? Have you come to terms with it now?'

'I think so.'

'And you're still in touch?'

'Not really, no.'

'A shame. But, then, I suppose it's better that way.'

He didn't answer immediately. 'It is for me.'

Sarah drank more of the gin and tonic that had replaced the sherry. 'You think I treated him badly, don't you? Your friend, Ben. What I did, the way I behaved, you think it was pretty inexcusable.'

Resnick shook his head. 'No. I don't think that. I think, at the time, I was sorry he was so hurt. But, you know, my job, it's hard to sit in judgement about what people do.'

'You surprise me. Seeing what you see, I should have thought you did that all the time. Pass judgement.'

'I know. Only that doesn't seem to be the way it works. What happens, most of the time anyway, whatever it is someone's done, somehow you come to understand. No way you could talk to them, else.' Resnick looked across at her. 'At some point in our lives, we're all capable of anything. I suppose that's what you learn most.'

Sarah sipped her drink. 'You don't know any more yet,' she said, 'about what happened to Peter? I mean, why or . . .'

'Not really, although . . .' He stopped, uncertain, and she leaned forward a little, waiting for him to carry on. 'There's a chance, just a chance, mind, we might have a lead, something to go on.'

Sarah set down her glass.. 'It's funny, isn't it? These days, you think, oh, people fooling around. Prostitution. Casual sex. Aids, that's what leaps to mind, isn't it? Aids, that's the danger. Not . . . not this.'

'I think,' Resnick said, 'if you're going to be okay, I ought to be moving.'

'Yes, of course, fine. You don't have to worry about me. I'm not about to do anything stupid.'

'I didn't imagine you would.'

She walked with him to the door. 'The funeral . . .'

'You'll let me know.'

'Of course.'

He was almost at the car, when she called him back. 'That girl, the one who was here with you the other day.'

'DC Kellogg. Lynn.'

'She's in love with you, you know.'

Thirty

'Thought you weren't coming,' Divine said, as Naylor materialised through the crowd. He had nabbed a seat to the side of the pub, close against the windows that looked out over the trees and sloping shadows of the park. Quiet half-hour with Sharon Garnett, who knew what might develop? But not now. 'Here,' he said, trying not to sound too grudging. 'You can just about squeeze in here.'

Naylor set down his own pint and the refill he had bought for Divine, and sat next to a youth in a cotton shirt with sleeves rolled back, who grudgingly made space for him.

'Sort out all the under-age drinkers amongst this lot,' Naylor said. 'Have the place to ourselves.'

'Aye, well. Better things to do, eh?'

'Happen.'

'How was Canada's feller-made-good?'

'Prick of the first water.'

Divine laughed. 'Maybe should've brought him along. There's women here, not seen a good shagging since Forest last won bloody Cup.'

Naylor nodded absent-mindedly and drank.

'Hey up, though. Here we go. There's one I'd not mind putting it to myself.'

Dressed in a black roll-neck, leather jacket and blue-black jeans, Sharon Garnett was making her way past the raised platform of the stage, where a tubby retread of Elton John was fiddling with the wiring of the electric piano and preparing to excite the crowd with a despairing version of 'Crocodile Rock'.

'What are you having?' Divine said, out of his seat and reaching for his wallet.

'A headache. I've heard this bloke before. What say we drink up and leave?'

A few minutes later they were walking along Arboretum Street and heading for Balmoral Road, a narrow cut-through that would take them to the Goose Fair site and the Forest Recreation Ground.

'This tart we're looking for,' Divine said, 'how well d'you know her?'

'Doris? Like I say, I've not been here long enough to know the girls well, but, yes, I've had words with her once or twice.'

'And?'

'She's all right. Straightforward enough. Honest.'

'Honest?'

'Yes. She doesn't make any bones about what she does. Doesn't make a fuss if she's nicked.'

'Back on the street the next night, probably carrying a dose of Aids.'

Sharon stopped walking. They were on the corner of Forest Road East, the cemetery that took up one corner of the recreation ground, off to their right. Immediately before them, open space dropped to near darkness and, beyond that, the lights of the terraced houses of Forest Fields. 'You don't know that,' Sharon said. 'And if she had, who gave it to her, answer me that?'

'A needle?' Kevin Naylor said.

'I don't reckon Doris does drugs,' said Sharon.

Divine laughed, the sound carrying on the wind. 'Makes her the only scrubber round here who doesn't.'

Doris Duke was short as Sharon was tall. They finally tracked her down some forty minutes later, climbing out

170

of a Mazda saloon in four-inch heels that still left her well below average in height. She was wearing a pink T-shirt that stopped between belly button and ribs, a waist-length nylon jacket, midnight blue, and a skirt which, when she backed out of the car, left little to the imagination. A small handbag hung from one shoulder by a gold chain.

'Doris.'

She almost smiled when she saw it was Sharon; a smile that fast turned sour when she saw the two men in her wake.

'Doris, we'd like to talk.'

'Oh, we would, would we?'

Divine wanted to slap the sneer from her face for a start.

'Yes, about your friend.'

'Which friend's that, then?'

'Marlene.'

'No.'

'Marlene Kinoulton. Don't let on you don't know who I mean.'

'I know who you mean, all right. Just she in't no friend of mine.'

'Since when?'

'Since she legged it with fifty quid she owed me.'

'And when was that, Doris?'

'Couple of days back.'

'And the fifty pounds?'

'Lent it her, didn't I? Slag never give it me back.'

'Why did she want the money?' Divine asked.

'I don't know, do I? Never asked.'

'Come on, expect us to believe you handed it over, just like that?'

'I don't give a toss whether you believe it or not. So happens it's the truth. One of your mates says they're short, you don't go through some sodding inquisition, right? If you've got it, you hand it over.'

Divine wasn't so sure.

'Even if it's fifty pounds?' Naylor asked.

Doris Duke laughed. 'Fifty? What's fifty quid? I can thumb down the next punter comes along here, earn that in twenty minutes.'

'Then why,' said Sharon, 'are you so steamed up about it?'

'Christ, you don't understand anything, do you? It's the principle of the sodding thing.'

They went to sit in Sharon's car to talk, Doris insisting that they drive well clear of the Forest first. 'Certain people see me sitting with you lot, they'd be less than well pleased.' Doris had grown up in the same part of east London that Sharon had lived in before striking out for the provinces, and because of that, and the fact that Sharon was clearly different – the Vice Squad wasn't exactly overflowing with blacks – Doris felt that, underneath it all, Sharon was all right.

But now it wasn't Sharon asking the questions.

'And you last saw Marlene when?' Divine said.

'I told you, Tuesday.'

'The day you lent her the money?'

'Yes.'

'Lunchtime. In the Queen.'

'Jesus, yes.'

'All right, Doris,' Naylor said, 'we only want to be sure we've got it right.'

'Oh, yes, I know,' sarcasm edging her voice.

'Don't want to put words into your mouth.'

Or anything else, Divine thought. Under the car's interior light, Doris's make-up was thick enough to chip and there was the clear residue of a bruise, dark above her left eye.

'And she didn't say anything about her plans? Taking off somewhere for a few days? We know she used to work

172

in Sheffield and Derby. That wasn't why she wanted the money? For the fare?'

'Look,' Doris said, her voice taking on the pained expression people reserve for children, the old or the very deaf, 'I don't know where she is. Don't even know where she's been. We were mates, yes, but we never lived out of one another's pockets. Sometimes she'll be off somewhere, weeks at a time; I don't see her around and then I do. This business, you don't ask too many questions. And the fifty . . .' She pulled open the ashtray beside the dashboard and stubbed out her cigarette. '. . . Most likely she owed someone. Either that or she just fancied going into town, buying herself a new dress.'

'Why would she do that?' Sharon asked.

'Why would you? Cheer herself up, of course.'

'Or make herself look smart.'

Doris gave it a moment's thought. 'Maybe.'

'So as to work the hotels.'

'Maybe.' Doris started rummaging for a cigarette in her bag and Sharon offered her one instead. 'Thanks,' angling her head towards the window as she lit it and exhaled.

'If you knew,' Sharon said, wishing that the two detectives weren't there, doing her best to exclude them with her voice. 'If you knew that was what Marlene was going to do, try the Victoria, say. The Royal. Maybe the Crest. If Marlene had told you that was what she had in mind and then you read about what happened to that man in his hotel room, well, I wouldn't blame you for keeping quiet.'

Doris looked at her, blinking through the veil of cigarette smoke. 'Yes, but I don't know that, do I? If she did that, I don't know nothing about it.'

Sharon gave a brief sigh and sat back. 'You're sure you don't know Marlene's new address?'

'Sure.'

'Okay,' Sharon said, swivelling round and snapping her

173

seat-belt into place. 'Why don't we take Doris back to work?'

They watched her walk away to join the knots of girls on the edge of the Forest. 'Wouldn't know the truth,' Divine said, 'if it jumped up and bit her in the arse.'

Naylor shook his head. 'I don't think she knows anything,' he said.

'I'm not so sure about that. I think she does,' Sharon said. 'And if I don't push too hard I think she might tell me, but I'd have to be on my own.'

'Aside from us, then,' Naylor asked, 'why wouldn't she open up now?'

'Partly, it's against her instincts. And I think she's frightened.'

'What of?'

'I don't know. And maybe it's not for herself, maybe it's on account of her friend.'

A car slowed as it neared them, the window rolled down on the driver's side. 'Get home to the wife,' Divine called. 'Before you get nicked.' The window went back up as the driver accelerated away.

'Why don't we call it a night?' Sharon said. 'I'll try Doris again tomorrow, all right? And we'll keep in touch.'

You run on, Divine wanted to say to Naylor, just run on ahead and let me give it a try. A drink some time, Sharon, how about that? Something to eat. Clubbing, maybe? Black Orchid's not too bad. But something in Sharon's eyes, the way she held herself, standing there and watching as they walked away, made him realise, no, it wasn't such a good idea after all.

Thirty-one

Slowing off the freeway, I can hear the sirens and already I'm thinking, hey, it's okay, how many times do you hear that in this city, night and day? Doesn't have to have anything to do with this case, anything to do with me.

But the closer I get to Fairlawn Avenue, the louder the wailing gets, not just the police, either. As I slow for the light, an ambulance shoots past me, causing traffic travelling on the cross street to swerve and brake. By the time I arrive at the house, my stomach is cramping fit to beat the band and I know what I will find.

Fifty yards away from the gathering furore and the flashing lights, I swing my car into someone's front yard and start to run. Paramedics are scuttling into the house with all their gear and a uniformed cop is standing guard on the sidewalk, while, behind him, two of his colleagues are threading out the famous yellow tape: Crime Scene, Do Not Cross. I show the cop my ID and can tell he isn't about to be impressed, when Lieutenant Daines appears on the square of trimmed lawn at the front of the house, badge clipped to the lapel of the black tux he must have been wearing when the call came through. His black tie is unfastened and hangs loose from the collar of his dress shirt and he has that look that homicide detectives get once in a while, no matter how long they've been in the job. The look that says, no matter how bad you thought it could get, it just got worse. Looking up, he sees me and waves me through.

Resnick turned down the corner to mark his place and set Cathy Jordan's book aside. A little more than two thirds of the way through and the body count was rising. Whoever had killed April Reigler at the end of chapter one, seemed to be working his or her way through April's college friends. Resnick thought it was an elaborate blind, a series of otherwise unnecessary crimes whose only purpose was to confuse the investigation and lead the police – and the redoubtable Annie Q. Jones – off along the wrong track. For his money, the answer lay closer to home. In his experience, that was usually the case. But he wasn't betting on it.

In the kitchen, he switched the radio on and swiftly off again. What was it about the BBC that the first few hours of Sunday morning were devoted so resolutely to pretending nothing had changed since 1950? From 'Morning has Broken' through to the Appeal for This Week's Good Cause, it was as though God were still benevolently in His heaven and all, in thought, word and deed, were right with the world. Even 'On Your Farm', which was allowed to interrupt the predominantly religious programmes, regularly featured one of its journalists sitting down to a trencherman's breakfast of sausage, bacon and eggs with commonsensical good-hearted country folk of the kind Resnick had long thought existed only in the minds and brochures of the English Tourist Board.

The clock above the dresser showed it was still shy of seven. He had been up since half past five, unable to sleep; had made two pots of coffee and now he was about to make a third. This time he would have toast and some of that marmalade he had bought at the Women's Institute market in the YWCA opposite Central police station. Wonderfully sweet and runny, the kind that always slid off the knife blade and on to your hand before you could hope to spread it on bread. Annie Q. Jones, he knew, would have already done her work-out to Cher's fitness video and would be standing with her coloured pens in front of the giant whiteboard on which she noted all the significant incidents in her current case; arrowing connections, circling clues. All Resnick could do, standing there waiting for the water to heat through, was allow the bits and pieces of the investigation to trundle round inside the washing machine of his brain. Turning the toast, he smiled, remembering how it had begun, the loneliness of the middle-aged runner with only one sock. One of the mysteries of the age, which neither he nor Annie Q. Jones would ever solve – why was it that whenever you took six pairs of socks to the laundry, nine times out of ten, you only got five and a half pairs back? Lynn? In love with him? What on earth had Sarah Farleigh been talking about?

Millington and his wife had this Sunday morning routine: as soon as the alarm sounded, Millington would push back his side of the duvet (John Lewis Partnership goose down, acquired only after his wife's careful perusal of comfort ratings and tog numbers in *Which?* magazine) and hurry downstairs, returning some fifteen minutes later with a tray, laden with tea (Waitrose organically grown Assam), slices of fresh granary bread (for which Madeleine had stood in line at Birds the Bakers the previous day), butter (now that the latest dietary reports had suggested a low level of dairy products was actually good for you, they were allowed butter) and Wilkin and Sons' 'Tiptree' morello cherry conserve. Not jam, conserve. And, for Madeleine, the *Mail on Sunday*.

Millington placed the tray in the centre of the bed, and prepared to climb back in, knowing full well no matter how circumspectly he did this, his wife would tell him to be more circumspect still.

'Careful, Graham,' she said. And, with Millington joining her in harmony, 'You'll spill the tea.'

Madeleine detached the sports pages from the paper and passed them across; that done, the drill was this: Graham would butter the bread, which he had already cut into two; Madeleine herself would add the jam. Graham would pour milk into the cups and she would pour the tea, now brewed to a good colour and strength. The only occasions he stirred in a little sugar was at the station, when he could be good and sure Madeleine wasn't looking.

'Ooh look, Graham, that writer, there's something about her in the paper.'

'Mmm? Where?'

The photographer had posed Cathy Jordan alongside the statue of Robin Hood beside the Castle wall, Cathy's hand reaching up to touch the bow. The headline: **MAKING CRIME PAY**.

'You know, Graham, I was thinking of going.'

'Where's that, love?'

'She's being interviewed this afternoon, by that woman from the box. The one I like, with the glasses, you know. From *The Late Show*. Oh, what is her name?'

'Don't ask me.'

'It was on the tip of my tongue just now.'

'Thought that were jam.'

'Oh, Graham, be serious.'

'So I am. Get your head over here and I'll lick it off.'

'Graham, don't! You'll upset the tray.'

'Not if we park it on the floor.'

'But I've not finished my tea.'

178

'Stewed by now. Any road, I can always nip back down later, mash some more.'

'Graham!'

'What now?'

'I shall have to go to the bathroom first.'

'Whatever for?'

'I shall just have to, that's all.'

'All right, then. If you must. But for heaven's sake, don't take all day about it.'

And Madeleine hurried into her dressing gown, leaving Millington to read about Notts' first innings against Middlesex, nibble another piece of bread and jam and hope the mood didn't desert him before she returned.

'Come on, Mum,' Lynn Kellogg was saying down the phone, 'that's just the way Auntie Jane is. You've been telling me that for years.'

And while her mother launched into another familiar family diatribe, Lynn, half-listening, sipped her Nescafé and struggled with seven down, four across in yesterday's crossword. At least, she thought, as long as her mother could find the energy to get worked up about her sister's failure, for the third year running, to send a birthday card, it meant there was nothing more urgent to worry about. Meaning Lynn's dad.

Not so long after Christmas, her father had had an operation to remove a small, cancerous growth from the bowel. 'We'll be keeping an eye on him, naturally,' the consultant had said, 'but so far, fingers crossed, it looks as though we might have nipped it in the bud.' And her father, slow to recuperate, shaken by everything that had happened – the strangeness of the hospital, the discomfort of endoscopy, the myth that no one who was ever admitted to an oncology ward lived more than a twelve-month after, the persistent threat of the knife – *was* getting better. When last Lynn had driven over to Norfolk to visit, he had been back out again, pottering between hen houses, cigarette hanging from his lips.

'Away with you, girl,' he had said, Lynn lecturing him for the umpteenth time about the dangers of cancer. 'There's not a thing wrong with these lungs of mine and you know it. Doctor told me so. So, less you see me pulling down these overalls and smoking out my backside, bugger all for you to get aerated about, is there?'

Lynn hoped he was right. She thought, hearing a bit of the old fire back in his voice, that probably he was.

'Yes, Mum,' she said now. And, 'No, Mum. That's okay. He's doing fine, just fine.'

A psychological process in which painful truths are forced out of an individual's consciousness – six letters. With her mother prattling on like that, Lynn couldn't, for the life of her, think what it was.

'Frank?'

Cathy Jordan rolled off her stomach and reached towards the clock radio, angling it in her direction. Jesus! She hadn't intended to sleep so late.

'Frank? You in the bathroom or what?'

No reply. Most likely he was off swimming, maybe found a gym downtown to press a few weights. Cathy eased herself up on to one elbow and dialled room service, ordered fresh orange juice and coffee, croissants and jam. If she was going to pig out most of the morning, she might as well enjoy it. Give some thought to what she was going to say that afternoon, not that it would be any different from what she'd said half a hundred times before.

The one thing Marius didn't like, the thing he could barely stand, the way she would introduce him as her nephew all the time. As if somehow she were ashamed of him, felt a need to explain. Secretary, that would have been something; personal assistant. She hardly referred to him by either of those titles any more, though, naturally, they explained what most people imagined his function was. And it was true. Dorothy's correspondence, he saw to that; appointments, meetings with publisher or agent, requests for interviews by the media, any and every little thing. Most people looked at him, accompanying her everywhere, helping her off and on with her coat, pulling out her chair, and they assumed one thing. About him. Poor Marius, camp as a clockwork sixpence, gay through and through. Well, if only they knew.

He had the oil ready now, a mixture of sweet almond and camellia, scented with dewberry, her favourite. It was just a matter of warming his hands. He knew she was waiting for him, towel spread over the sheet, face down, patient. Undemanding. Most of the world, Marius thought, didn't realise how beautiful old people could be. Their skin. Lightly freckled, the delicacy of fine lines patterned like honeycomb: he thought Dorothy had lovely skin.

Thirty-two

When Resnick's wife had entered into an affair, she had been driven to it; driven by what had disappeared from their own lives, by passion. It had also been a sign: clear, not negotiable. This is over for us; I want out. Of course, it had not been clean, nor without pain. It rarely is. But clear, yes, that's what it had been.

Whether passion had driven Jack Skelton beyond the bounds of propriety with the self-possessed DI Helen Siddons during her brief sojourn in the city, Resnick had no way of knowing. He had only seen the looks, the late-night conversations conducted in corners, the lingering glances. What the superintendent would have seen in her, attractiveness and intelligence, both well honed, was easier to judge; aside from the fact that Skelton was her senior officer, what might Siddons have seen in him? She was not, Resnick thought, the kind of person to commit to any action unless it contained an advantage. And if passion was what had been at stake there, would passion for Jolly Jack have been enough? Enough for her to risk losing her footing on the fast track towards the top? Not too many points for engaging with a superior in an extra-marital affair; not unless that superior was of the rank of assistant chief constable at the very least.

God, Charlie, Resnick thought, as he approached the Skelton house, you're getting cynical in your old age. It must be Sundays, that's what it is. All that bell-ringing and sanctimonious ill will. All those cars queuing to get into DIY centres.

He was pleased finally to have arrived, to have parked behind the Volvo in Skelton's drive, climbed out and automatically locked the door, walked towards the house in his response to the superintendent's early summons.

'Had breakfast, Charlie?'

Resnick nodded, yes.

'You'll have some coffee, though?'

'Thanks.'

Skelton's daughter, Kate, was sitting with her feet drawn up under her, in one of the easy chairs in the L-shaped living room. Walkman in place, the usual tinny whispers escaping, she sat reading an A-level textbook, occasionally scribbling a biroed note in the margin. His wife, Alice, with an expression for which the word sour could have been invented, had barely stopped to greet Resnick as he entered; hurrying on past him and up the stairs to the first floor, from whence the whining suck and bump of the vacuum cleaner could now be heard.

All the little nudges, Resnick thought, that make a home, that make a marriage.

He and Skelton sat on stools in the kitchen, alongside what Resnick guessed the brochures called a breakfast bar; the smell of grilled bacon was tantalising on the air and a scrambled egg pan had been left in the sink to soak. Resnick tried to remember the last time he had seen the superintendent unshaven.

'Sure you won't have anything?'

'No, thanks. I'm fine.' Resnick accepted the coffee and drank some without tasting.

'You've seen the Sundays?' Skelton asked.

Resnick shook his head. 'Always try hard not to.'

'What with this bloody crime festival being here, and now the murder, they're having a field day. Already got us down as the most violent city in the country. Load of bollocks! Give a roomful of monkeys a set of statistics and

183

a computer and they'll prove bloody anything. Anyway, goes without saying, the chief constable's been breathing down my neck for a result. Invited Alice and myself out to his place this afternoon, high tea.'

Resnick smiled; the thought of Alice Skelton having to put on her best frock *and* be polite to people she probably despised, was something he'd rather imagine than actually see.

'Laugh all you want, Charlie, while they're carving into the Yorkshire ham on the lawn, I'm going to be carpeted inside, good and proper. Unless you've got something you've yet to tell me.'

Resnick wished he had. 'Marlene Kinoulton, she's still our best shot. About the only shot we've got.'

'And she's disappeared.'

Resnick shrugged. 'May not mean a great deal. Sounds as if she's never in one place for long. You know how it is with these girls, some of them, all over the shop.'

'If I could say we had confirmation of her identity, that would be something, but so far not a bloody thing.'

Resnick drank some more coffee. 'It's amazing to me, though I suppose by now it shouldn't be, just how unobservant most people are. Close on sixty potential witnesses we've questioned so far. Vast majority of them, couldn't even place Farleigh as being there at all, despite the fact he must have spent a total of over two hours that evening, downstairs in the hotel, either in the restaurant or the bar. Of those that did remember him, half of them have no recollection of his having been with a woman, and those that do . . . well, it's a lottery if she was fair or dark, caucasian or Chinese.'

Skelton reached up towards one of the fitted cupboards, lifted out a bottle of cooking brandy, tipped a shot into what was left of his coffee and pushed the bottle in Resnick's direction, where it stayed, untouched. Little early in the day for his boss to be hitting the hard stuff, Resnick thought. He said nothing.

Skelton said, 'At least that business with the letters, threats to that woman, Jordan, that seems to have died down.'

Muffled but on cue, Resnick's bleeper began to sound.

Cathy Jordan had fallen back to sleep. One of those shimmering dreams that refused to touch ground. Railway carriages, aeroplanes, other people's bathrooms. Silk. Steel. Slivers of skin. She woke with the undersheet wound tight between her legs and her hair plastered to her scalp with sweat. 'Frank?' Frank was still not back. Breakfast? The breakfast didn't seem to have arrived. If room service had knocked, they had got no answer and gone away. Cathy prised herself from the bed and made it, less than steadily, to the shower.

Testing the temperature of the water with her hand, she stepped beneath the shower, letting the water stream over her neck and shoulders and as, eyes closed, she lifted her face towards it, she felt braced, revived.

Ten minutes later, Cathy briskly towelled herself down. Through the curtains, she saw it was another fine day. Not exactly sunny, but fine. Better than she had anticipated. Maybe she'd laze around a little longer, take a look at the Sunday papers. Wasn't that interview she'd done being printed today?

She glanced around. Frank could have taken the newspaper with him when he went out, but that seemed unlikely. Probably, they were still outside in the corridor.

Wrapping a towel around her, Cathy pulled back the door and looked out. There they were, and a full breakfast trolley, too. A glass cafetière with silver trim, juice, several pots of honey and jam, a bread basket covered with a starched white cloth. Oh, well, the coffee would be cold, but nothing was wrong with orange juice and a couple of cold croissants. Cathy wheeled the trolley back inside and snapped the door closed with her hip. Letting the towel fall to the floor at her feet, she flicked back the cloth from the basket and screamed.

Where she had expected croissants, a baby nestled snugly, its limbs, where they showed through its baby clothes, skinned and streaked with blood.

Thirty-three

The flesh was rabbit, not the supermarket kind, but bought fresh and skinned, none too expertly at that. The blood, it seemed, had been squeezed from a pound or so of liver, the richness of the smell suggesting pig as the most likely source. Baby clothes, otherwise new, had been purchased at Mothercare. The face, cherubic and brittle, had been detached from a child's doll, the old-fashioned kind.

It was not until later, when the trolley was being carefully checked and searched, that the note was found, a single sheet inside a small envelope which had been slipped between two napkins, folded beneath an empty glass.

'You don't want to see it,' Resnick said.

'Yes, I do.'

'There's no point, not now. Why don't you wait?'

'Till when?' Cathy Jordan had laughed. 'Till I'm feeling better?'

When Resnick had first arrived, she had been standing by the window, dressed in denim shirt and jeans, an absence of colour in her face. Someone from the hotel had brought her black coffee and brandy and she had drunk the latter, allowed the coffee to get bitter and cold. The trolley and its contents were where she had left them, towards the centre of the room.

Frank Carlucci had arrived back from the pool a little after Resnick, unaware that anything was wrong. Immediately, Cathy had rounded on him, shouting, where in God's name had he been, why the fuck was he never there

187

when she needed him? Once, hard, she had pounded her fist against the meat of his shoulder and Frank had lowered his head, eyes closed, bracing himself for her to strike him again. 'Can't someone, for Christ's sake, get me some fresh coffee up here?' she had said, turning away, letting her hands fall by her sides.

Since then she had been quiet, almost controlled, patient while Resnick made calls, issued orders, people came and silently went. Conversations were held in hushed tones beyond the door.

Handling the edges carefully with gloves, Resnick held the note towards Cathy Jordan's face. It had been typed on an ill-fitting ribbon, black shadowing into red:

> *How do you like this? The only misbegotten child you're likely to have.*

Cathy read it slowly, again and again, tears filling her eyes until she could no longer see. Blindly, she moved towards the bathroom, banging her shin against the low table laden with magazines. When Frank went to help her, she pushed him angrily away.

The two men looked at one another, Resnick replacing the note inside its envelope.

'What kind of a sick bastard does something like this?' Frank asked.

'I don't know,' Resnick said. All the while thinking, this weekend the city is full of them, writers, film-makers, people for whom thinking up things like this is meat and drink.

'Frank,' Cathy said, coming back, tiredness replacing the shock in her eyes, 'would you be a sweetheart, see what's happened to that coffee?'

'Sure.'

As Frank picked up the phone, Mollie Hansen appeared in the doorway and Resnick motioned for her to stay where she was, walking over and leading her into the corridor outside.

'I only just heard,' Mollie said. Her face, usually unblemished and even, was beginning to show signs of strain. 'I'm not sure I know everything that happened.'

Concisely, Resnick told her all she needed to know.

'How's she taking it?' Mollie asked.

'She's angry, upset, pretty much what you'd expect.'

'And those threatening letters she had – do you think this is the same person?'

'It's possible. As yet there's no way of knowing. At first sight, the note doesn't seem to have been written on the same machine. But that might not mean a thing.'

'And you don't imagine . . .'

'What?'

'Well, that business with the paint. This couldn't be another stunt to get publicity for their cause?'

'Vivienne Plant and her friends? I don't know. I'd have thought she'd have had a photographer on hand, at least. But we'll talk to her, all the same.'

'Good.' They were standing near the lift doors, opposite a lithograph of trees and a beach, shaded pink. 'Can I talk to her? Cathy?' Mollie asked.

'From my point of view, no reason why you shouldn't. But you might leave it a while longer. Give her some time to settle down.'

Mollie sighed, looked at her watch. 'I suppose so. It's just she's got this interview this evening with Sarah Dunant. If she isn't going to be able to go ahead with it, I ought to let Sarah know.'

'Why don't you give her half an hour?' Resnick said. 'I can let her know you're around. If she says she wants to talk to you now, I'll let you know.'

'Fine,' Mollie smiled tiredly. 'Thanks.'

Behind her, the lift shushed to a halt and Lynn Kellogg

stepped out, Kevin Naylor immediately behind her. 'Thought you could use a little help,' Lynn said.

Resnick nodded his thanks and set them both to work.

Susan Tyrell stood in the centre of the kitchen, door open to the garden, whisking meringue and wondering how long it had been since she and David had made love. Probably it had been Christmas, that squeaky bed in her parents' spare room, several bottles of cheap champagne and some good port enough to stir a little life into David's libido. Even then, he had called out the name of some movie star at the point of climax. His and not hers. Hers had been an altogether quieter, more private affair, later.

Since then it had been a cuddle last thing at night, those long moments before falling into sleep, David's last waking act to turn away from her arms.

'Why do you stay with him?' her friend, Beatrice, had asked.

Susan had sat there like a contestant on *Mastermind*, stumped for the right answer.

'This damned festival,' Tyrell said, coming into the kitchen, cellphone in his hand, 'is getting more like a Quentin Tarantino screenplay every day.'

Terrific, Susan thought, blood and gore and bad seventies pop songs, continuing to stir the meringue as he relayed the events at the hotel.

'You are coming to the show this afternoon?' Tyrell asked.

'Oh, yes, I expect so.'

'You should. Aside from one screening at the Electric in 1982, *Dark Corridor* hasn't been shown in this country since the fifties. And Curtis himself hasn't set eyes on a print of *Cry Murder* since he was still in the States.'

'Really?' Susan said with barely feigned interest. The meringue was just stiff enough now to cover the pie. She

190

could have got into an argument about rarity not always equalling quality – if the damn films were any good, *why* hadn't some enterprising programmer shown them? – but she lacked the energy. Umpteen eleven- to eighteen-year-olds, nine till four, Monday to Friday, she knew well enough to reserve her strength for what really mattered.

Back at the hotel, Lynn Kellogg and Kevin Naylor were questioning as many of the staff and guests as they could find. Resnick had phoned Skelton and arranged to meet him back at the station to make his report; he had promised to talk with Cathy again later. Frank sat in the chair before a silent television, watching a ball game that, for all its apparent similarities to baseball, he just didn't understand.

Cathy Jordan lay on the bed, fully dressed, staring up at the ceiling with blank, blue eyes.

Thirty-four

'I guess when I married Frank, that was more or less my last chance. Kids, I mean. Oh, we talked about it, back and forth, you know. Frank he would have been keen, keener than me, if you want to know the truth, but, well, the time never did seem right. This book to be finished, that book; another damn tour. In the end, I suppose the idea just ran out of steam.'

Cathy Jordan had wanted to get away, clear her head, and Resnick had brought her to Wollaton Park, green slopes and a golf course, ornamental gardens round an old ancestral pile and down below where deer were grazing, the lake they were walking around.

'You have kids?' Cathy asked.

Resnick shook his head.

'But you're married, right?'

'I was. Not any more.'

'I'm sorry.' She laughed. 'I say that, sorry, automatically, you know, without thinking. Truth is, half the friends I've got are divorced and most of the others wish they were, so . . .'

They emerged between brightly coloured rhododendron bushes at the far end of the lake, a middle-aged couple walking amongst other couples who were exercising their dogs, simply enjoying the sunshine. Here and there, men sat transfixed beside fishing rods, immovable as stone.

'Mostly, now, I never think about it. Kids, I mean. Then something happens like today – well, never *like* today, not, thank God, exactly like that – and somehow it starts up again . . .' Her voice trailed away and it was a good few moments before either of them spoke. A pair of Canada geese skidded noisily on to the water, scattering blue. 'I guess it gets easier, right? I mean, the point finally has to come, you accept it: I am not going to be a parent.'

Resnick shrugged. 'Maybe,' he said, not believing it was so. Even now it would lurch at him, unsuspected, out from the darkest corner of the house or through the glare of a midsummer street – the urge to have a child of his own.

'Well, I tell you,' Cathy was saying, 'I'm from a big family and whenever we get together, nephews and nieces every which way, I get home after one of those things and I'm glad of the rest.' She laughed. 'I've got three sisters, five cousins, seems they pop another one out whenever they stop to take a breath.'

Resnick smiled and together they walked on past the lake's edge and up the slow incline towards the Hall. By the time they had turned through the gateway past the stables and the small agricultural museum, it was time to drive the short distance back to the city.

'You going to be okay?' Resnick asked. They were standing beside the car in the hotel forecourt, motor idling. 'Mollie seemed concerned about this interview you have to do.'

Cathy gestured dismissively with her hand. 'I'll be fine. And listen, thanks for this afternoon. Most people wouldn't have taken the time. I'm only sorry I wasn't better company.'

'That isn't true.'

She threw back her head and laughed. 'Along with everything else, I'm fucking premenstrual!'

Resnick watched her walk towards the doors. 'Take

care,' he said, then climbed back in the car and drove to the station.

Millington's wife was spending the afternoon rehearsing *The Merry Widow* and he had come in to the office in an open-neck shirt and his third-best sports jacket, the one with the leather-patched sleeves, and was threading his way, painstakingly, back through the statements that pertained to Peter Farleigh's murder. Something whose importance they had failed to grasp, a connection they had missed – if it were there, so far it had eluded him.

'Call for you from the wife,' Millington said, seeing Resnick walk in.

Resnick's stomach went cold; without reason, his first thought was of Elaine.

'Ex-wife, that is,' Millington went on. 'Widow. Farleigh's.'

'Sarah,' Resnick said.

'Yes, that's it. Wants to know, once the inquest is over, will we be prepared to release the body?'

Resnick's breathing was back to normal. 'I'll talk to her, thanks.' He looked down at the material on the sergeant's desk. 'Anything?'

Millington shook his head. 'About as enlightening as shovelling shit.'

Resnick nodded and moved away.

'Boss.' He turned again at the sound of Divine's voice; Mark coming into the room with a slice of part-eaten ham and pineapple pizza folding around his hand. Lunch, Resnick thought, I knew there was something. 'Had a bell from Garnett. Says she's going to have another go at Kinoulton's mate later, reckons as how she knows more'n she's letting on.'

'You think she's right?'

'Could be. Let's face it – some bugger's got to know something.'

194

'Okay,' Resnick said. 'Keep on top of it.'

Sharon Garnett, Divine thought, I shouldn't mind. Tilting back his head as he lifted the pointed end of pizza to his mouth, he wandered over towards his desk.

In the corner near the kettle, Resnick found the remnants of a packet of chocolate digestives and dunked them in lukewarm tea. He was considering phoning Sarah Farleigh, still wondering exactly what he might say, when Kevin Naylor and Lynn Kellogg got back from Cathy Jordan's hotel.

Naylor had talked to the room service staff on duty, the young woman who had prepared Cathy Jordan's breakfast tray, the man who had taken it up to her room, knocked, received no reply and left it on the trolley outside the door. He had talked to the maid who had been changing bed linen and towels on that floor. Everyone had followed procedure; no one had noticed anything amiss. Unless one of the staff were lying, and Naylor didn't think this was the case, the most likely scenario was that the macabre 'baby' had been exchanged for the proper contents of the basket while the trolley was outside the room. Which raised the question – since, presumably, the thing had required planning, and since whoever was responsible could hardly have been sure the breakfast trolley would be so conveniently standing there – what other means had been envisaged for its delivery?

After helping Naylor a while at the hotel, Lynn had gone off in search of Vivienne Plant, who, after a few obligatory warnings about harassment, had been only too happy to give the names and addresses of three witnesses who could testify that she had been engaged in a fortnightly badminton game that morning, after which she and her friends had progressed to Russell's bar for a good, unhealthy fry-up brunch.

'Okay,' Resnick said, having listened to their reports.

'Without getting into a lot of lengthy forensics and committing more hours than we can afford, that may be as far as we can go. For now, anyway.'

'That's okay, then,' Naylor said, walking with Lynn across the CID room. 'We can get back to doing something important.'

Lynn stopped in her tracks. 'What?'

'Well, you know. Not as if there was any real harm done,' Naylor said.

'No harm?'

'You know what I mean. It's not as if anything actually happened.'

'Something happened all right,' Lynn said.

'Yes,' Naylor agreed, digging an even deeper hole for himself, 'but not serious.'

'Suppose it had been Debbie, though, Kevin, how would you feel, then? How would she feel, d'you think?'

'She'd be upset, course she would . . .'

'Upset?'

'Yes, but she'd get over it.'

'Which means it's not worth our bothering with?'

'Not as much as some other things, no.'

'If she'd been hit, though? Physically attacked, raped even?'

'Then, of course, that'd be different.'

Lynn laughed, more a snort than a laugh. 'Fact you can't see wounds and bruises, Kevin, doesn't mean a person hasn't been damaged. Hurt. Doesn't have to mean it's less serious.'

Thirty-five

Doris Duke didn't look as if she were working. Instead of high heels, she was wearing a pair of scuffed trainers and there was a hole at the back of her black tights big enough to slip a hand through. Aside from what still stuck, haphazardly, to her face from the previous night, she wore no make-up. Her hair had been pulled back from her head and hung raggedly down, secured by a couple of pins and a rubber band. There was a cigarette in her hand.

Sharon eased the car over to intercept her and Doris's head instinctively turned; she wasn't out looking for business, but she wasn't going to shunt it away.

As soon as she recognised Sharon, she knew it was business of a different kind. 'What d'you want now?' she asked, trying to summon up a belligerence that wasn't really there.

Sharon set the handbrake, slipped the car into neutral. 'Talk.'

'Oh, yeah? What about now?'

'This and that?'

'Pay for my time, will you?'

Sharon smiled. 'You've been watching too many of those TV movies, Doris. That's the only place girls like you get paid to talk to the likes of me.'

Doris stood uneasily, shifting her weight from one foot to the other, cigarette cupped in her hand. 'From what I've seen, your sort are either looking to bang you up and slap the hell out of you, or they're sniffing round for freebies.'

She gave Sharon a look that was meant to be provocative. 'Which is it with you?'

'Neither. I told you. I just want to talk.'

'And I said, what about?'

'Marlene.'

Doris dropped her cigarette to the pavement, quickly ground it out and began to walk away.

'Doris . . .'

'No,' she called over her shoulder. 'I already told you everything I know.'

Sharon released the handbrake and let the car coast after her. 'All right,' she said through the window, 'we'll talk about something else.'

'Yeah? Like what? Swap recipes and tips on chipping away old nail polish?'

'If you like, yes. Why not?'

'You know sodding well why not!'

Sharon let the car roll on down the hill, Doris, head down, crossing the road behind her. By the time Sharon had stopped the car and got out, they were level.

'Come on, Doris. A deal.'

'Yeah? What's that?'

'I'll buy you a meal and we'll talk and if you don't want to say anything more about Marlene, that's fine.'

'I thought I didn't get paid for my time?'

Sharon was standing next to her now, taller, having to stoop down; Sharon wearing a leather jacket, unzipped, over her souvenir T-shirt from a Prince concert, blue jeans and a pair of ankle-high Kickers, green with a grease mark on one heel. 'This isn't buying your time, it's buying you lunch.'

'Lunch?'

'Tea, dinner, whatever. Come on, when did you last eat?'

'That's where I was going now.'

'So fine. Where to?'

Doris grinned, just a little, not giving it too much. 'McDonald's. Got these vouchers I've been saving from the *Post*. Two McChicken sandwiches for a couple of quid.'

'Okay,' Sharon said. 'Why don't we go in the car? That way, we could go to the one by the canal, what do you say?'

Sharon told Doris to keep her McChicken vouchers for another occasion and splashed out on two Big Macs, fries, apple pies, cola. They had stopped at the paper shop on Lenton Boulevard so that Doris could buy another twenty Bensons, king size. There was a seat by the window, and although they couldn't actually see the canal from there, they could work out where it was, across the other side of Sainsbury's car park, to the right of Homebase.

Doris picked out most of the middle of her Big Mac, toying with the bun but never really eating it. The fries she dunked in a generous puddle of red sauce. Sharon ate slowly, saying little, trying to make the younger woman feel at ease.

Doris told her about a childhood bounded by Hackney Marshes and Homerton Hospital; Dalston, Clapton, Hackney, Leyton. A familiar enough story, familiar to Sharon certainly, not so very different from her own; the same story many of the working girls had to tell. When it was told at all. And Doris, not a product of what sociologists and politicians called a broken home; no one-parent family hers. Her father, on the dole, had always been there. Always. Through the unbroken veil of cigarette smoke, beneath the slow-fading bruise, Sharon looked for the child in Doris's eighteen-year-old face but it had long been driven out.

    she says:
    if only I could be

199

three again, struggling with my shoe laces;
start all over, go back to the beginning

shake my mother

abuse my father

'You reckon her for it, don't you?' Doris said suddenly, pushing away the carapace of her apple pie. 'That bloke got himself knifed. You reckon her for that.'

'Do you know where she was, Doris? That evening? Where she was working? Was it the hotels?'

'I already told you, I hadn't seen her since the Tuesday.'

'Tuesday afternoon.'

'Right.'

'When you lent her the money. The fifty pounds you never got back.'

Doris mouthed an oath. Sharon reached for her cola and drank a little more. Doris lit another cigarette. Two lads walking past outside shouted something they could neither of them make out and one of the lads went into a swagger, cupping non-existent breasts. His mate laughed so much he nearly got clipped by a passing car.

'She wanted it for drugs, didn't she?' Sharon said.

Doris nodded. 'Crack.'

'How bad is she?'

It seemed a long time before Doris answered. 'Look, you know as well as what I do, there's girls out there, they don't keep high, they go crazy and once it gets like that, there's nothing they won't do to score. These dealers, they play 'em along, let 'em get in debt, serious now, hundreds I'm talking, easy. Once it's like that, they can do what they like with them. Sex shows, dyke stuff, animals. This one bloke, charged his mates a tenner each to wank off over this girl while his alsatian licked her out.' Doris shuddered and made a face. 'Marlene, though, she wasn't like that. She was bright, dead clever. Older, too. Been around, but it didn't show. That's how come she could work the hotels. Me, now, I walk in and they've got me walking right out again, regular revolving door. Not Marlene. That's why I was surprised when she started doing crack. Oh, we'd have the odd spliff once in a while, who doesn't? But crack.' Doris shook her head. 'First, it was just weekends, fifteen, twenty quid a rock. You know, when we was busy. Never ends up like that, though, does it? Marlene, she could see what was happening to her. Kept trying to kick. Even went to that place, you know, down by the Square. What's it called? Crack Awareness, something like that. Got worse anyway. Got so she hated what she was doing, couldn't stand being touched. Being with some bloke, any bloke, but, of course, that's what she had to do. Keep earning, more and more, trying to stay ahead.'

In another part of the restaurant, twenty or so eight- and nine-year-olds were having a party, flicking Chicken McNuggets across the tables, wearing cardboard cut-out hats.

'How much,' Sharon asked, 'had she got to hate it?'

'She used to say, next man who touches me, I'm going to kill him.'

'And you thought she was serious? You thought she meant it?'

'No, don't be bloody stupid, course I didn't! We say that all the time.'

'Then what?' Sharon said.

Doris took a long drag on her cigarette. 'Week or so back, the night that other bloke was done, you know, stabbed. It was in the paper, found him starkers in the road.'

Sharon waited, Doris taking her time.

'I ran into Marlene,' Doris said, 'she was leaning on this wall off Forest Road, looked like she'd just been throwing up. There was blood all down her front. Up her hand and arm.'

To an almighty roar from the children, one of the McDonalds staff jumped up on to the middle of their table dressed as Mr McChicken, and started flapping his wings.

Sharon bided her time.

'Who did she cop from, Doris?'

Doris blinked at her across the smoke from her cigarette. 'Richie. I don't know ... I don't know where, but yes, Richie that's the only one I ever heard her mention. That's who she said.'

Thirty-six

Dorothy Birdwell's fingers fumbled with her water glass, almost sending it tumbling, and for once Marius was not poised to intervene and set everything to rights. Marius, in fact, was nowhere to be seen. It gave her a pinched feeling in the back of the throat, making it difficult to breathe. And as for talking . . .

Dorothy steadied herself and, with almost exaggerated care, brought the glass to her lips. The forty or so people who had gathered to hear her thoughts on Christianity and the crime novel, with special attention to the work of Dorothy L. Sayers, watched and waited patiently. After all, she could sense them thinking, at her age you can't expect too much.

Well, expectations were strange things. She reached out towards the small table at her side and lifted her copy of *Such a Strange Lady* into her lap.

'As we can be only too aware,' she began, 'living as we do in these particular times, it is difficult not to see the art of biography and the wish of the individual for privacy as being incompatible. Think then only of a young woman, an only child, born at Christchurch Cathedral Choir School, a Christian scholar whose second book of poems was titled *Catholic Tales and Christian Songs*, and yet who nevertheless became pregnant out of wedlock and secretly gave birth to an illegitimate son. How irreconcilable the gulf between the life that is apparent and expected and the life that is actually lived.'

She paused and caught her breath. If only she had not

been forced to have words with Marius earlier that afternoon – some of them, she would have had to agree, significantly less than Christian. If only Marius had not stalked off in such high dudgeon, no word of where he was going or when he might return.

Dorothy looked out at her audience and continued. 'In her religious play *The Devil to Pay*, Dorothy Sayers explicitly deals with Faustian themes, the extent to we are all of us prepared to go, the amount we will pay for happiness on this earth even though it might mean we risk damnation in the next . . .'

'How about a couple of drinks, honey?' Cathy Jordan said in a mock-seductive, mid-Western voice. 'One way or another, I reckon we've earned them.' She was leaning against the frame of the bathroom door, a towel wrapped around the middle of her body. A tumbler of tap water, with the aid of which she had just swallowed aspirin, was held lightly in her right hand, wrist resting on the swell of her hip.

'Go to hell, Cathy, why don't you?' Frank said, flipping over the pages of the magazine he was reading – a copy of *Première* he'd picked up at the airport, everything you ever wanted to know about Demi Moore except what does she ever see in that asshole actor.

'What does she ever see in that asshole actor?' Frank asked.

'Which particular one did you have in mind?'

'Demi Moore. You know. The one with Demi Moore.'

'Oh, him.'

'Yes, him.'

'He was great in *Pulp Fiction*.'

'Didn't catch it.'

'Just terrific.'

'I still don't see . . .'

She lifted the magazine from his hand and then dropped

it back down. 'They're a partnership, that's what it is. That's why it works.' Playful, she nudged him with her bare toes. 'She works. He works. Simple. A partnership.' She threw him a face and headed back towards the bathroom door. 'We should try it some time.'

'What?'

'Nothing.'

'What the fuck was that about?'

He was on his feet now, close behind her, and Cathy turned to face him. 'Work it out for yourself.'

'Every cent you earned this last year, I earned as much.'

Cathy shrugged. 'I had a bad year.'

'Bitch!'

'Sure, Frank. Love you too.'

For an instant, she flinched and closed her eyes, thinking he was going to strike her, but what he did was jerk the towel from around her, so that she stood before him, naked.

Her breasts were heavier than when he had first seen her, the skin across her belly less taut, but there was nothing to deflect from the fact that she was still a beautiful woman; more beautiful as she stood there now, unclothed, than in her boots, bright shirts and jeans. Most women Frank knew, the reverse would be true.

'Well?' Cathy gave him a look that said, what now? and he didn't know. She held out the glass towards him and automatically he reached to take it. Swiftly, she stepped back inside the bathroom and shut the door, flicking the bolt across.

Mollie Hansen was sitting in the Broadway Cinema CaféBar, nibbling at a portion of cabbage stuffed with peppers and drinking Red Raw ginger beer. Slides of scenes from various forties *films noirs* were being projected on to the far wall, and she was idly checking them off as she ate: *Mildred Pierce, Gilda, The Lady from Shanghai.*

'Hi, Mollie.' Susan Tyrell was standing at her shoulder, an empty glass in one hand, a bottle of Cabernet-Shiraz in the other. 'Okay if I join you?'

'Sure.'

Susan pulled out a chair and sat down.

'In for a long wait?' Mollie said with a grin, indicating the bottle.

Susan's eyes rolled upwards. 'David's just getting going on Hollywood *femmes fatales*. Stepping out of the shadows in tight black dresses with guns in their hands.' She filled the glass to within a quarter-inch of the rim and brought it to her mouth without spilling a drop. 'Once he gets started on that little fantasy, I might as well be invisible.'

Mollie forked up some more stuffed cabbage. Larger than life on the wall, Joan Crawford, in poor lighting and a fur coat, stood over the dead body of Zachary Scott.

'You see what I mean?' Susan asked, 'Who ever paid any attention to her when she was just plain old married Mildred, wearing an apron morning till night and baking pies?'

Mollie waited for the laugh, but it didn't come. 'That's a movie,' she said. 'Not real life.'

Susan drained her glass and began pouring another. 'Try telling that to David.'

Mollie looked at her seriously. 'Then maybe it's time to get out of the kitchen?' she said.

Susan looked away. 'Yes, well, I'm afraid that time is long past.' And then she did laugh, but it was loud and forced. 'Listen to me, carrying on. Complaining about David to you of all people.'

Mollie leaned closer and covered Susan's hand with her own. 'If you feel this bad, you've got to sit him down and talk to him. Make him listen.'

'Really. And when did you last succeed in doing that?'

Marius Gooding had let himself back into the hotel suite he had been sharing with Dorothy Birdwell and locked the door. Pulling the blinds, he stripped down to his undershorts and vest. 'Bitch!' he said, as he pulled out drawer after drawer of her neatly folded clothes and spilled them across the floor. 'Bitch!' as he jerked her satin and taffeta dress from its padded hanger and tore it neck to hem. *Bitch!* he scrawled across the photograph in the back of her new book. *Bitch!* in black felt-tip on the centre of the sheet. *Bitch!* on the wall above the bed. *Bitch!* along one arm, the inside of his legs, across his face, and all around his head. *Bitch! Bitch! Bitch! Bitch!* Marius curled up on the floor, knees to his chest, head in his arms, and cried.

Thirty-seven

Frank didn't recognise the woman sitting up at the bar; no reason that he should. It was early yet, early for serious drinking, and the place, long and narrow with stairs leading to a high balcony at the rear, was quiet. Music – which he recognised as Joe Sample, Frank having been a major fan of the Crusaders since seventy-two, 'Street Life' one of his favourite records of all time, the one he always instructed DJs to play when he and Cathy hosted parties of their own – was pumping quietly from large speakers suspended from the ceiling. The barman, fresh-faced and possibly as young as he seemed, set aside the newspaper he was reading and asked Frank what he wanted. The answer was a whisky sour, large, a little salt on the glass; iced water on the side. And something to pick on. He hadn't eaten since lunch and reasoned this was the start of what might prove a long night.

'Nachos,' the barman suggested. 'Chicken wings? Potato skins? Onion rings?'

'Forget the nachos and the onion rings. Let me have the chicken and the potato skins, okay?'

'Sir.' The barman passed Frank's order through to the kitchen and began to slice the lemon, fresh, for his whisky sour.

Frank toyed with the drink when it came, checking the temptation to swallow it right down; ever since the talk with Cathy down by the canal, he'd felt like he was walking on the proverbial eggshells. He laughed and the woman four seats along turned her head; never understood what that meant before, eggshells, what it was like. Now he thought if it was going to crack and let him tumble through, why not take a hammer to it, smash it first himself? Do unto others instead of being done to.

He finished his drink and called along the bar for another. The woman, sipping what Frank thought was some kind of rum cocktail, rum collins, cuba libra, one of those, glanced at him again. Not giving it too much. Still light outside, in the bar it was cool and dark. There were rings on the fingers of both the woman's hands, Frank noticed; dark hair which fell past her face due to the way she was sitting, partly shielding her from his gaze. Thirty-five, Frank thought, forty. Waiting for a friend. Nothing to get worked up about.

'Your whisky sour, sir.'

'Sure,' Frank said. 'Thanks.'

When Cathy arrived outside the main convention room for her interview, she had managed to patch up most of the damage, though the skin around her eyes was darker than usual and her face was pinched as if she were suffering from too little sleep. Which was partly the truth.

'You okay?' Mollie asked, concerned, stepping forward to greet her.

Cathy nodded: fine.

And from anything other than close up, she did look good: a cream linen suit with wide lapels, a green satin shirt and, poking out from beneath slightly flared trousers, the ubiquitous boots.

'Cathy, I think you know Sarah Dunant.'

'Sure. We met at the Edgars last year.'

The two women smiled and brushed cheeks and set off towards the platform, Mollie leading the way.

'So which part of the States are you from?' the woman was saying.

And, 'How long are you over for?'

And, 'Oh, interesting.'

Frank all the while hearing Cathy's voice – *I wonder if that isn't long enough?* Eight years. Close to. Saying it, it didn't seem so long. But living it. He shook his head. Some days he could scarcely remember when there had been anything else.

'Sorry,' Frank leaned sideways towards the woman's stool. 'I didn't catch what you said.'

'I said, do you want another drink here or are you ready to move on somewhere else?'

The music had shifted again, back from some guitar band that reminded Frank of the Byrds, back to the Crusaders, the album they made – eighty-one, eighty-two? – with Joe Cocker.

'I'm okay here,' Frank said. 'Unless you're getting restless?'

She shook her head and slid her empty glass towards his; all this time they'd been talking and he still hadn't got a good look at her face.

'Two more,' Frank called along to the barman. 'Same as before.'

The convention room was comfortably full, without being overcrowded. Mollie had been able to spot a few of the more vocal feminists, identified them from previous events she had helped to organise. *Representations of Women in the Media. Melodrama and the Family.* She had talked to quite a few of them at length, respected what they had to say. Liked them.

After a brief introduction in which Sarah Dunant had placed Cathy Jordan's work within the context of post-seventies crime fiction, she led her through a series of questions about her career, its false starts and now its successes. Dunant then summarised the prevailing politically correct readings of crime fiction and asked Cathy for her opinions. There were questions from the floor, searching rather than hostile, and then the interview was over: polite, professional, non-contentious.

Cathy had opted to close the session with a reading and she chose the opening chapter from *Dead Weight*. Instantly, the caustic, slightly self-deprecating voice of Annie Q. Jones buttonholed the audience and when she finished it was to warm applause.

Mollie came on to the platform to thank both women formally and bring the proceedings to a confident close. Now she could take them to the hotel bar, buy them a drink, make her excuses, take herself home and rest, thankful that the evening had passed without incident.

Still in the bar, Frank was explaining the difference between a latte and a mocha, though he wasn't sure if his companion were still listening and if she were, whether she had understood. Where previously there had been several feet of space behind them, now they were constantly being banged against and jostled by one or other of the young people who stood in groups around them, smoking and drinking and laughing. The volume of the stereo had increased four-fold and whatever was being played now seemed to consist of a thumping bass and very little else.

'You want to try somewhere else?' Frank asked, mouth close against her hair.

'I thought you weren't interested?'

'I'm interested.' He wondered how long her hand had been on his knee.

'Then let's go back to your place.'

'How d'you mean?'

'You've got a room, haven't you? You're staying at a hotel?'

Frank shook his head. Now that he could see her, he

liked what he saw. Liked her breath, slightly sweet, upon his face. 'We can't go there.'

'I thought you were here on your own. Have you got a wife or something?'

'That doesn't matter. We just can't go back to my room, that's all.' He let his hand cover hers, where it was still resting, high on his thigh. 'What's wrong with your place?'

'We'll go to another hotel,' she said, and smiled. 'As long as your credit card's good for it.'

'Hey, don't worry about the money. But d'you think we'll get into somewhere this late? Town strikes me as pretty busy.'

'Don't worry about that,' she said, getting carefully down from her stool. 'Just trust me.'

Thirty-eight

The first time Resnick had seen Sharon Garnett, the sun had been showing weakly through winter clouds and the earth beneath their feet had been coarse with frost. All around them, the high stink of pig food and pig shit. Other officers, silent, as they lifted a stretcher across the ruts, the body of a young woman sealed beneath thick plastic that was spotted here and there with mud.

Now, as she pushed her way through the bar towards him, Resnick realised that she was both taller than he had remembered and likely older too. The only black face in the Sir John Borlace Warren.

'Your local?'

Resnick grinned. 'Not exactly.'

After Sharon had rung him with the information about Marlene Kinoulton's probable drug supplier, he had put through a call to Norman Mann at Central Station and the choice of meeting place had been the Drugs Squad officer's shout.

'Pint?' Sharon asked.

'Guinness, thanks. Half.'

By the time she had been served, Norman Mann had joined them, lager in hand, dark hair thick on his head and curling up over the collar of what had clearly been bought from a job lot of black leather jackets.

Resnick shook his hand and did the introductions.

'This Richie,' Mann said, once they had elbowed their way into a corner, 'had our eye on him for quite a while. There's a blues he does his drinking some nights. No sense looking for him there too early, but by the time we've supped a couple of these, we could wander down. See what's what.'

'You think he'll talk?' Sharon asked. 'Give us anything we need to know?'

Norman Mann winked broadly. 'Always a chance. Smoked enough weed, we'll be lucky to shut the bastard up.'

The room was small and, in the way of most hotel rooms, anonymously airless. Frank had tried to kiss the woman as she leant back against the door, clicking the lock, but she had swerved her head aside. Then, as he had reached towards the light switch, she had caught hold of his arm and ducked beneath it, twisting him round till he was hard against her. She had kissed him then, her mouth slippery over his, teeth blocking out his tongue.

'At least now you're going to tell me your name?' he said.

'Why? Isn't it better like this?'

'In the dark?'

'Yes.'

But it was not quite that, the curtains only partly pulled across and light enough from the city shining through; he touched her face and she shuddered, almost before the touch, as if anticipating something else. His skin against hers was surprisingly soft. At first, she squirrelled the tip of her tongue into his palm and then drew her teeth down and around one of his fingers, nipping it a little at the knuckles before drawing her lips back along it so slowly that he moaned. With a laugh, she bit down into the fleshy round beneath his thumb.

'Hey!'

'Hmm?'

Frank fumbled her open at the front and bent his head into her neck, squeezing her breasts. Whatever moment he might have pulled back at had long passed. She touched him and, arching back his head, he closed his eyes.

'Frank?'

'Yeah?'

'Let's go to bed.'

Soon she was kneeling over him, kissing him, deft pecks like a bird's, delicate and sharp. His trousers had been pushed and kicked down to his ankles, shirt thrown sideways to the floor; his boxer shorts were tight across his thighs.

'Like me, Frank?'

'Sure I like you.'

'I mean me. Really me.'

'Sure.'

'You're lying, Frank.'

'I'm not.'

'Lying.'

'Look, I swear to God . . .'

'Anyone, Frank. I could be any woman in the whole wide fucking world. Any woman, Frank. Any cunt in a storm.'

He made to roll aside and she leaned her weight against his arms, surprisingly strong. 'What's the matter, Frank? Don't want me any more? Huh? Don't fancy me?'

Head sideways below the pillow, he didn't answer.

'Don't you like it when a cunt talks back, Frank? That the problem?'

'There's no problem,' he mumbled, only just audible above the hum of the air conditioning.

'What?' Her face lowered close to him, laughter in her voice, teasing.

'I said there's no fucking problem.'

'Temper,' she scolded. 'Temper.' And rocking back on his hips, she reached a hand behind and between his legs and he could sense rather than see her smile. 'You're right, Frank. No problem at all.'

She moved again, her buttocks lower on his thighs, the front of her pale-coloured briefs against his balls. Spreading his hands, straightening his arms, he raised his face towards hers and she kissed him, he kissed her, her fingers tugging at his hair.

'Wait,' she said, minutes later. 'Wait.'

'What for?' His breathing was harsh.

'What do you think?' Swivelling off him. 'I have to go to the bathroom, of course.'

He watched her dart away, pale, no longer slender, saw the shimmer of electric light before the bathroom door closed it out. With a slow sigh, he lay back down, rested an arm across his face and once more closed his eyes.

A blues club in Radford or Hyson Green didn't mean laidback, Mississippi Delta bottleneck, the kind that might grace TV advertisements for beer or jeans; it didn't even mean second- or third-generation bump and grind, juke blues, South Side Chicago, T-Bone Walker or Otis Rush. It meant after-hours drinking, Red Stripe and rum, the sweet scent of marijuana drifting in lazy spirals down the stairs.

They were illegal, of course, and the police knew where they were and who ran them, and those that ran them knew the police knew and, unless something exceptional happened to upset the racial apple cart, that was how it stayed.

This particular club was off the Radford Road, more or less across from where the Hyson Green flats used to be, until they had been bulldozed down and the land leased to house another supermarket. Perish the thought the Council would build more homes. The fact that the club was above the premises of what had been some kind of outreach office of the Probation Service, only added a little extra piquancy.

Norman Mann paused at the foot of the stairs and drew

in a deep, long breath. 'What d'you reckon, Charlie? Worth inhaling, eh?'

Smelled a sight better than a lot of things illegal, Resnick thought, and likely did a lot less harm, but that was as far as he was prepared to go.

The treads on the stairs were cracked in places and bare. As they climbed higher the bass from recorded reggae made the walls vibrate. Norman Mann motioned for Resnick and Sharon to stay at the end of the landing, went to the door and knocked. There followed a long and fairly tortuous conversation Resnick couldn't hear.

'We'll wait down there,' Mann said, when the head he'd been talking to withdrew and the door was sharply closed.

In what had once been the Probation office, a forty-watt bulb hung from a length of fraying flex. Miraculously, it still worked. What it cast light on were an old desk, empty boxes, balls of dust, a stack of forms waiting forever to be filled in and signed – those that hadn't been shredded by the mice for their nests. A hungry cat would have thought it had died and gone to heaven. Next time Dizzy nips my trouserleg because he thinks I've put him on short rations, Resnick thought, I'll bring him down here and lock him in.

Richie made them wait. When he finally appeared in the doorway, he was wearing a skinny-ribbed V-neck jumper in bright colours and tight trousers which, even in that dim light, shone when he moved. He was slightly built and about as pale as a black man can be without becoming Michael Jackson. He stood lounging against the door frame with a can of lager in his hand.

'Who's these?' he said, indicating Resnick and Sharon with a nod of the head.

Norman Mann made the introductions.

'Marlene Kinoulton,' Resnick said. 'We'd like to find her.'

'Slag! I'd like to find she first.' The syntax was right, but at root the accent was no more Caribbean than if he'd gone down the pit at sixteen – which conceivably he might have done, except that by then they were already closing them down.

'She owe you?' Norman Mann asked.

'She owe everybody.'

'That why she's keeping her head down? Maybe skipped town?'

'She not even got the sense to do that. I saw her fat white ass only this afternoon.'

'You sure?' Resnick asked.

'I not blind.'

'Then you would have had a word with her,' Norman Mann said. 'Her owing you, and all.'

'She getting into this car, in't she?'

'Which car?'

'I don't know. Big white car. She's working, in't she? Doing business. Drive off before I can say a thing.'

'No way you could have been mistaken? You're positive it was her?'

'Yeah.'

'Where?'

'Round near her place.'

'You got an address for her then?' Resnick said.

'What's it worth?'

Both men stared at him and Richie stared back for long enough to show no way were they going to intimidate him. Then he gave his can a little chug.

'How about peace of mind?' Norman Mann said. 'Good will.'

'What you want she for?' Richie asked. He was looking at Resnick.

'Something serious,' Resnick said. 'Nothing that would affect you, I can promise you that.'

'Promise?' Richie drained the can and tossed it into the nearest corner. 'What's that?'

Over their heads, someone had turned up the volume and the ceiling had started to shake.

'That gives way,' Norman Mann said, glancing up, 'going to be a lot of people hurt bad. Crying shame.'

'Forest Fields,' Richie said. 'She have a room, Harcourt Road.'

'Number?'

'Top end, corner house.'

'Which side?'

Richie grinned. 'Depend which way you looking, don't it?' And then, addressing Sharon directly for the first time, ' 'stead of hangin' out with these guys, get your black ass down here some night, show it a good time.'

Thirty-nine

Frank Carlucci couldn't be certain how long he had lain there before he realised the woman wasn't coming back. However much sexual anticipation he was experiencing, the effect of innumerable whisky sours had meant that the meeting between his head and a pair of the hotel's comfortable pillows had so far resulted in one thing only. The woman was, he seemed to remember thinking, taking one hell of a long time in the bathroom, but aside from that, he didn't recall very much at all. A sound that, he now realised, might have been that of the room door opening or closing, and that was all.

Sitting up – first quickly, and then, as his head informed him speed was ill-advised, cautiously – he looked at his watch. Too dark too see. Reaching across, he snapped on the bedside lamp. Blinking, then squinting, he tried again. A quarter past one. He had scarcely been asleep any time at all.

Easing himself off the bed, he checked the bathroom, the door to which was wide open and, of course, it was empty. Only then, with sinking desperation, did he scrabble on the floor for his jacket and fumble his wallet out into the light. He knew what remained of his English cash and all his credit cards would be gone, but, contradicting him, they were there, the money, as far as he could tell, intact.

Back in the bathroom, he splashed cold water in his face and then wondered why he was bothering. Cathy was bound to be asleep in their own room by now, another hotel across the city, and what was to be gained from waking her, he didn't know. Better to face her the next day with a fresh face and a good story.

Frank hung the *Do Not Disturb* sign outside the door, climbed back into bed and inside five minutes he was snoring, first lightly, then loudly.

They had been parked across the street some ten minutes, Norman Mann smoking two Bensons while he and Resnick listened to one of Sharon's anecdotes about policing deepest Lincolnshire. 'Go into some of those places,' Sharon said, 'and I'd know how my relatives felt, getting off the boat at Tilbury in the 1950s.' Or mine, Resnick, thought, in 1938. Except, of course, that they'd been white.

'Well, what d'you think, Charlie? Shall we give it a pull?'

Resnick pushed open the car door and stepped out on to uneven paving stones. Apart from a stereo playing too loud a half-dozen doors down, the street was quiet. The end terrace to the right, facing north, had stone cladding on the front and side walls, window frames and ledges which had been newly painted, yellow, and a small sign attached to the front door to show that the householders were members of the local Neighbourhood Watch. The house opposite had a derelict washing machine upside down outside in the scrubby front garden, one of its upper windows covered in heavy-duty plastic where the glass had been broken and not replaced, and at least a dozen milk bottles beside the front door, each containing a varying amount of mould and algae.

'So, Charlie – no call to be much of a detective here, eh?'

'Give me a minute,' Sharon said at the space where the front gate should have been. 'I'll get round the back.'

Once she had disappeared from sight, the two men

slowly walked towards the door. When Resnick rang the bell it failed to work; he knocked and no one answered, but from the sound of the television they knew somebody was at home. Norman Mann leaned past him, turned the handle and pushed and the door swung grudgingly inwards.

'Thanks very much,' he said with a wink, 'we'd love to come in.'

They followed the sound of amplified voices into the front room.

Three youths, status unemployed, were watching a video of *Naked Gun 2½* amongst a plethora of beer cans and empty pizza boxes and the faint scent of dope.

'What the fuck?'

Resnick showed them his identification, while Norman Mann walked past them towards the television set and switched it off.

'Hey! You can't . . .'

'You live here?' Mann asked.

'Yeah.'

'All of you?'

'Yeah.'

'Who else?' Resnick asked.

One of the youths, his head partly shaven, a trio of silver rings close in one ear, got awkwardly to his feet. 'Look, you gonna tell us what's going on? What the fuck this is all about?'

'Easy,' Mann said. 'We ask questions, you answer them. So, now – who else is there, living in the house?'

The youth looked round at his mates before responding. 'There's Terry, right, up on the first floor at the front . . .'

'He's not here now,' put in one of the others. 'Off home to see his old man.'

'Who else?' Resnick said.

Two of them exchanged quick glances; the one with the

shaven head stared at a stain in the carpet, one amongst many. 'You won't let on?' he finally said.

'To who?' Norman Mann asked. 'And about what?'

'The landlord. See, the bloke as was up there moved out and he left it to us to let out the room.' A few more shifty looks wove back and forth. 'On his behalf, like.'

'And you forgot?'

'No, well, we got someone in, all right . . .'

Norman Mann laughed. 'Just a bit slow in letting the landlord in on it?'

'Something like that.'

'Well, I know how it is, lads,' Mann said. 'Busy life like yours. Going down the video shop, cadging fags, jerking off, signing on. Understandable, really, you've never quite found the time.' One of the youths sniggered; the others did not.

'This unofficial tenant,' Resnick said. 'Got a name?'

'Marlene.'

'Kinoulton?'

'Yeah, that's right. Yes.'

There were footsteps outside and then Sharon walked into the room. 'Back door was open. Didn't reckon anyone was about to do a runner.'

'Here,' said the shaven youth. 'How many more of you are there?'

'Hundreds,' Norman Mann grinned. 'Thousands. We're taking over the fucking earth!'

The room Marlene Kinoulton had rented was on the first floor at the back. No lights showed under the door and when Resnick knocked there was no response. A hasp had been fitted across the door and a padlock secured.

'Have that off in two ticks,' Norman Mann said, flicking it up with his forefinger.

'And have anything we find ruled inadmissible by the

court,' Resnick said. 'Let's wait for the morning, get a warrant.'

'Suit yourself.' Norman Mann looked quite disappointed. He was more of a knock-'em-down-and-reckon-the-consequences-afterwards man himself.

'I'll babysit the place the rest of the night,' Sharon offered, once they were back downstairs. 'If she's around, she might come back.'

'Good,' Resnick said. 'Thanks. I'll send Divine round to relieve you first thing. Meantime, I'll chase up a warrant. See what she's got in there, worth keeping a lock on.'

In the front room, Norman Mann took a swallow at the can of lager he'd popped open and set it back down with a grimace. 'What you're scrounging off the DSS, ought to be able to afford better than that.' Reaching round, he switched the TV set back on. 'Thanks, lads. Thanks for inviting us into your home.'

Forty

Cathy Jordan woke early, with the creamy taste of another late-night supper still rich in her mouth. She lay without moving, aware of Frank's absence, accepting it without surprise. They had tried, in the time they had been together, handling her enforced absences, these trips to the conventions and booksellers of the world, in a number of ways. At root, however, there were two alternatives: he went with her or he stayed home. Cathy liked to claim she left the choice to him.

If Frank waved her off at the airport with a hug and a kiss and a see-you-in-six-weeks, within days he would be calling her erratically around the clock, unable to settle; and she would return to smiles and flowers and rumours of drunken nights and drunken days and always there would be messages from women Cathy had never previously heard of, backing up on the answering machine.

Or he travelled with her, bemoaning the cappuccinos and gymnasia of the free world; frequently bored, listless, quick to take offence and give it. And there were mornings like this, Cathy waking to one side of the bed, the other unslept in and unsullied, and later, around lunchtime, Frank would reappear, without explanation, his expression daring her to ask. Which at first she had, and, of course, he had lied; or she had made assumptions, right or wrong, and he had responded with counter-accusation and attack. It was after one of these, she had finally said, 'Frank, I don't give a flying fuck what you do or who you do it to, but if I ever contract as much as the tiniest vaginal wart as a result of your fooling around, I will never – and I mean, never – speak to you again.'

Sniping aside, not a great many words had been exchanged on the subject since.

Cathy sat up and surprised herself by not wincing when her feet made contact with the hotel carpet. It had been past midnight when Curtis Woolfe had insisted on buying several bottles of champagne and then doctoring everyone's glass with four-star brandy. For the umpteenth time he proposed a toast to David Tyrell and thanked him for, as he put it, restoring his life's work to the light of a new day. It didn't seem as if Curtis was going to be a recluse any longer. Amongst the other rumours which abounded was one that he had been asked to film Elmore Leonard's non-crime novel *Touch*, with Johnny Depp as Juvenal, the beautiful healer, bleeding from five stigmata on prime-time television and Winona Ryder as the record promoter who falls in love with him.

Cathy, who to date had fielded approaches, official and unofficial, from Kim Basinger, Sharon Stone, Amanda Donohoe, Melanie Griffith, Phoebe Cates, Jamie Lee Curtis, Michelle Pfeiffer, Bridget Fonda and Jennifer Jason Leigh to play Annie Q. Jones, had leaned across and warned Curtis not to hold his breath. In most cases, it was far better to bank the option fee and pray no one ever got around to making the movie.

She was about to get into the shower when the phone rang and she lost her footing to the sudden thought that it was someone calling with the news that something had happened to Frank. Something bad. The skin along her arms pricked cold as she lifted the receiver. Frank, out on the town in a town where men where getting stabbed and worse.

It wasn't Frank, or anything about him; it was Dorothy Birdwell, asking if Cathy would consider joining her for breakfast.

Cathy drew breath. 'Sure, Dorothy. Why not?' And she returned to the shower, relieved, surprised, wondering if there was a certain British etiquette to these occasions she was supposed to observe.

Skelton and his wife were making brittle conversation over the toast and marmalade. Frank Carlucci had not been the only person to stay out all night unannounced. At a little after seven, Kate had phoned from Newark and said she was sorry, but she'd got stuck, missed the last train, missed the bus, there'd been some confusion and she'd missed her lift; it had been all right, though, she'd been able to stay with friends. She hoped they hadn't been too worried. Why, Skelton had asked, his temper conspicuously under wraps, had she not called to tell them this earlier, before the worrying had begun? Kate's explanation had been too complicated and devious to believe or follow.

'What on earth was she doing in Newark in the first place?' Alice had demanded, tightening the belt to her dressing gown.

Skelton had shaken his head; aside from a vague idea that they sold antiques, he had never been certain what people did in Newark anyway.

'What time did she say she would be back?' Alice asked.

'She didn't.'

He had been pouring another cup of rather tired tea, when the doorbell sounded.

'There she is now,' said Alice. 'And she's forgotten her key.'

But it was Resnick, braving another episode of happy families in order to persuade Skelton to apply for a search warrant for the end terrace in Harcourt Road.

'The whole house?' Skelton asked, when he had listened to Resnick's explanations.

'Might as well. While we're about it.'

While Cathy Jordan's breakfast was heavy on the grains and fruit, heavy on the coffee, Dorothy Birdwell's order, carefully enunciated, was for one poached egg – 'And that's poached, mind, properly poached, not steamed' – on dry wholemeal toast and a pot of Assam tea.

'Cathy,' Dorothy Birdwell said, once her egg had been delivered (a poor, shrivelled thing, in Cathy's opinion) to the table. 'I may call you Cathy, may I?'

'Sure, Dottie. That's fine.' She could tell Dorothy didn't like *that*, but the older woman took it in her stride.

'You know, dear, I am not the greatest fan of the kind of thing that you write.'

'Dorothy, I know.'

'In fact, I would go so far as to say, in a way I find it quite pernicious. I mean, this may be old-fashioned of me, I'm sure that it is, but I do think there are certain standards we have a moral obligation to maintain.'

'Standards?' Great, Cathy thought, she's invited me down to receive a lecture, a *grande-dame* rap across the knuckles.

'Yes, dear. A certain morality.'

Cathy speared a prune. 'Let me get this straight. Are we talking sex here?'

'My dear, you mustn't think me a prude. Sex is fine, in its place, I'm sure we would both agree to that.' (We would? Cathy thought, surprised.) 'But its most intimate details, well, I don't think we need to have those spelled out for us, you see. Not in all their personal intricacies, at least. And the violence we most certainly inflict upon one another, if I wish to learn of that, I can always read the newspaper – though, of course, I prefer not to – I do not wish to find myself confronting it inside an otherwise charming work of entertainment. You do see my point, dear?'

In polite company, Cathy wondered, what did you do with a prune stone? Spit it out into your hand, or push it under your tongue and risk being accused of speaking with your mouth full. Either way, it didn't matter. Dorothy's question had been rhetorical.

'But I do want to say that I think the way those ghastly women have been ganging up on you is perfectly dreadful. And in no way could I ever bring myself to support their actions.' She fluttered her hands above the remains of her poached egg. 'That silly business with the paint.'

Cathy nodded. 'To say nothing of the rabbit.'

Dorothy inclined her head forward. 'Yes, dear. It was about that I most particularly wanted to talk.'

'You did?' The antennae in Cathy's brain were beginning to stand up and point, but she couldn't yet tell in which direction. She set down her spoon and fork and waited.

'Marius,' Dorothy said earnestly, 'has always been such a sweet boy, so single-minded in his attentions. I really couldn't begin to tell you all the things he has done for me.' For a moment, Dorothy paused and dabbed at her mouth with a napkin. 'But, I now realise, there are times when he has allowed his – I suppose the only word I can use is devotion – his devotion for me to, well, blind his judgement.' She sipped her tea, grimaced in a ladylike way and added just a touch more milk. 'I am sorry, dear.'

Cathy didn't say anything: she couldn't immediately think of anything – aside from the scatological and the profane – to say. She stared across the table at the older writer instead and, in return, Dorothy Birdwell smiled one of her perfunctory smiles and tipped some more hot water from the metal jug into the teapot.

'Are you telling me,' Cathy finally got out, whispering because she was afraid anything else would be a shout, 'that it was Marius pulled that gross stunt with the rabbit dolled up as a fucking baby?'

It was no good, the whispering hadn't worked; she was shouting now, not quite at the top of her voice, but loud enough to have half the dining room turning round and an assistant manager heading towards them at a fast trot.

'Yes,' Dorothy said, head bowed, 'and I'm afraid that is not all.'

'Not all? Not all? Jesus, what's the little creep done now?'

'My dear, I can only assure you, you have my deepest sympathy and apologies.'

'Sympathy? Apologies?' Cathy was on her feet now, stepping back. 'With all due respect, Dorothy, your apologies, my ass!'

'Really, dear, I don't think this kind of a scene . . .'

'No? Well, I don't give a fuck what you think. What I do give a fuck for is where in sweet hell is your little lapdog, Marius?'

'I dismissed him, of course. I'm afraid there was quite a little scene. He was very upset. Very. But in the circumstances, there was no way in which I could change my mind.' Again, she paused. 'I am sorry, dear, believe me.'

'Where,' Cathy said, 'is Marius now?'

'I can only imagine he's gone to the station . . .'

'Train station? He's heading for where? London? Where?'

'Is everything all right?' the assistant manager asked. 'Is there anything I can do?'

'Keep out of my face,' Cathy snapped.

'Manchester,' Dorothy Birdwell said. 'He has a friend, I think, in Manchester.'

'Thanks,' Cathy said, 'for the breakfast. Thanks,' over her shoulder, as she hurried off towards the nearest phone, 'for everything.'

Resnick had just got back to his office, warrant signed and

delivered into his hand, when Millington beckoned him towards the phone he was holding.

'Cathy Jordan, for you. Likely wants to know if you've finished her book.'

'Hello,' Resnick said, and then listened. After not too many moments, he asked Cathy to stop, take several deep breaths and start again. Slowly. 'Right,' he said when she had finished. 'Right. Yes.' And, 'Right.' He passed the receiver back into Millington's hand. 'Graham,' Resnick said, 'get on to the station. Manchester train, I think it's the one comes across from Norwich. Have it stopped.' He swivelled round to see who was available in the office. 'Lynn, pick up this bloke at the railway station, I'll arrange back-up. Marius Gooding. Late thirties, five seven or eight, shortish hair, dark. Smart in an old-fashioned kind of way. Maybe a blue blazer. Keep it low key, just ask him in for questioning, that's all.'

'What if he refuses?'

'Arrest him.'

'What charge?'

'Threatening behaviour, that'll do. Okay?'

'Right.'

Millington was still talking to the stationmaster; any immediate developments he could handle here. Divine and Naylor had already gone out to relieve Sharon at the house where Marlene Kinoulton had her room. As he left to follow them, Resnick patted his inside pocket, making sure the search warrant was in place.

Forty-one

They found: one three-quarter-length coat, navy blue; one leather jacket, hip-length, black, badly scuffed along one sleeve; five skirts, three short, one calf-length, one long; two sweaters; one white, ruffle-front shirt; one black-beaded fishnet top with fringing; eight other assorted tops, including two T-shirts and a blue silk blouse with what looked like blood on one sleeve; one black velvet suit; two pairs of jeans, Levi red tab and Gap denim; three pairs of ski pants, one badly torn, possibly cut; five pairs of ribbed woollen tights; seven pairs of regular tights, one red, one blue, mostly laddered or holed; three pairs of stockings, all black, two with seams; two pairs of cotton socks, off-white; eleven pairs of briefs, two of them crotchless; one black suspender belt; three brassières; one bustier; one nurse's uniform, badly stained; one school gymslip, bottle green.

Two pairs of ankle boots, a brown and a bright red; one pair of black leather lace-up boots, knee-length; two pairs of trainers, Reebok and Adidas; seven pairs of shoes.

Condoms: Durex Featherlite and Elite and Mates liquorice ribbed.

K-Y lubricating jelly, three tubes.

Vaseline.

Body Shop body massage oil.

Cotton buds. Smoker's toothpaste. Safeway frequency wash shampoo. A diaphragm. A pregnancy testing kit, unused. Soap. Boots face cream. Nail polish, seven different shades. Nail polish remover. One Philips electric razor, lady's model. One set of make-up brushes. Navy eyeliner. Green mascara. Dejoria hand and body lotion. Aloe hair gel. Max Factor Brush-On Satin Blush. Princess Marcella Borghese Pink Marabu Blusher, hot pink. Three kohl pencils. Three bottles of aspirin. One packet of Nurofen. Lipsticks, seven ranging from Coral Reef to Vermilion. Panty liners. One box of tampons, extra absorbency, five remaining. Perfume. One plastic bottle of Tesco antiseptic mouthwash, peppermint flavour, family size.

Paperback books: *Dark Angel* by Sally Beauman; *The Silence of the Lambs* by Thomas Harris; *Rosemary Conley's Hip and Thigh Diet*; *Rosemary's Baby* by Ira Levin; *Tess of the D'Urbervilles* by Thomas Hardy.

Assorted copies of *Elle*, *Vanity Fair*, *She*, *Cosmopolitan*, *Fiesta* and *Men Only*.

One video tape of *Sex Kittens Go Hawaii*.

Kleenex.

An Aiwa radio-cassette player, with a copy of the Eurythmics' *Greatest Hits* inside. Assorted cassettes by Phil Collins, Chris Rea, Chris deBurgh and Tina Turner.

One medium-size suitcase, a tan handbag, two imitation leather shoulder bags. Inside one of the bags, a purse containing forty-seven pence in change, several used tissues, a torn half-ticket for the Showcase cinema and a strip of four coloured head-and-shoulder photographs of an unsmiling Marlene Kinoulton.

In a drawer, one Coke can, a hole punched through approximately one inch from the end, around which there were signs of burning. Two boxes of matches. A container of aluminium foil.

In a buckled metal dustbin in the back yard, and partly covered by grey-black ashes, several fragments of dark material – synthetic mixed with cotton – singed, but not burnt.

In the kitchen on the ground floor, somehow stuffed

down behind the piece of narrow, laminated board that separated the washing machine from the swing-top rubbish bin, one dark blue, Ralph Lauren, wool and cotton mix sock with a red polo player logo.

Forty-two

On its way to Liverpool, via Manchester, the twin-carriage train stopped at Langley Mill, Alfreton and Mansfield Parkway, Bolsover, Sheffield, Edale and Stockport. At that moment, it had stopped within sight of the station, small knots of would-be passengers staring along the track towards it, checking their watches, the overhead clock, the monitor screens on which the slightly flickering green lettering announced no delay and clearly lied.

Lynn almost approached the wrong man, before she spotted Marius, standing close to the window of the buffet, glancing distractedly at the copy of the *Telegraph* folded in his hand. He was wearing a blue blazer, grey trousers with a deep crease, black brogue shoes that shone. There was a smart, double-strapped, leather suitcase at his side.

'Marius?' Lynn said softly, so softly that he only just heard.

'Hmm? I'm sorry?' He looked at a youngish woman, with brown hair cut, he thought, rather savagely short. A round face that seemed, somehow, to have sunk, like early-punctured fruit.

'Is your name Marius?'

'Marius Gooding. Yes, why? Have we met? You'll have to forgive me, I don't remember.'

What she was taking from her pocket was her warrant card. 'I'm a police officer. Detective Constable Kellogg. I . . .'

He was still smiling his well-mannered, tentative smile

when he struck out, the arm that held the newspaper jerking towards her face. For an instant, Lynn was lost in tall pages of newsprint, crisp and self-righteous editorials, as Marius followed up his blow with a push and took to his heels. Twenty yards along the platform, heading for the stairs, he collided with an elderly couple, loaded down with walking boots, binoculars and rucksacks, off for a day in the Peaks. Spinning around, close to losing his footing, Marius started off again in the opposite direction, aiming for the far side of the buffet, the steps that would take him up to the bridge and the open car park, the streets beyond.

Lynn positioned herself well, feet firmly set; she made a grab for his upper arm, ducking beneath his open hand as he made to fend her off. Her fingers grasped the sleeve of his coat and held fast. Marius's impetus rocked Lynn back, but not totally off-balance. Buttons sprang free as threads snapped.

Most of the people waiting on the platform had ceased worrying about their train. Fingers pointed; cries of 'There!' 'There!' and 'Look!' A black porter, white-haired, too small for his blue-black uniform, hovered anxiously, wanting to do something but unsure what.

Lynn ducked again under a flailing arm and tightened her grip on Marius's opposite wrist, forcing it high towards the middle of his back.

Marius gasped with sudden pain.

'Go on, duck,' someone called admiringly. 'You show 'im right and proper.'

Releasing one of her hands, but not the pressure, Lynn caught hold of Marius's hair, just long enough at the back to give her leverage. Marius cried out as first one knee, then the other struck the concrete platform.

'Nesh bugger!' a voice came dismissively. 'Be scraightin' next, you see if he ain't.'

And, in truth, there were tears in the corners of Marius's eyes.

'Marius Gooding,' Lynn said, a little short of breath, 'I'm arresting you on suspicion of threatening behaviour . . .'

'That's ridiculous! When did I ever threaten . . . ?'

'For assaulting a police officer and resisting arrest.'

The socks matched: a perfect fit. The youth with the earrings and the shaved head had remembered finding the second sock, the one that Naylor had triumphantly discovered in the kitchen, but not exactly where. Somewhere on the stairs, he thought? Out in the yard? Anyway, he had assumed it belonged to one of the other lads (knowing it not to be his, his came from a stall in the market or at Christmas and birthdays from Marks and Spencer, via his parents) and had stuffed it in the washing machine along with an accumulated load. How it had ended up wedged where Naylor had found it, he had no idea, except, socks, well, almost as if they had a mind of their own.

The Coke can still contained minute traces of what Resnick was certain would prove to be crack cocaine.

And the blood on the silk blouse? If blood indeed were what it was? Forensic tests would be carried out with as much haste as urgent calls from Resnick himself and Jack Skelton could engender. If the blood proved to match that of the late Peter Farleigh, they were as good as there, home free. If not . . .

'So, Charlie,' Skelton said, turning away from the window behind his desk, clear blue sky beyond the edge of the building outside. 'Are we there, do you think, or what?'

'Nudging close. Got to be. Business with the sock, could be coincidence, but that's asking a lot. Circumstantial, though, at best.'

'This, er, friend of hers – Doris Duke. She'd give

evidence about seeing the blood on Kinoulton's clothing, as well as her deteriorating mental state?'

Resnick shifted his weight in the chair. Close and yet still far. 'Maybe, though what credence the jury'd give to her, I don't know. Something concrete, that's what we need. Positively linking Kinoulton with the attacks, any one of them. That's what we still don't have. If Farleigh's hotel room had given up a clearer print that'd be a start, but no. Smudge and fudge. I can lean on McKimber again, but he's got his own reasons for not wanting to get dragged in too far. Desperate to get back with his wife and kids, poor bugger.'

Skelton coughed, a sudden, sharp attack and Resnick waited while it subsided.

'Course, if we could lay our hands on Kinoulton herself, ask her some questions direct, it might be a different picture.'

Skelton nodded neat agreement and flicked out the sides of his suit jacket before sitting back down. 'Not to fret, Charlie; something'll turn up.'

Once his panic and anger had subsided, Marius Gooding had apologised so abjectly, his tongue must have tasted of the interview room floor. Over and over. You have to believe, I've never done such a thing in my life. Never struck anybody at all, never mind a member of the opposite sex, a woman. No, Lynn, had observed, but you have done other things.

'What? What other things?'

One by one, she showed him the Polaroids that had been taken inside Dorothy Birdwell's hotel suite. *Bitch! Bitch! Bitch!*

Without further hesitation, Marius had demanded a phone call and a solicitor. The call was to Dorothy Birdwell, who listened patiently to his pleading and then hung up without answering.

The solicitor who arrived was actually a solicitor's clerk, Heather Jardine; a forty-three-year-old Scot, divorced with two teenage children, who had abandoned a stuttering career as a playwright and enrolled in evening classes in law. She knew Lynn Kellogg fairly well – they had been through this and similar procedures before – and the two women treated one another with more than grudging respect.

Jardine made sure her client was aware of his rights, had been fairly treated and asked if he might not have a cup of tea.

Lynn waited for Kevin Naylor to join her and set the tape rolling, identifying those present in the room and the time.

'All right, Marius, why don't we talk about the incident with the rabbit first off?'

After a less than ten minutes of prevarication, Marius asked if he could speak to Heather Jardine alone. This allowed, he admitted the incident with the breakfast trolley, said that he had got it ready the previous day and had intended to leave it outside Cathy Jordan's door; seeing the trolley there, waiting to be taken into the room, he had elaborated his plans accordingly.

'And what was the point?' Lynn asked. 'I mean, why go through all of this rigamorole?'

Marius didn't reply immediately. Instead, he swivelled his head and asked Heather Jardine if he had to answer, and she said, no, he did not. Another few moments and he answered anyway. 'It was a symbol,' he said. 'Of what I think of her work.'

'A symbol?' Lynn repeated carefully.

'Yes.'

'Perhaps you'd best explain.'

'Oh, if you'd read any, you'd know.'

'In fact, I have,' Lynn said. 'A little.'

'Then you'll know the awful things she does; little

239

children tortured, abused, defiled.' His face was a mask of disgust.

'Do you have children, Mr Gooding? Yourself?' Lynn asked.

'I don't see what on earth . . .'

'I was interested, that's all.'

'Well, no, then. No, I don't.'

'But it's something you feel strongly about?'

'Yes. Yes, of course. I mean, it's only natural. At least, that's what you would think. And the fact that she's a woman. That it's a woman, perpetrating these things . . .'

'Not exactly, Mr Gooding.'

'What do you mean?'

'I mean, Ms Jordan isn't actually *doing* any of these things. She isn't *doing* anything. Other than writing books. Isn't that so?'

'Yes, but . . .'

'Let me be clear here,' Naylor said, leaning forward for the first time. 'The business with the rabbit, that was to teach Miss Jordan a lesson, frighten her into stopping writing, what?'

'Huh, she's never going to stop, is she? Not with a formula like that. Raking it in. God knows what she must have earned, the last few years. Though, of course, she hasn't got the respect. Not from the critics, nor the affection of her readers. True affection, like Dorothy.'

'That was what you had for Ms Birdwell? Yourself, I mean. Affection and respect?'

'Of course, yes. Why I . . .'

'Then why this?' Lynn's finger hovered over the first of the photographs. 'Or this? Or this?'

Marius closed his eyes. 'I was upset. I . . .'

'You seem to get upset a lot,' Lynn observed quietly.

'I thought . . . I know it was stupid and foolish and very, very wrong . . . but I thought she didn't . . . Dorothy didn't . . . after everything that had happened between us, all the time we had spent together . . .' His body was racked by a sudden sob. 'I thought she didn't love me any more. And I am deeply, deeply ashamed.'

The faint whir of the tape machinery aside, the clipped clicking of the clock, the only sounds were the contortions of Marius's ragged breathing as he struggled to recover himself, regain some element of control. Heather Jardine looked at the notepad on her lap and wished she could light up a cigarette; Kevin Naylor simply looked embarrassed. It was Lynn whose eyes never wavered. If ever anyone was in need of therapy, she was thinking, it's this poor, pathetic bastard and not me.

'These feelings you had about Cathy Jordan,' Lynn asked, 'about her work. Would you say that Ms Birdwell shared those?'

'Most strongly, yes.'

'But she didn't approve of the methods you used to express what you felt?'

'*Grand guignol* was the term she used. Over-theatrical. Too close for Dorothy's liking to the kind of thing you can imagine Jordan doing herself. Though, of course, that was the point.'

'She was happier with the letters, then, was she?' Lynn asked, making a leap of faith.

Marius's face was a picture.

Reaching down for the folder that was leaning against one leg of the table, Lynn extracted copies of the threatening letters Cathy Jordan had received and set them carefully down along the length of the table.

'The letters,' Lynn said. 'Have a good look. Remind yourself.'

Marius wobbled a little in his seat.

'I think,' Heather Jardine said, rising to her feet, 'my client is in need of a break.'

'This interview,' Lynn said, face angled towards the

tape recorder, 'suspended at seventeen minutes past twelve.'

At four minutes to two, Alison and Shane Charlton rang the buzzer at the Enquiries desk below and asked if they could speak to somebody about the Peter Farleigh murder.

Forty-three

'We had a message,' Alison Charlton said, 'you wanted us to get in touch. We've been away, you see. The weekend.' She smiled at her husband, who smiled, a touch self-consciously, back. 'We came in as soon as we heard.' The wedding rings, Resnick noticed, were shiny and new on their hands.

'The man who died,' Shane Charlton said, 'Alison's mother had saved his picture from the paper. She knew we'd been staying there that night. The same hotel.'

'It was Shane's firm's do,' Alison explained.

'I recognised him, we recognised him right off,' Shane said. 'Didn't we, Ali?'

'Oh, yes.' Her face, bright already, brightened still further. 'We were right facing him, him and her. Going up in the lift. Must have been – I was saying to Shane, wasn't I, Shane? – after that that it happened.'

'What time was this?' Resnick asked. 'Can you remember?'

'It would have been round eleven thirty,' Shane said.

'Nearer quarter past,' Alison said.

'You said, him and her,' Resnick reminded her.

'The woman . . .'

'The woman he was with . . .'

'Nice looking, she was. Well, quite . . .'

'Considering.'

'Like you say, considering. And I think she'd been drinking, don't you, Shane?'

'Didn't act drunk, though, did she? Not exactly.'

243

'No, it was what she said.'

Shane nodded, remembering.

'Come right out with it, didn't she? We might as well not've been there, might we? For all she cared. Well, I'd never've had the guts to have said it. Not the way she did. One hundred and fifty pounds, she said, just like she was talking about, oh, you know, the weather. A hundred and fifty pounds, to spend the night. I said to Shane after, when we was in our room, would he, like, if he was off on business and on his own, without us being married, of course, would he ever spend that amount of money. And you said you might, d'you remember, but only if she looked like me. I thought that was really sweet.'

She giggled and Shane, embarrassed, fidgeted in his seat.

'Could you describe her?' Resnick asked. 'The woman.'

They looked at one another before Alison answered. 'She was, well, she wasn't young.'

'She was never old,' Shane said.

'Thirty-five, should you say, Shane?'

Shane shrugged. 'Something like that.'

'And she was dressed, you know, not tarty. Smart, I suppose you'd say. She had this black, button-through dress. Satiny, sort of. Sleeveless. A blouse underneath.'

'Colour?'

'Blue. It was, wasn't it, Shane? Quite a dark shade of blue.'

'I don't know. I don't think I ever noticed.'

'I'm sure it was. Midnight blue, I think that's what you'd call it. Midnight blue.'

'How about her hair?' Resnick asked. 'What do you remember about that?'

'Well, it was dark. Definitely dark. And she wore it up like this . . .' Alison demonstrated as best she could with her own hair, even though it was too short to give the proper effect. '. . . pinned, at the back.'

'She had one of those things,' Shane said.

'What things?'

'I don't know, those things you put in your hair.'

'A ribbon? She didn't have a ribbon.'

'No, not that. One of those plastic thingummies . . .'

'A comb?' suggested Alison.

'She wasn't just standing there with a comb in her hair, don't be daft.'

'That's what they're called, though. Combs.'

'Don't you remember?' Shane said.

Alison shook her head.

'It was on the right-hand side,' Shane said.

'Well, that was over towards you. Where you were standing.'

'That's right.'

'What colour was it?' Resnick asked, hanging on to his patience. 'This comb.'

'White. Off-white.' And, as though plucking the name from the air, smile on his face as if his answer had just won a prize. 'Ivory.'

Alison smiled for him.

'I'd like you to look at some photographs,' Resnick said. 'Down at Central Station. The Intelligence Bureau. I'll get someone to drive you down.'

'Oh, great,' Alison exclaimed. 'We'd like that, wouldn't we, Shane?'

The officer set out the photograph of Marlene Kinoulton along with eleven others of similar colouring and general age and appearance. Neither Alison nor Shane picked her out immediately, but when they did, there was little or no uncertainty.

'It was the hair that threw me, wasn't it you, Shane?'

245

Alison said. 'She didn't have it down when we saw her. Like I told the other policeman . . .'

'Inspector Resnick,' Shane said.

'Inspector Resnick, yes. Like I told him, her hair was up then. Made her look quite a bit different. Bit older, of course, but smarter. I'd wear it like that all the time, if I were her.'

Heather Jardine and Lynn Kellogg were standing out at the rear of the station building, the ground around them dark and slick from the quick summer shower. Heather Jardine was having her second cigarette in succession, all the more necessary having given up smoking from New Year's Eve until a week ago last Friday. Now, it was as if she couldn't get the nicotine back into her bloodstream fast enough.

'So how's it been?' she asked and they both knew what she was referring to, Lynn standing there with a polystyrene cup of lukewarm coffee in her hand, not wanting to talk about the kidnapping and its aftermath, not at all, but understanding the other woman's need to ask, the concern.

'Not so bad,' Lynn said. 'You know . . .' Letting it hang.

'I don't suppose,' Heather said, 'it's the kind of thing you ever really forget.'

Lynn swallowed a mouthful more coffee; though the sun had come back out, the recent rain had left a nip in the air and she caught herself wishing she had worn a cardigan, some kind of a sweater.

'He's not come up for trial yet, either, has he?'

Lynn shook her head.

Heather drew smoke in heavily and held it in her mouth before exhaling. 'These letters, they're pretty nasty, I know. Threatening, it's true. But even if you could prove

246

in court he actually did send them, there's never any real sense he was intending to carry any of those threats out.'

Lynn let her continue.

'I suppose if you took some of it literally, there might be a charge of threat to kill, but well . . . I don't think the CPS would be over the moon about that, do you? Without that, unless the woman wants to press charges herself, take out a civil action, where are you?'

Lynn smiled wearily. 'Public Order Act, section five.'

'Ah, you'd not bother. Most your boss is likely to press for, bung him up before the magistrate and have him bound over.'

Lynn had a mouthful more coffee and tipped the remainder out on to the wet ground. 'And what about all the rest?'

'Resisting arrest?'

'Assault.'

Heather stubbed out the butt of her cigarette on the sole of her shoe. 'First offence, no record, previous good behaviour. I'd be surprised if it got anywhere near court, and if it did, any barrister worth half his fee would argue a hole through the prosecution a mile wide.'

'Maybe.'

'If I'm wrong,' Heather laughed, 'I'll buy you a bottle of twenty-year Macallan.'

Not really a drinker, Lynn took this to be an impressive offer. 'Shall we go back in? At least, we can make him wriggle and squirm a bit longer.' She shuddered, not from the cold. 'It's not just his public-school accent or that pathetic little moustache, don't know what it is, but there's something about him, makes my skin crawl.'

Involuntarily, Heather had begun scratching her thigh. 'Mine, too.'

Skelton was standing behind his desk, about as close to being at ease as he ever seemed to get. 'Pulled in all the extra bodies I can, Charlie. Go through the city tonight like a fine-tooth comb. If she's still here, we'll find her.'

'If not?' Resnick asked.

'Then we'll release her picture in the morning.'

Forty-four

'. . . Police today took the unusual step of releasing a photograph of a woman they wish to interview in connection with a number of attacks on men, including the murder of Peter Farleigh, whose body was found with fatal stab wounds . . .'

Susan Tyrell reached over and pushed one of several preset buttons, switching the radio to Classic-FM. 'Did you see the picture, David?'

'Mm? Sorry, which picture?' He was standing by the microwave, concentrating on the controls; one second too many and the croissants would be reduced to slime. Close by stood the matt black espresso machine he had talked Susan into buying him the Christmas before last and which he had never learned to use.

'In the paper,' Susan said. 'The woman they think's been stabbing all those men.'

'On the game, isn't she?'

'So it says.'

The microwave pinged and David slid the warm croissants on to plates. It was warm enough again for them to sit out in the garden, make use of the deckchairs Susan had picked up on sale at Homebase. He picked up the paper from where Susan had left it and carried it back to his chair. Centre columns, page three. 'Marlene Kinoulton, doesn't have much of a ring to it, does it? Not exactly stunning, either. Can't quite imagine who'd want to shell out for her.'

'Really?' Susan said, pouring the coffee. 'I should have thought she was just your type.'

David laughed. 'What on earth's that supposed to mean?'

'Oh, you know, one of those raddled creatures you fantasise about, short on morals and long on hearts of gold. I can remember you dragging me off to see *Cutter's Way* ...'

'Jeff Bridges.'

'... just for the scene where Lisa Eichhorn looks so pained and awful after he's walked out on her. What did you say? You'd never seen a woman looking so bereft ...'

'Or beautiful.'

'Right.' Susan broke into the croissant with her fingers. 'And then she gets killed.'

David raised an eyebrow and passed her the jam. 'Goes with the territory.'

'Prostitutes and whores, you mean? Victims.'

'I suppose.'

Susan looked at him hard. 'I wonder why they're always the ones you fancy so much?'

A butterfly landed for an instant on David's sleeve, then fluttered off towards the cotoneaster. 'I liked Julie Andrews once.'

'You were seven. And you're avoiding the issue.'

'Is it an issue?'

Susan brushed crumbs from the front of her blouse. 'It might be.'

David wriggled his lean body against the striped canvas. Just when he was having a nice, relaxing morning for a change. 'Then I suppose it's to do with – oh, you know what it's to do with – fallen angels, forbidden fruit.'

'Like her?' Susan said, nodding in the direction of Marlene Kinoulton's picture in the newspaper. 'But you don't fancy her.'

'That's different.'

'Why? Because she's not pretty, screen-star pretty?'

'For God's sake, Susan, because she's real. And because what goes with her is real.'

'Such as?'

'How long a list do you want? Herpes, gonorrhoea, Aids.'

'Oh,' Susan said, 'for a moment I thought you were talking about commitment.'

'Commitment? To a whore?'

'Yes. Why not? That's what it is, after all. You start off fancying her, you decide to pay for her, you end up sticking a condom on your cock and sticking it inside her. I'd say that called for quite a lot of commitment, wouldn't you?'

David had jerked to his feet, spilling coffee down one leg of his trousers and across the seat of the deckchair. 'Christ, Susan, what's this all about?' He couldn't remember her so animated, so angry.

Susan put down her cup and plate, folded her hands across her lap. 'The night before last, I went out and picked up a man.'

David stared at her, mouth slightly open. Just stared. As if hearing it for the first time, he heard the harsh, bright call of the magpie on the overhanging branch of their neighbour's pear tree.

'I picked him up in a bar and we went to a hotel.'

David turned towards the bottom of the garden, walked five paces, turned back around. 'Look, Susan, I'm sorry, I can't deal with this now. I have to go.'

All she could do was shake her head from side to side and laugh.

Hurrying past her into the house, David froze at the entrance to the hall. Where was his briefcase? Where were his keys? What was going on with his life?

'David,' Susan touched his arm and he flinched.

251

'David, look at me.' And she leaned back against the front door the way she thought Claire Trevor might have done, Barbara Stanwyck or Jane Greer. 'I didn't tell you so that you could deal with it. It's done. Over. I just wanted you to know.'

As he tried to push past her, reaching for the handle to the door, she added, close to his ear, 'I thought you might look at me differently, that's all.'

He hesitated for a second before tugging at the door and Susan stepped to one side, letting him go.

She was still standing in the hallway when she heard the car start, tyres spinning a little as it sped away. She hadn't told him exactly how drunk she had needed to be, the way excitement and revulsion had tasted in her mouth; nor about the way her face had looked in the bathroom mirror before she had decided to cut and run.

Susan looked at her watch: nine seventeen. They would have realised at school by now she wasn't coming in. She was surprised they hadn't phoned. In the living room, she poured herself a generous glass of gin, lit a cigarette: isn't that the kind of thing Lisa Eichhorn would do? Claire Trevor. Barbara Stanwyck. Jane Greer. All those women who rarely made it in one piece, through to the final reel?

Forty-five

Resnick sat at the coffee stall, taking his time through his second espresso of the morning. A sudden shower had surprised him as he was walking his way down from the Woodborough Road and he had ducked into the market by the rear entrance.

Marlene Kinoulton's photograph was prominently displayed on the front page of the local paper. All of the previous night's searching had brought them nothing but sore feet and abuse. Urgent messages had gone out to Leicester, Sheffield, Derby, the other cities where it was known she had worked. It was too early to gauge the extent and accuracy of public response, though early signs were far from promising; what had come through via the information room so far had been patchy and poor. Nowadays, it seemed, unless you went on television, *Crimewatch UK* or one of those, chances of lighting a fire under the public were poor. And he supposed, in time, if Kinoulton weren't traced, that was what would happen. Actors and a film crew and a researcher asking to interview him so that they could get it just right. '*Later tonight, on* Crimewatch UK, *the intriguing story of the missing prostitute and the hotel-room murder . . .*'

A woman with a child of under two clinging to her skirt, climbed on to the vacant stool next to him, lifted the child into her lap and stuck a dummy in its mouth. Directly across from where he was sitting, a man he had put away for two stretches for burglary, joked with one of the Asian stallholders over a cup of tea. He did not acknowledge Resnick, nor Resnick him. When the festival was over and all the visitors and writers and film-makers had returned to wherever they had come from, this was what it would come back to. People who lived here; who did what and to whom?

'Another espresso, inspector?'

'Thanks. Better not.' Lifting the small cup to his mouth, he swallowed down what was left. Dark and bitter, why was it so good?

Cathy Jordan and Frank Carlucci had tiptoed around each other, exchanging no more words than were necessary. Neither of them wished to begin a conversation that could reopen old wounds and, in all probability, inflict new ones. Mollie Hansen had phoned earlier to enquire whether Cathy were happy to be interviewed on *Kaleidoscope* that evening, she had to ring John Goudie back and let him know.

Now Mollie was there at the hotel, making sure that the travel arrangements to London were clear; after the radio programme, there was a book signing in the Charing Cross Road at Murder One, at which point the publicist working for Cathy's UK publisher would take over and Mollie was in the clear. That is, she could get on with attending to the rest of the festival.

She was leaning against the counter at reception, just through speaking to Cathy on the internal phone, when Resnick came in.

'Not more trouble?' she asked, intercepting him with a guarded smile.

'No.' He realised he was staring at her and looked away.

Mollie laughed. 'My God! You don't like it, do you?'

'What?'

'And now you're embarrassed to have noticed.' She

254

had had a small stone fitted in the right side of her nostril, bright blue.

'Not at all,' Resnick blushed.

'You don't approve, body adornment?'

He shook his head. 'I don't suppose I've ever thought about it. I was surprised, that's all.'

Mollie smiled. 'Do you like it, though? Be honest. I'd like to know what you think.'

'I think you looked fine before.'

It was Mollie's turn, almost, to flush. 'You're here to see Cathy?'

He nodded. 'Just quickly. I shan't be long.'

'If I hang on,' Mollie said, 'I don't suppose I could scrounge a lift?'

'If I had the car with me you could.'

'Never mind. Some other time maybe?'

'Maybe.'

'Well,' backing away, 'see you around, I guess. Come to a movie, why don't you?'

'I'll try.'

Mollie raised a hand, fingers spread, and turned towards the doors. By the time she had walked from sight, Resnick was standing by the lifts, watching the numbers descend.

When Resnick got out of the lift on Cathy Jordan's floor, Frank Carlucci was waiting to get in. The two men exchanged cursory nods before Frank, hands in pockets and ample shoulders hunched, stepped inside and the doors closed behind him.

Cathy opened the door on Resnick's first knock and was surprised to see him standing there and not Frank.

'Sorry. Figured you for the penitent husband, back to crave forgiveness.'

'Does he have something to be forgiven for?'

Cathy's mouth turned upwards into a smile. 'Don't we

all? And wouldn't life be a deadly bore if we did not?' She moved aside to let Resnick enter. 'But in Frank's case, this particular case, I have no idea.' She shrugged. 'Going on his track record, I'm prepared to give him the benefit of the doubt.'

'Innocent as charged.'

Cathy grinned. 'Guilty.'

'Marius likewise.'

'He owned up?'

Resnick nodded.

'The letters as well?'

'Yes.'

Cathy's fist punched the air. 'The bastard! The snivelling lousy bastard!'

'He got a friend in the States to send the letters for him; everything that happened over here was down to him. He swears he never had any intention of carrying any of it through. Just wanted to frighten you, shake you up; make you think about what you were doing.'

'Frighten me?'

'Yes.'

'The little shit!'

'As far as it's possible to tell, my guess is he's telling the truth. It's difficult to see him as actually dangerous, more of a nuisance.'

'If I didn't know better, I'd think you were building up to telling me you're about to let him go.'

Resnick stood there looking at her.

'Jesus! You are! You're going to give him a friendly pat on the head and a warning. Be a good slimebag and don't do it again.' She turned, shaking her head. 'I can't believe it. I can't fucking believe it!'

'Dorothy Birdwell insists she won't press charges. Also, she's paid to have the room set back to rights and the hotel's keen to avoid any adverse publicity.'

Cathy's face was white with anger. 'Which just leaves

me, right? And who the fuck am I, that you should give a good god-damn?'

Resnick took a pace towards her, then a pace back. 'Cathy,' he said.

'What?'

'Whatever you decide to do, it's unlikely, given all the circumstances, that the CPS will recommend prosecution.'

'Shit!' Cathy crossed the room to the whisky bottle, poured a stiff shot and carried it back with her to the settee. 'So what will happen to him? Exactly.'

'Most likely, he'll be bound over not to repeat this or any other behaviour.'

'And then he'll walk?'

Resnick nodded. 'Yes.'

Cathy took one sip at her Scotch and then another. 'Where is he now? You've still got him in custody?'

'Yes, why?'

All energy, Cathy jumped to her feet. 'Fine. I want to see him.'

'I don't know ...'

'Come on, just see him, right? One final time. Tell him goodbye.'

Resnick looked a long way short of convinced.

'Inspector ... Charlie ... Surely it's the least you can do? After all, I'm not exactly about to stick a knife in him, pull out a gun.'

'I still don't know ...'

'Please.'

'All right. But just five minutes. No more. And I shall have to be there all the time.'

Cathy smiled at him with sweetness dropped in acid. 'But of course.'

The police cells were full so Naylor had stuck Marius Gooding in one of the interview rooms and turned the key.

'Half an hour,' he had said. 'Forty-five minutes. Tops.'

Marius had been there for not far short of three hours. Silent, a uniformed officer had brought him a cup of tea and a copy of a three-day-old *Daily Mail*, which Marius had read through several times, cover to cover.

When Resnick entered, he was quickly on his feet, a protest forming on his lips; then, when he saw who was with him, he remained silent.

'Hello, Marius,' Cathy Jordan said, not halting until she was an arm's length away. 'Been treating you okay, have they?'

Marius looked at her, eyes refusing to focus; Resnick had remained near the door and was picking at something that seemed to have lodged on the cuff of his shirt.

'I just wanted to see what you looked like, remember you, in case there was any chance I might have the misfortune of running into you again. And to thank you. No, really, I mean it. Thank you for showing me how low a piece of phlegm like you can go. Exciting, though, was it, Marius? Give you a little hard-on? Thinking up all that stuff in those letters you sent me. Writing about it. What had happened to those women. Those kids.' A fleck of spittle had landed on Cathy's chin and with the back of a hand she wiped it away. 'Must have known those books of mine pretty well, Marius, to quote them so well. So accurately.'

Marius didn't want to look at her, but he wasn't able to look away.

'Might make a point of asking your therapist about that, your fascination with all those nasty incidents you profess to hate. That is, after you talk to him about your mother, your relationship with her.'

He flinched as if he had been struck and clenched both hands fast by his sides.

'Got to be something there, right? Explain this thing you've got for old women.'

'Cathy,' Resnick said, moving forward. 'I think that's enough.'

'No,' shaking her head. 'No, it's not nearly enough.'

Lightly, he placed a hand on her shoulder. 'It'll have to do.'

She tilted her head towards him and smiled. 'Okay. Okay, Marius. No hard feelings, maybe. Well, not too many. And I do hope, whoever the shrink is you go to see, he can help you sort yourself out.'

She looked at him and the first vestiges of a grateful smile appeared at the edges of Marius's eyes. 'Here,' Cathy said softly. 'Have this to remember me by.' And, with a fast swing of the arm, she hit him hard across the face and he rocked backwards, the ring on her finger opening a cut deep below his eye.

Resnick grabbed her but she was already stepping away. 'Well,' she said, 'let's see if your DPP or whatever it is, reckons it's worth prosecuting me for that.'

Releasing her, Resnick pulled a handkerchief from his pocket and gave it to Marius to hold against his face. Then he opened the door and called along the corridor for someone to administer first aid.

Cathy paused in the doorway. 'Then there's a tooth for a tooth, Marius. You remember that one, don't you?'

They stood on the steps outside the police station, watching the traffic playing ducks and drakes with the traffic lights around Canning Circus.

'I tricked you,' Cathy saaid. 'For that, I'm sorry.'

'You had that in your mind all the time?'

'Pretty much.'

'I should have known.'

Quickly, she glanced at him. 'Maybe you did.'

Resnick didn't reply.

A pair of uniformed officers exited behind them and walked around the corner to the official car park.

Cathy offered Resnick her hand and he took it in a firm grip. 'That book of mine,' Cathy said, 'if you ever finish it, you could always drop me a line, let me know what you think.'

'Of course.'

They both knew, whatever his intentions, he most probably would not. Cathy gave him her card regardless and he slipped it down into the top pocket of his coat.

'See you then.'

'Yes, see you.'

For some minutes he stood and watched her go, a tall woman with cropped red hair, wearing a red silk shirt, blue jeans and heeled boots, walking away.

Forty-six

At a little short of nine the next morning, Sarah Farleigh was sitting in Resnick's office, black leather handbag resting in her lap. She was wearing a black suit that looked new, hemline stretched across her knees.

'Asked to see you, sir,' Naylor explained outside. 'In the circumstances, I thought you'd not mind.'

'Okay, Kevin. That's fine.'

There was a moment to look at her, through the glass, before she turned. One of her hands moving distractedly from her side to the brooch on the lapel of her coat, from the corner of her mouth to a stray twist of hair.

'Sarah.' As he entered she rose and came towards him and, although he held out his hand, she moved inside it and gave him a brief hug. Where her face had rested on his sleeve, it had left a smudge of make-up and, stepping back, she brushed it away.

'Is there any news?'

'News?'

'The woman – have you caught her?'

'Not yet.' Resnick went round behind his desk and sat down.

'I don't suppose you've any idea why she did it?'

'Not really. Not till we talk to her.'

'And if you don't?'

'We will.'

'You sound sure.'

'Murders,' Resnick said, 'one area where our clear-up rate is good.'

261

'I thought that was usually the – what do you call it? – family ones?'

'Domestics. Yes, I suppose it is. More often than not.'

Sarah had resumed her seat and retrieved her bag from the floor. Now she opened it and took out a photograph, square and a little creased, bent at the edges. 'I don't know what I was doing, looking through stuff of Peter's, I suppose, and I found this.' She leaned forward and placed it on the desk, for Resnick to swivel round.

It showed Sarah and Ben Riley in a rowing boat, Sarah leaning back, her face, sharper-featured than now, smiling out from beneath the brim of a large, white sun-hat. Ben had the oars in his hands, a cigarette dangling from one side of his mouth. He looked – the phrase leapt immediately to Resnick's mind, somewhat archaic, but appropriate – as pleased as Punch.

'You know where that was taken, don't you?'

Resnick looked again. There was a small, curved bridge in the background, flowering shrubs. 'It's up by the university, isn't it? The lake?'

'That's right. And you know who's behind the camera.'

'No, I don't think so.'

'It's you.'

He looked at it once more, trying to cast back. 'I'm sorry, I'm afraid I don't remember.' He made to give the photograph back to her, but she held up her hand and shook her head. 'Keep it.'

'Well, I . . .'

'I thought you might like it. You never know, you might see Ben some time. Or write . . .'

'Okay. Thanks.' Resnick glanced at it again before sliding it into the drawer to the right of his desk.

'If you don't find her, this woman, I mean, suppose it takes a long time – it could now, couldn't it? – what happens about the body?'

262

'As I told you when I phoned, it remains the property of the coroner.'

'But not forever. What if you never find her?'

'Sarah, I don't think that'll be the case. Believe me.'

'So I can't bury him?'

'Not yet. I'm sorry.'

For several moments, she closed her eyes; body held taut. 'A memorial service, then. That's what I'll do. There'll have to be something.'

Resnick was on his feet. 'As long as you think you're up to it, that sounds a good idea.'

'Thanks.' This time, she was the one offering her hand and he took it. 'You will come?' she said.

'Of course.'

Sarah smiled her thanks.

'I'll see you out.'

'Nice car,' Resnick said, as Sarah unlocked the Volvo. He said it as much to make conversation as anything else; since leaving his office, she had fallen quiet. Not that that surprised him; he was glad to see her coping as well as she seemed to be.

'It was Peter's. I've got an old Fiat, just for nipping about, locally. Longer distances, I use this if I can. It's a lot more reliable.'

'Well, take care, Sarah. Drive safely. And you will let me know about the memorial service?'

Millington met him on the stairs. 'Call from Sheffield, possible sighting of the Kinoulton woman; sounds promising. Local CID're running it down.'

'Good.'

'Oh, and the report's in on that blouse found at the house. It was blood. And it is the same group as Farleigh's.'

'Let's hope Sheffield turn up trumps, then. Put this one away before it gets too long in the tooth.'

Forty-seven

Sheffield, not for the first time, was a wash-out. As were Birmingham, Bradford, the Chapeltown district of Leeds. There was a twice-confirmed rumour that Marlene Kinoulton had been working the streets of Butetown, down near the Cardiff docks. A Vice Squad officer had warned her off, only recognising her from the circulated description when it was too late; a bevy of the local girls had backed her into a corner and given her a tongue-lashing, warned her to piss off out of their territory or they'd get one of the pimps to see to her face and legs.

Millington and Divine drove down to Cardiff; Mark Divine pleased at the chance to make a rugby player's pilgrimage to Cardiff Arms Park. It was about the only part of the trip that worked out well. The co-operation which the local force had promised was dissipated in a miasma of broken promises and missed appointments. They did persuade one of the runners working for a high-flown dealer to talk to them over a late-night biriani and chips. Marlene Kinoulton he swore he'd seen just two nights before, sold her the last two rocks he'd had.

Millington and Divine stayed another couple of days and, as far as they were able, turned the underbelly of the city upside down. Afterwards, only one thing seemed certain: Marlene Kinoulton had been there and now she had gone.

Resnick allowed Marian Witczak to talk him into accompanying her to a midsummer dance at the Polish Club and, after several generous glasses of bison grass vodka, remembered how to polka. A card from Cathy Jordan, a street scene in Dublin, reminded him that he had still to finish *Dead Weight* and, between other things, he got not quite to the end, but almost.

Debbie Naylor waylaid Kevin one night with a bottle of wine and something racy she'd bought from an advertisement in the back of the Sunday paper and now she woke in the mornings with carry-cots and Babygros dancing before her eyes.

Kate Skelton, who not so long before had driven her parents close to despair, shoplifting to pay for her drug problem, astonished them by getting three good A levels and applying to university.

Sharon Garnett applied to be transferred from the Vice Squad into CID and her application was turned down.

Lynn Kellogg came into Resnick's office one morning at the end of July and told him she was seriously thinking about moving back to East Anglia and had been sounding out an old friend about a vacancy in a Norwich force.

'Can we talk about this?' Resnick said. He felt as if something solid was being pulled out from beneath his feet. He felt something he didn't understand.

'Of course,' Lynn said, and waited.

'I meant, I suppose I meant, not here.'

'You're busy.' His desk was the usual clutter of reports and forms, empty sandwich bags.

'Yes. No. It's not that. I suppose . . . well, to be honest, you've taken me by surprise.'

'Yes, well, it's nothing definite yet, although . . .' She stopped, reminded of the look that had come into her father's eyes, the first time she had told him she was applying to join the police. 'How about a drink then?' she said. 'If you want to talk it through.'

'It's a long time since you were at the coffee stall,'

Resnick said. 'They've just about given up asking where you've got to.'

Lynn smiled; just a little, not too much; just with the eyes. 'All right.'

Amongst the other things on Resnick's desk, unopened, the invitation to the service at Wymeswold Church dedicated to the memory of Peter Farleigh.

He thought she'd changed her mind. Several of the stallholders had taken in the goods that hung around the outside of their sections and pulled down the metal sides. Resnick had read the cricket report in the local paper twice.

'Sorry,' Lynn said, a little out of breath, her cheeks flushed with colour for the first time in weeks. 'Something cropped up.'

'Important?'

'No, just fiddly.'

'Here,' the assistant said, setting down a cappuccino, 'for you the first one free.'

'Thanks,' Lynn said, 'but best not.' She pushed a pound coin across the counter and grinned. 'Probably consitutes a bribe.'

Now they were there, there was no rush to talk. Resnick sipped his espresso as Lynn tasted the chocolatey froth from a cheap metal spoon. With a thump and clatter, another stall was locked away for the night.

'Your dad,' Resnick finally said. 'Is that the problem?'

'How d'you mean?'

'The reason you're thinking of moving back.'

'Oh, partly, yes. In a way.'

'I thought he was better. Doing okay. Stable, at least.'

'He is. But cancer, you know, so hard not to think, whatever the doctors say, it's not going to come back. Somewhere else.'

'There's no sign, though?'

267

'No, not yet. No. Touch wood.' She glanced around. The couple who ran the corner vegetable stall were laughing together, lighting up, just for a moment holding hands. 'It's my mum, more.'

'She's not ill?'

Lynn shook her head. 'Just works herself up into such a state.'

Resnick finished his coffee; wondered if there were time for one more. 'That's the reason, then? To be near your mother, close?'

Lynn drank some of her cappuccino. 'Not really, no.'

Something had begun pressing against the inside of Resnick's left temple, urgent, hard.

Lynn tried to choose her words with care. 'Ever since what happened. When I was ... taken prisoner. I can't stop, haven't been able to stop myself, well, thinking ...'

'That's only natural ...'

'I know. Yes, I know. And Petra says ... That's my doctor. Petra Carey. She says I have to take time, open myself to it; she says there's a lot I have to talk myself through.'

'Like what?'

'Like you.'

Resnick's left eye blinked. If the assistant turned around, he would order another espresso, but, of course, the man continued stubbornly washing down the counter at the other side.

Lynn was speaking again, her voice measured, trying to talk the way she would to Petra Carey if Petra Carey were there. 'Tied up there at night, in the caravan, never knowing when he might come in. Knowing what had happened to that other girl, knowing what he'd done, what he might do. I was scared, of course I was scared. Terrified. Though I knew the last thing I could afford to do was show it. To him. And underneath it all, somehow – I'm not sure, I was dreaming a lot of the time, I think I must have been; trying not to let myself fall asleep, but not being able to stop myself – but somehow there was always this idea that it would be all right, that someone – no, you – that you would come and – God, it sounds pathetic now, doesn't it, hearing myself say this – but that you would come and save me.' For a moment, Lynn pressed her face into her hands and closed her eyes. 'Except,' she went on, 'it wasn't always you. It wasn't as straightforward as that. Sometimes, I would think it was you but then when I saw your face, it was my dad. You were ... my dad.' She shook her head, low towards her hands, which were folded over one another now, beside her cup. 'It isn't even that simple. There are things, other things, I can't, I don't want to say.'

Resnick put one hand over hers, ready to retract it if she pulled away.

'I haven't been able to talk to you,' Lynn said, not looking at him, looking away. 'Not really talk, not since it happened.'

'I know.'

'I just haven't felt comfortable, being with you.'

'No.'

'And it's difficult. So bloody difficult!' With surprise, the assistant looked round at her raised voice. 'And I hate it.'

'Yes,' Resnick said, taking away his hand. And then, 'So this is why you want to go; this rather than your mother, anything at home.'

'Oh, they want me back there, of course. My dad doesn't say so, but my mum, she'd love it. But if it wasn't for this other business, no, I don't think I'd go.'

'And you don't think we could work it out. Somehow, between us, I mean. Maybe, now you've started talking about it?'

'That's what Petra says.'

'That you, we, should talk it over?'

269

Lynn nodded, still not looking at him. 'Yes.' And when Resnick was silent, she asked him what he was thinking.

'I was wondering why you hadn't felt able to come to me before?'

'You're hurt, aren't you?'

'By that? Yes, I suppose I am.'

'She said you would be. But, I don't know, I just couldn't.'

'You were afraid of what I'd say?'

'No. What I would.'

Resnick's intention, that evening, had been to go along to the refurbished Old Vic and listen to the new Stan Tracey Duo. But by the time he'd fed the cats, fiddled around with a smoked ham and stilton sandwich, he didn't seem to feel like going out. Sitting on the back step with a bottle of Czech Budweiser, he found out how Annie Q. Jones was getting on, embroiled in plot and counter-plot in the last fifty pages of *Dead Weight*. Poor Annie, sapped on the head from behind, going down a narrow side street in pitch darkness – at least she had her lover to provide a little comfort in the small hours.

His neighbours, also enjoying the light, pleasantly warm evening, had thrown open their windows and were treating him to muffled television laughter and the smell of chicken frying. Resnick finished his beer, took the book back inside, page at the start of the final chapter folded down, and set off to walk down into the city.

He arrived at the pub in time for the last two numbers. Stan Tracey, hunched over the keyboard, angularly manoeuvring his way through 'Sophisticated Lady', taking the tune into seemingly impossible blind alleys and then escaping through a mixture of finesse and sheer power. Finally, Tracey and an absurdly young-looking Gerard Presencer on trumpet had elided their way along a

John Coltrane blues, the audacity of Presencer's imagination more than matched by his technique.

Just once, in the middle of the trumpeter's solo, eyes closed, Resnick had seen a perfect vision of Lynn, her face, round and open and close to his. And then it had gone. While the applause was still trickling away, he lifted his empty glass and set it down by the end of the bar, nodded towards the landlord, and made his way towards the door.

Back home again, Bud nestled in beside his feet, Resnick finished the book:

> *I know that Reigler has suffered another stroke, but still I'm not prepared for what I find. One side of his body seems totally paralysed, the same side of his face sunken and lined, one dark eye staring out. His speech is slurred, but I get the jist. As confessions go this one's pretty simple and to the point. He nods when he's finished and I switch off the tape that's been resting on one arm of his wheelchair.*
>
> *Seems he's got one more request.*
>
> *I don't know why I should raise a finger for him and then I find out what it is.*
>
> *The gun is in the drawer and I'm careful only to handle it with the gloves I conveniently have in the pocket of my coat. There's a wind got up from the ocean and the temperature has plummeted. There's one shell in the chamber and just a moment of doubt when I think it might be intended for me, but one more look at his wrecked body and I know that's not the case.*
>
> *The trigger mechanism seems light, though even so, I'm not convinced, the state that he's in, he's going to be able to find enough*

pressure, but I figure that's his problem, not mine.

I hear the gunshot as I'm climbing into my car, and I guess it's worked out all right. I don't go back. There'll be a call box on my way home and I can pull over and perform my anonymous civic duty. I risk the last ten miles way above the limit. I know Diane's going to have something ready, maybe even something we can eat in bed, and I don't want to keep her waiting.

Well, no longer than she finds enjoyable.

So that was how it ended, he thought, clear-cut and happy, no loose ends. With a wry smile, Resnick closed the book and reached across to switch off the light.

Forty-eight

The church was small and most of the pews were filled with the Farleigh family and neighbours, Peter Farleigh's colleagues from work and a few representatives of organisations he had regularly supplied. After several hymns, carefully chosen but randomly sung, the vicar spoke with a pious briskness of Peter's devotion as husband and father, his dedication and selflessness as a breadwinner, the admiration and respect with which he was held within the community. The managing director of Farleigh's firm, who turned out to be Japanese, talked briefly and in perfect, Oxford-accented English of his late-lamented model employee. Then the youngest Farleigh daughter, wearing a long, loose-skirted floral dress, sang 'Where Have All the Flowers Gone', accompanying herself on the guitar.

People cried.

Resnick stood in line to grasp Sarah's hand and kiss her on the cheek, express his condolences to her children, strung out awkwardly beside her. 'You will come back to the house afterwards?' He looked into her red-rimmed eyes and agreed.

There were scarcely more than a dozen there when Resnick arrived: immediate family, and the vicar, exchanging pieties with Peter's mother, who had the good fortune to be profoundly deaf.

Resnick ate several skimpy sandwiches, making them more palatable by taking separate triangles of tongue and cheese and pressing them together. He chatted in a

273

desultory manner with Peter and Sarah's son, who replied in monotones and couldn't wait to get away.

'I don't know what she's looking so sad about,' the older daughter spat out towards Resnick, glancing over to where her mother was standing. 'It wasn't as if she loved him anyway.'

Overhearing this, her younger sister burst into tears.

Once he noticed people beginning to slip away, Resnick retreated to the kitchen and rolled up his sleeves, stacking and washing up the glasses, cups and plates. The son borrowed his mother's Fiat to drive his grandparents to the station and the two sisters, reconciled, went for a walk.

'Thanks for staying, Charlie,' Sarah said, when she had seen the last visitor off. 'And for doing all of that.'

'It's nothing. Glad to be of help.'

'Well, it's sweet of you. And now I need a drink. You?'

'No, thanks.'

'Driving?'

'That's right.'

Sarah smiled, the first he had seen all day. 'You were always that way, Charlie. I remember. Careful to the point of being almost boring. Ben, now, he didn't care. Not that much. I've driven back with him when he probably wasn't safe at all.'

'Sarah,' Resnick said, more sharply than he had perhaps intended.

'What?'

'Stop it. For heaven's sake.' He wiped suds and water from his hands with the tea towel and dropped it on the counter beside the sink.

'Charlie. I'm sorry, I don't understand. I was only . . .'

'I know what you were doing. Bringing up Ben again and again, pretending we were forever doing things together, one big happy trio.'

'Elaine, too . . .'

'Sarah, aside from that time at the lake I doubt if we

274

spent more than a couple of dozen hours together, all told.'

'Charlie, I don't know, is that true? It certainly isn't the way I remember it. I . . . Oh, Charlie, I just keep thinking about him, that's all. All day today, when I should have been thinking about Peter . . .'

'You had your chance to marry him and you turned him down.'

'And I made a mistake.'

'I'm sorry.'

'God, Charlie, I was wrong. You're not the way you used to be. You've changed. You've become hard, mean.'

'Maybe that's the way I have to be.'

She drank some of her sherry, barely tasting it, then set the glass back down. 'To do this?'

'Yes.'

She walked into the living room and he followed her through; the French windows into the garden had been left open and there was a breeze. A cat, ginger and black, that Resnick had not noticed before, was curled up on one of the armchairs.

'Yours?'

She shook her head. 'Next door's.'

For an instant the words caught at the back of Resnick's throat. 'You used his car, didn't you?' he said.

Sarah looked back at him. 'Yes,' she said. She seemed smaller already, as if she had shrunken a little inside her smartly tailored suit. Her green eyes had ceased to glow.

'There was a list on the computer, vehicles that had checked into the hotel garage. When I saw the number had been traced through to Peter as owner, I assumed he had been using it himself.' Resnick looked across at her, but whatever she had focused on was way down the garden, beyond the shrubbery. 'It took a while for all our routine checks on the car hire returns to go through the computer, but when they did, there was a Ford Granada under Peter's name.'

'Two and two then, was it, Charlie?' She had turned to face him now, moved towards him; the shine was back in her eyes but it was of quite a different nature than before.

'Most of the prints we lifted from the hotel room were too smudged to be of any use; there was one inside the rim of the bath, only partial, but enough to get a match off the invitation you sent me . . .'

'You bastard!'

'Not enough in itself.'

'Too bad. Too bloody bad!' She turned her back to him, leaned her head and arm against the mantelpiece and started to cry. Resnick left her to it. After a while, she pulled a small handkerchief from her sleeve and dabbed at her eyes.

'He phoned me that morning, telling me to take the car to the garage; as if I needed reminding, like a complete child. And would I run around the house after him, picking up his dry cleaning and take that in as well?' She blew her nose. 'He said he'd ring me that evening, but, of course, he didn't. He rarely did, when he was away, and I knew why. I knew what he would be doing, some cheap little tart or other, some whore. And, of course, I was right. I was right.'

She started to cry again, really cry this time, and Resnick went over to her and placed his hands, lightly, on her upper arms.

'I was outside, in the corridor, when she left. I can even describe her for you, if you want. Except that her hair was up, she was pretty much like her photograph. In the paper. When I went in, Peter was on the floor, just past the end of the bed. He was crawling towards the bathroom, crawling on his hands and belly and leaving these trails, like a snail, except they were red, all along the floor. I felt sick. I couldn't stop watching him. It was horrible, disgusting.

He got himself up on to the side of the bath and then stopped, Collapsed. Unconscious. The knife, the one she'd stabbed him with, it was still on the bed; I could see the handle sticking out from the sheet. Maybe she'd looked for it and not found it, I don't know. Anyway, I took it and went into the bathroom. Peter still hadn't moved. I thought I could still hear his breathing, but I couldn't be sure. I remember his buttocks were all flabby and loose, almost white except for these purple spots. And the awful flab of his belly, pushed out on both sides by the bath.' Resnick felt, rather than saw, her shake against his hands. 'I only stabbed him once, in the side. I couldn't believe how easily the blade went in.'

Resnick had heard the car pull up a while since, back along the road. He wondered how long they had been out in the garden, how much they had overheard? He called out and Millington and Lynn Kellogg stepped inside.

'Sarah Farleigh,' he said, 'I am arresting you for the murder of Peter Farleigh...' He was glad she was looking away again, not directly up at him; glad to have got the business done before the children returned.

Curtis Woolfe

FILMOGRAPHY

Death by Night
RKO, 1994
Photography: Nicholas Musuraca
Screenplay: Albert Maltz and Warren Duff
Jean Brooks, Lawrence Tierney, Paul Lukas

Angel Eyes
Republic, 1945
Photography: John Alton
Screenplay: Curtis Woolfe and Steve Fisher
Bill Elliott, Albert Dekker, Martha MacVicar

Dark Corridor
RKO, 1946
Photography: Robert De Grasse
Screenplay: Lawrence Kimble and Daniel Mainwaring
(uncredited)
Gail Russell, Albert Dekker, Kent Smith

Cry Murder
Republic, 1947
Photography: John Alton
Screenplay: Curtis Woolfe and Doris Miller
Dane Clark, Coleen Gray, Luther Adler

Dead Ringer
Monogram, 1948
Photography: Mack Stengler
Screenplay: Steve Fisher
Steve Brodie, Jennifer Holt, Myron Healey

High Tension
Allied Artists, 1952
Photography: Joseph F. Biroc
Screenplay: Curtis Woolfe and Warren Douglas
Dan Duryea, Dorothy Malone, Charles McGraw

Lone Justice
Allied Artists, 1953
Photography: Ernest Miller
Screenplay: Steve Fisher
Bill Elliott, Coleen Gray, Myron Healey

The Last Gun
Allied Artists, 1954
Photography: Ernest Miller
Screenplay: Daniel Mainwaring (as Geoffrey Homes)
Bill Elliott, Peggie Castle, Dorothy Malone

Days of the Gunfighter (I Giorni des Pistoleros)
BRC Produzione Film/Estela Films, 1965
Photography: Francisco Marin
Screenplay: Jesus Navarro
Rod Cameron, Hally Hammond (Lorella de Luca), Henry
Silva

Second Unit Director (uncredited)

A Long Ride From Hell (Vivo per la tua Morte)
Cinerama Releasing Corporation, 1968
Director: Alex Burks (Camillo Bazzoni)
Screenplay: Steve Reeves, Camillo Bazzoni
Steve Reeves, Wayde Preston, Silvana Venturelli

Cathy Jordan

BIBLIOGRAPHY

Annie Q. Jones Mysteries

Angels at Rest (1989)
Uneasy Prey (1990)
Sleeping Fools Lie (1991)
Shallow Grave (1993)
Dead Weight (1995)
Living Proof (scheduled for publication, 1996)

Other Fiction

Family Affairs (1982)
Rimrock (1984)
From Shore to Shore (1987)

Shots in the Dark

Thanks are due to Adrian Wootton, Programme Director of *Shots in the Dark*, and his committee, for the assistance and co-operation which made it possible to set this novel in and around the festival.

Thanks are also due to those writers and others who have allowed themselves to be cast in the margins of the action, adding verisimilitude and texture.

SHOTS IN THE DARK
Nottingham's International Mystery and Thriller Festival
incorporating
SHOTS ON THE PAGE
Crime Writing Convention
is held annually at the Broadway Media Centre
14 Broad Street, Nottingham, NG1 3AL, England